"HERE THEY COME AGAIN, LIEUTENANT!"

Kincaid turned and looked again through the gun slit. The battle had raged for nearly three hours, and the house, with windows shuttered and doors barred, had become increasingly hot and stifling.

It was with bitterness and determination that Kincaid leveled his sights on the warrior in the front rank. "Choose your targets carefully, men," he called out. "Make every shot count. Let's take as many with us as we can."

He squeezed the trigger and the battle was on again. But not for long...

"We're out of ammunition, Lieutenant," Richardson raged, jerking his empty weapon from the gun port. "Request permission to take them on hand to hand, sir..."

EASY COMPANY

EASY COMPANY
AND THE ENGINEERS

JOHN WESLEY HOWARD

A JOVE BOOK

EASY COMPANY AND THE ENGINEERS

First Jove edition published December 1981

First printing

Printed in the United States of America

Jove books are published by Jove Publications, Inc.,
200 Madison Avenue, New York, NY 10016

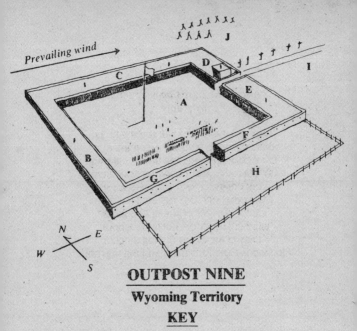

Prevailing wind →

N E
W
S

OUTPOST NINE
Wyoming Territory
KEY

A. Parade and flagstaff

B. Officers' quarters ("officers' country")

C. Enlisted men's quarters: barracks, day room, and mess

D. Kitchen, quartermaster supplies, ordnance shop, guardhouse

E. Suttler's store and other shops, tack room, and smithy

F. Stables

G. Quarters for dependents and guests; communal kitchen

H. Paddock

I. Road and telegraph line to regimental headquarters

J. Indian camp occupied by transient "friendlies"

INTERIOR   OUTSIDE

OUTPOST NUMBER NINE
(DETAIL)

Outpost Number Nine is a typical High Plains military outpost of the days following the Battle of the Little Big Horn, and is the home of Easy Company. It is not a "fort"; an official fort is the headquarters of a regiment. However, it resembles a fort in its construction.

The birdseye view shows the general layout and orientation of Outpost Number Nine; features are explained in the Key.

The detail shows a cross-section through the outpost's double walls, which ingeniously combine the functions of fortification and shelter.

The walls are constructed of sod, dug from the prairie on which Outpost Number Nine stands, and are sturdy enough to withstand an assault by anything less than artillery. The roof is of log beams covered by planking, tarpaper, and a top layer of sod. It also provides a parapet from which the outpost's defenders can fire down on an attacking force.

one ─────────────

Crystal-clear water, crisp and fresh, gurgled in the sparkling sunlight as it wound along the course of the stream known as Cole Creek, named after the homesteader who had been found lying facedown in its upper origins many years before. His scalp had been taken and a Sioux war arrow, with its unmistakable yellow and red stripes, had been found lodged between his shoulder blades. His hat had drifted downstream, flowing with the meandering stream bed on the High Plains waterway in Montana Territory, and the place where it had been found, lodged against the bank, had come to be known as Lost Hat Crossing.

Six riders sat their mounts at that crossing now, while their horses nuzzled the icy water, and they were a hard-looking gang of men. Colt revolvers hung from their narrow hips, stocks of Winchesters protruded from their saddle scabbards, and stock ropes hung in coiled loops from their saddlehorns.

The eldest man, and obviously their leader, had a stern but strangely appealing ruggedness about him. In his early fifties, John Cole wore his years well, even though his swarthy face

1

was weather-creased from years of exposure to wind and sun. A full but neatly tended mustache was prominent on his upper lip, and its gray coloring matched the long sideburns visible beneath a wide-brimmed Stetson hat. A fur-lined jacket covered his broad shoulders, and there was a wiry leanness about him that bespoke a lifetime of hard labor. But it was the eyes that were the most prominent thing about him as he stared into the meandering stream bed. Azure blue, they had a cold depth to them, the deep look of bitterness and heartbreaking loss, the look of a man who had loved once in his lifetime, but who would never love again.

The man beside him, Jason Cole, was nearly an exact replica of his father, sans mustache and gray hair. At twenty years of age, hard years on the plains had left no mark on him, and the youthful vitality in his tanned face contrasted sharply with the rigid determination of the older man. Jason watched his father in silence and there was a look of deep compassion in his eyes as John Cole slowly removed his hat and held it by his side.

"You can't ever come here without remembering her, can you, Pa?" Jason said softly.

The elder Cole's thick, whitish-gray hair was brilliant in the strong morning sunlight, and he continued to stare down as though he had not heard what his son had said. Finally he spoke without looking up, and his words were muted, as if being uttered over the grave of a loved one.

"No I can't, son. Your ma was the most beautiful woman in the world and I loved her more than anything I've ever known, before or since. I still can't believe she's dead."

"It's been eighteen years now, Pa. You're going to have to get over her sometime."

"No, don't think so. You were only two years old when we lost her, so I can understand how you might forget. But—"

"I didn't say I forgot, Pa. What I meant was, it's time to accept the fact that Ma's never coming back to us."

John Cole slowly replaced his hat, tore his eyes from the stream bed, and stared upriver. "Eighteen years ago your grandpa was killed by the Sioux. We know that 'cause his body was found. I had taken you and your sister into Garderville with me for supplies, 'cause both you little tykes loved to ride up on the seat of the wagon with me. When we got back home your ma was gone, the homestead burned down, and all the

2

stock killed. No trace of your ma has ever been seen since that time."

Cole paused, rubbing an old knee injury with one hand and remembering the past. "I rebuilt the place in your ma's memory. Everything is just the way it was when I last saw her. And someday I'll find her and bring her home and it'll be just like she'd never left. Maybe like she was coming downstairs from a nap or something."

"If she wasn't killed, Pa, she was taken by the Sioux," Jason said gently. "She could never live with them for eighteen years."

"She was a strong-willed woman, your ma. If there was a way to survive, she'd find it. Just like I have, even when they put that Sioux reservation next to my land. God knows how I hate them, but I've learned to live with it."

Jason studied the stream bed. "It's a little ironic, isn't it, the government using Cole Creek as the boundary between our property and the reservation?"

"Yes it is. I didn't like it, but there wasn't anything I could do about it. This stream is our life's blood. That's why your grandpa and me chose this place. Without the water we get from this creek for our stock, the Grace Land spread, which I named after your ma, would be just another piece of useless prairie soil. That old creek there cuts through our ground, then into the reservation, runs along here, forming a boundary, and then back onto our place again. Even though I don't wish them well of any kind, Cole Creek here helps the Sioux just as much as it does us. And they need it just as bad."

"Well, they've never given us any trouble over it in the past, so maybe it's one thing we can share. Just as long as they stay on their side and we stay on ours, this water's free for anybody to use."

"I'm aware of that. That's why I come here every so often, to make sure—" .

"John? Look over yonder," said a hired hand named Mike Reeves, raising his gloved hand and pointing to the northwest. "Looks like about twenty of 'em to me."

Cole's eyes snapped in the direction indicated, and the hard look instantly returned to his face. A band of Sioux warriors sat their ponies on the crest of a prairie swell at a distance of possibly a hundred yards. They were uniformly dressed in

3

moccasins, tanned leggings, and vests; feathers dangled from their braided black hair. Each had a rifle across his lap, and there was a stoic silence about them, as if they had been frozen in time and were more a painting or a sculpture than living, breathing human beings.

Even though hatred instantly boiled in Cole's heart, he couldn't help but admire how magnificently wild and fierce the Sioux looked, and they reminded him of a herd of splendid antelope, swift and free.

"Son of bitches," he said under his breath. "Don't anybody move. I've never seen them this close to our ground before. If they want a fight, we'll give 'em one, but let them make the first move."

The two sides stared at each other in silence, separated only by the lush growth of greasy grass shifting in rhythm with the wafting breeze. The only alien sound was the drifting cry of a prairie falcon, shrieking primeval rage at a target missed. A minute, then two, elapsed before a lone warrior moved forward and walked his mount down the hill at a leisurely, almost unconcerned pace. They could see he was fairly young, possibly twenty, but his countenance was that of a man who had fought many battles and to whom the humility of defeat was an unknown phenomenon. When he stopped his horse at the edge of the stream, which was twenty yards wide at the crossing, a ragged scar was visible across his chest and exposed through the open buckskin vest. There was an air of nonchalant pride about the Sioux warrior, but his lean body was taut and poised like a man prepared to leap suddenly away from some danger yet unseen. He held his rifle in his right hand and gripped the hackamore in his left, jerking the pony's head up and denying it a drink of the water coursing past its hooves. He looked at the white men across from him with unflinching eyes and spoke in a controlled tone:

"Hear me! I am Black Eagle, chief of the Lakota. I will meet one of you at the middle of the stream. I have words that you must hear."

Jason immediately lifted his reins, then pulled his horse back at a gesture from his father. "You stay here, son. I'll go. If anything happens, put a bullet through his brain for your ma."

Urging his horse into the stream, Cole spoke as the animal moved toward the center of the creek through fetlock-deep

4

water. "My name is John Cole. I own the Grace Land spread and every damned head of cattle on it."

The Indian had matched Cole's move, and they stopped their horses at midstream, with the animals' heads not five feet apart. There was absolute silence between them as they stared evenly at one another while water gurgled around their horses' hooves. Finally, Cole spoke with bitter, contempt-encrusted words.

"You said you wanted to talk to me. I'm here. Let's get on with it."

The warrior's lips curled into a sneer and he nodded toward the far bank. "Why do they send one so old? Is the young one afraid of a Lakota warrior?"

"No, he's not afraid," Cole replied. "He's just not used to the putrid smell of bear grease. Say your piece."

"Peace? The white man says that word so easily. And always with the same result. You have taken Lakota land. And now you would take Lakota Minni as well."

"Minni?" Cole asked, genuinely confused. "I don't know what the hell you're talking about."

Black Eagle gestured downward with his rifle barrel. "Wakan Tonka has given this to us. No white man will take it away."

Cole glanced down and then back at the Sioux. "You mean water?"

"That's what I mean."

"Hell, boy, we don't want your water. This stream belongs to all of us, and nobody can take it away. Not me and not you."

"You are wrong. The Lakota do not wish to take it away from you. But you white men will take it away from us, like the flat-tailed one with the teeth."

Again, Cole was confused. "Do you mean beaver? Like a beaver dam?"

Black Eagle nodded, and there was hot contempt in his eyes. "*Heya*. You call them beaver. There were many, like buffalo, until the white man came."

"So what's this about a dam?" Cole asked, tiring of the confrontation.

"And you know nothing of it?"

"Not a goddamned thing."

"It is known that you hate the Lakota. I believe you wish

5

to take our water. The big chief in Wa-sha-tung will listen to you. He sends white men here to take our Minni."

Cole's eyes narrowed as he studied the young warrior, trying to figure out the meaning of his words. "What the hell are you talking about, boy?"

"Without Minni-Tonka we will have no game to hunt. We will be slaves of the agency, waiting for food that never comes." Black Eagle's chest swelled and he squared his shoulders. "The Lakota will make war first."

"Don't be rattlin' your saber too loud in my direction, son. If it's war you want, it's war you'll get. Now what the hell is all this bullshit about a dam? I don't want this creek dammed up any more than you do. I haven't talked to anybody in Washington about it, but I damned sure will if one is built. What say you knock off the bragging about making war and try to talk a little sense?"

A contemptuous sneer curled across Black Eagle's lips. "The white man talks with two tongues and you are no different. In the direction from which the darkness comes, where the Minni-Tonka cuts deep into the earth, they build this dam of yours. They are the men with the hairy ears, and they are many."

Cole fell silent, studying the Indian's words. He knew "the men with the hairy ears" was a reference to the Army Corps of Engineers, and he assumed the place where they were building was the one called Ryan's Ravine, which would be the only logical place for a dam. It was roughly a two-hour ride east from Lost Hat Crossing, and Cole felt a sense of dread fill his heart. If they actually were starting to build a dam, as it appeared they were, he knew it must be for some long-range purpose that could in no way be beneficial to his interest. Dams meant civilization, and civilization meant people. People equated to more homesteads and the loss of the federal land upon which he now had permits to graze his cattle. Not to mention the increased demands on an already limited water supply and tighter government control, which Cole hated even more than he did the Sioux. He had been watching the young warrior during the fleeting seconds it had taken for these thoughts to race through his mind, and now he lifted his reins, pulled his horse's head up, and prepared to turn away.

"Have you anything else to say to me?" he asked.

"*Heya*. If the Minni is taken away from us, all whites will die. I have spoken."

The two men stared at each other in extended silence, and Cole noticed a strange, disturbingly familiar look about the Sioux's eyes. Then he turned the horse toward the opposite bank.

"Spare me your threats, Black Eagle, or whoever in hell you are. You and your people won't be dealing with an old man and an unarmed woman this time. We're ready anytime you are."

He heard the clatter of hooves on rock behind him, and the splashing sounds of a horse running through water, and he knew the warrior was galloping his mount from the stream bed. Cole reined in before his son and turned to watch the band of Sioux vanish on the far side of the rolling prairie swell.

"What was that all about, Pa?" Jason Cole asked.

Cole turned to look at his son. "Two things, mostly. That young buck there says he's going to kill all of us. And it seems the damned fool government is going to dam up Cole Creek."

"Dam it up? Why?"

"Well, me and that lad didn't get into specifics, but for whatever reason it is, I'm not likin' it. Let's ride on over to Ryan's Ravine and have a look for ourselves. Any dams built on this creek will be built over my dead body."

Major Brian Sacke rose from the cot in his tent and studied his image in a hand-held mirror. Even though he was thirty-five years of age, he had not had much luck with the sideburns that had earned his branch of the service the appellation of "hairy ears," and he thought he looked just slightly ridiculous with his thick-lensed, gold-rimmed glasses and sparse blond mustache. But he hoped the addition of the mustache and traditional hairstyle would give him a degree of much-needed respect from the men of his command and provide an air of authority. At six feet tall, with a lean, sparsely built frame, Sacke was aware of his nickname—"beanpole with windows"—and even though it was never uttered in his presence, it still rankled on him.

At the sound of approaching footsteps, he quickly shoved the mirror under his cot and assumed an authoritative position at the field desk on one side of the command tent.

"Major Sacke?" a voice demanded while the tent flap was

7

thrown aside, and it was obvious the visitor had no intention of observing military courtesy.

Sacke turned to see the tall, rugged-looking captain who was five years his senior. "Yes, Captain Edgerton? What is it?"

"Where the hell's that mounted infantry unit that was supposed to be sent here to protect my men?"

Sacke noticed the customary lack of deference to rank, and he brushed his fledgling mustache with a nervous motion. "They should arrive any day now, Captain," he said, striving for an authoritative, confident tone and failing. "Is there some sort of problem?"

"Not now, Major, but there damned well might be. A band of about twenty featherheads was watching the timber detail this morning. Every damned one of 'em had a rifle, and the men said there was no question but that they were prepared to use them. Their leader, a young buck with a scar across his chest, damned near trampled Private Swanson when they rode away. I won't put up with that kind of shit, Major. We were sent here to build a dam, and even though this is a piss-poor place for one, that's just what we'll do."

There had long been a feeling of animosity between the captain and Major Sacke. Call it jealousy of rank, pure contempt, or absolute lack of respect, but whatever it was, the major had always tried to keep as much distance between them as possible and, in so doing, hide his fear of Edgerton. Sacke cleared his throat unnecessarily.

"Well, ah, Captain, I certainly won't have my men harassed," he said, remembering that he had forgotten to send a message notifying Captain Conway at Outpost Number Nine of his arrival at Garderville. "I'll send another dispatch immediately and tell that infantry captain to get his ass and his troops up here on the double. As you know, I'm not one to mince words when a direct order is disobeyed."

The captain smiled coldly. "No, I'm sure you're not. And I'm not one to have my men double-crossed. Personally, I hate the sight of a blue-leg, or anybody else who can't handle a plumb line, but it sounds to me like those Sioux were just part of a bigger war party, and I haven't got time to kick the shit out of them and stay on schedule too."

"No, that's true. We have a job to do and we weren't sent out here to fight."

8

"Hell, there's nothing I like better than a good scrap, Major. But there's a time and place for everything. My boys and I always seem to find time to squeeze in a little brawl along the way."

Without saluting, the captain spun on his heel and stalked away. Sacke watched him go, wondering how he had ever wound up in a roughneck outfit like a field unit of the Army Corps of Engineers. Sure, he allowed as he watched the vacant doorway, it was true he had earned an engineering degree in college, and it was equally true that he had experienced no desire to be assigned to a combat unit when he'd joined the army. But he had envisioned a staff position in planning and management back in Washington, where the cut of his uniform would turn the ladies' heads and the dirt would be under someone else's fingernails. Such a position had been his until that fateful night when he had been caught in the bedroom of the daughter of the senator from Delaware.

Everything had gone to hell for him after that, Sacke remembered, absently tapping a pencil on the desktop. He had been shipped out West to locate, survey, and initiate construction on several proposed dams. The Garderville dam was to be the first, and the major had been less than enthusiastic upon selecting the site and settling in under what were, to him, barbaric living conditions to wait out the construction process. What the hell, he had thought when he packed his transom away that final time nearly a month before, out in this godforsaken land, a dam's a dam.

Major Sacke rose dejectedly, peeked through the tent flap, then turned and produced a flask of whiskey from a lower drawer and poured generously into a glass. He sighed as the glass moved toward his lips and mumbled to himself, "What the hell is a man like me doing in a shithole like Garderville? It wouldn't even make a decent slum back in Wash—"

"Major Sacke?" came a hard voice from outside the tent, which the major immediately recognized as that of First Sergeant Fred Hatcher. Hatcher was a burly man, scarred from countless fights, and one who seemed to tolerate the major strictly through military necessity. "There's somebody out here to see you."

"Just—just a minute, Sergeant," Sacke replied, hastily downing the whiskey, wiping his lips, and replacing the bottle in the drawer. "I'll be right out!"

9

Sacke straightened, adjusted his uniform, belched discreetly, and then marched toward the tent flap like a man propelled through great motivation. As he stepped into the sunlight he adjusted his hat and looked up at the six mounted range hands staring down at him.

"Major, this man here calls himself John Cole," Hatcher said, pointing a blunt finger at the lead rider. "He don't seem to be too fond of our little project here. You talk to him. I've got work to do," the sergeant concluded, moving off toward the ravine.

Major Sacke stepped forward with a somewhat nervous smile and offered his hand upward. "Good afternoon, sir. I am Major Brian Sacke, battalion commander. What can I do for you?"

Cole hesitated, watching the major's face for long moments before finally accepting the handshake.

"Like your man there said, I'm John Cole. I own a cattle spread about ten miles from here." Cole spoke in a slow but emphatic voice and folded his hands across the saddlehorn while staring at Sacke with cold, hard eyes. "My cows sometimes get a terrible fondness for water, and they're used to drinkin' when the urge strikes them."

"So? What has that to do with me, Mr. Cole?"

Cole looked toward the ravine, where soldiers with picks and shovels were already preparing the escarpment of the dam, and then his attention shifted to another crew that was busily digging a ditch at an oblique angle to the northwest. After his gaze drifted over the men felling timber on the distant horizon, he looked again at Sacke.

"Everything," he said flatly. "Whose decision was it to build a dam here?"

Sacke cleared his throat and adjusted his glasses. "Well, I guess it was mine, sir. I selected the site and am in complete charge of construction."

"Then you're the idiot that I want to talk to."

"That's fairly strong language, Mr. Cole. I'm sure you intend to explain."

"You're damned right I do. Obviously some of your men are digging a channel over there to divert the water, isn't that right?"

"That is correct. There is a natural stream bed just over that rise—"

"And that one isn't?" Cole snapped, jabbing a finger toward Cole Creek.

"Please let me continue, Mr. Cole. That other natural stream bed," Sacke said with the pride of great knowledge, "is utilized only during the winter rains. On its boundaries lie some of the best land with farming potential in this area, if only water could be provided year 'round. Which it will be, once this dam is completed."

"Farming land!" Cole boomed. "Hell, boy, this is cattle country, and there ain't been a plow stuck in the ground yet!"

"It is the intention of the United States Government to see that that oversight is corrected," Sacke said cautiously.

"And it is the intention of John Cole to see that it isn't. My pappy died to build a homestead for his family here, and I'll damned sure die to see that it isn't taken away."

"No one is talking of taking your homestead away, Mr. Cole."

"Like hell you're not! Do you know the course of that 'natural streambed,' as you call it?"

"Certainly I do. I have mapped and charted all the land in this area." Sacke turned slightly and gestured toward the tent. "Would you care to see the maps?"

"I don't need to see any maps, boy. I was ridin' over this ground when you were still just a twinkle in your daddy's eye. I know every inch of it, every buffalo wallow, prairie dog town, and water hole." The stockman's eyes narrowed as he said the last words. "And I also know that Cole Creek is the only reliable source of water in this entire goddamned area."

"Precisely why it was selected for damming, sir, and if you don't mind my saying so, I think you're getting a bit overexcited."

"Overexcited, your ass! When you were making your fancy maps and charts, did you happen to notice where that other stream bed crosses my property?"

Sacke hesitated. "Well, I didn't actually visit the location, but from the natural direction of travel, through geological necessity, I'd say it would have to cross somewhere near the northeast corner."

"The *extreme* northeast corner, young feller. As she runs now, Cole Creek provides a natural boundary between my ground and the Sioux reservation. My cattle very rarely cross, 'cause the graze is just as good on my side as on the other.

11

They just go to the creek, get their drink, and then wander on back the way they came. Cattle are creatures of habit, Major, and if that stream isn't where they found it, they'll cross onto the Sioux reservation and I'm gonna have myself a war with a young buck named Black Eagle. That's the long of it. The short is, I've got just as much right to that water as anybody else, if not more."

"And your rights will not be impinged upon, Mr. Cole. As you just stated, the new stream will *cross* your property," Sacke said with a weak smile.

"At a point where it won't do me any more damned good than trying to fill a bucket with a spoon. And that's a little job I don't plan to take on."

"Well, I'm terribly sorry if this project is going to cause you some inconvenience, Mr. Cole, but there is little that can be done. The money has already been appropriated by Congress, the plans have been approved by the Department of the Interior, and considerable time and money have already been spent. It is the viewpoint of the current administration that the entire Western frontier should be opened up for additional settlers and not left dormant for a select few who happen to be in the cattle business. We in the Corps of Engineers have been entrusted with the responsibility to see that those objectives are met."

There was a hard glitter in Cole's eyes as he took up his reins again and shifted to a more comfortable position in the saddle. "Those few of us who happen to be in the cattle business provide damned near every scrap of meat eaten by the folks back East, Major. They have done that in the past and they will continue to do it in the future, and no four-eyed army major is going to change that. We settled this land, Major, when no one else had the guts to come out here. Our people died—men, women, and children alike—and we paid a terrible price to build what we have. There are other men just like myself further on down the line who depend on Cole Creek as much as I do. If you continue with this ridiculous project, you're going to have a hell of a lot more than just me and my men to contend with."

"Is that a threat, Mr. Cole?" Sacke asked, striving for authority in his tone.

"It's more than that, son. It's a promise."

"Any interference from you will be handled through proper

12

legal channels, sir. I have my orders and I intend to follow them out."

"Then good luck to you." Cole started to turn his horse around, but stopped and smiled down at Sacke. "I might as well let you know, you're going to have two sides to fight before this thing is settled."

A confused look crossed Sacke's face. "Two sides? I'm afraid I don't understand."

"When you were drawing your little lines and circles on those maps of yours, did you happen to follow the entire course of this proposed new creek?"

"Well, ah, not exactly. Why?"

"Because your stream is going to flow right through the center of the Sioux' summer campground. They'll be up to their asses in water every time they go into their tipis."

"Then . . . then . . ." Sacke stammered, "we'll just move them."

Cole's smile broadened. "Don't think you're going to get off that easy, Major. Those people have been moved about all they plan to be. They've got habits and traditions just like the rest of us. And one of the things they get the most riled up about is someone fooling with their burial grounds."

"Burial grounds? I have no intention to desecrate their burial grounds."

"You don't, huh?" Cole asked with a nod toward the tents spread out across the plains. "Just behind your tents there, maybe a couple hundred yards from where you're standing, is a place where the Sioux have buried their dead since the beginning of time. I wouldn't be surprised if, when your boys dug their shit trenches, they turned up a bone or two. You ain't real popular with Black Eagle right now, I suspect, and it's going to get worse."

Sacke glanced nervously in the direction indicated before looking up at Cole again. "Worse? How do you mean?"

"There's going to be a lake behind your dam, isn't there, Major?"

"Yes, of course. That's the purpose of the whole thing."

"And there's your problem. Those Sioux aren't going to appreciate having to dive down twenty feet just to visit the graves of their ancestors. Which they'll have to do, because their entire burial ground is going to be covered with water." Cole smiled again and touched the brim of his hat with two fingers while flicking spurs against his horse's flanks. "Like I said, Major, good luck."

A sinking, dejected feeling swept through Sacke as he watched the six horses gallop away. Then, turning, he scurried toward his tent, stepped inside, and began hurriedly to scrawl out the message to be sent to Outpost Number Nine.

two

"Sergeant? Could you come in here a minute, please?"

"Yes, sir. Just one second."

Captain Warner Conway pursed his lips and continued to survey the inspection report in his hands. He was a tall, distinguished-looking man in his mid-forties, with hair slightly graying at the temples, and the blue uniform with its captain's bars looked impressive on him. In spite of long years and numerous campaigns, his body was still trim and there was a look of confidence about him, the look of a man born to command, yet self-assured enough to understand the meaning of compassion. Born a Virginian, he had served as a lieutenant colonel under General Grant during the Civil War, and even though he'd been reduced in rank at the end of the conflict and was overdue for promotion now, there was not the slightest indication of bitterness about him.

Now he served as commanding officer of Outpost Number Nine, which was manned by Easy Company, a mounted infantry outfit. Located on the High Plains of Wyoming Territory, the outpost was situated to protect the vital communications

15

link known as the South Pass over the Rocky Mountains.

The door opened and Acting First Sergeant Ben Cohen poked his head inside.

"You wanted to see me, sir?"

"Yes, Ben. Come on in. Have a seat."

Ben Cohen stepped through the doorway, which framed his broad shoulders, thick neck, barrel chest, and powerful forearms, at the ends of which hung hamlike fists with scarred knuckles that gave silent testimony to behind-the-barracks discipline meted out in the past. Cohen took a seat in a chair before the desk while Conway glanced up from the report.

"What's the book on this new recruit, Private Greer? From what I've seen here, he isn't exactly blue-ribbon material, if you know what I mean."

"He isn't, sir. More of the same shit we've wound up with before. A young kid, big for his age but dumber than a brick, probably run away from home and didn't have anyplace else to go but the army."

"Can he soldier?"

"Don't think so, sir. I never thought we'd get anybody out here worse than Malone, but I'm afraid we have."

"Oh, Malone's all right, Ben. He'd probably be a damned good soldier if we never paid him and kept him restricted to the post."

"They go together like hand and glove, sir. Pay, pass, drunk, fight, and restriction. But Greer's an entirely different matter."

"In what way?" Conway asked, selecting a cigar from the box on his desk, lighting it, and then leaning back in his chair.

"In just about every way, sir, except with regard to intelligence. He doesn't drink, I don't think he's ever been in a fight in his life, and he kind of holds back, doesn't say much, and seems to prefer being by himself."

"That doesn't make him a bad soldier, Ben," Conway offered gently.

"No it doesn't, sir. But it does make him a misfit, and the other men are starting to needle him a little bit more than usual. Especially after last payday."

"What happened then?"

"He turned down his pass into town, gave ten of his thirteen dollars to me for safekeeping, and volunteered for stable duty. Horses seem to be the one thing he cares about, and he'd rather be around them instead of the other men."

16

Cohen hesitated, watching the captain. "And women in town as well."

"What's your point? Are you saying you think he's a homosexual?"

"I have no idea. But the men in his barracks are beginning to call him 'Queer Greer.' And they've labeled him a kiss-ass for turning down leave time and volunteering for extra duty."

Conway considered this briefly. "Yes, that could be trouble. Keep an eye on him and give me an opinion when you can. We can't have dissension within the ranks, no matter how slight. Also, refuse him extra duty. If he doesn't want to take his passes as they come up, that's fine. He can stay here on post and lie on his bunk if that's what he wants to do."

"I agree, sir, and I would have mentioned it if you hadn't. These regular soldiers of ours are hard men, Captain. They've been through a lot and haven't broken yet and they don't take too kindly to anyone that they think might be a sissy. They know their life might depend on his ability to fight some day."

Conway blew out a stream of smoke and contemplated the moist tobacco at the end of his cigar. "It very well might. But Greer hasn't been tested in the field yet. Who knows? He might surprise us all."

"I hope so, sir. For his sake."

"We'll just have to wait and see, I guess. In the meantime—"

The captain's words were interrupted by a knocking on the door followed by the words, "Excuse me, sir. But I've got a telegram here that you should see as quickly as possible."

"Come on in, Matt," Conway replied.

The door swung to one side and First Lieutenant Matt Kincaid stepped into the room. Kincaid was broad-shouldered, narrow at the hips. With his tall, lean build, the blue uniform, accented with light blue piping, gave him an air of authority and he walked like a man prepared to meet any challenge that might confront him.

"Morning, Sarge," Kincaid said with an easy smile as he crossed the room and stopped before Conway's desk.

"Good morning, sir," Cohen replied, eyeing the dispatch envelope in the officer's hand. "Why is it that I feel suddenly tired every time I see one of those damned things?"

"Because all that's ever in these envelopes is bad news. This one is no exception." Kincaid looked at the captain. "Do

17

you remember that telegram we received about three weeks ago from Washington? The one telling us there was an engineering outfit on its way out here to build a dam, and that we should be prepared to give support if requested?"

"Yes, Matt, I do. Is that the request there in your hand?"

"Yes it is, sir," Kincaid replied, handing the message across the desk to the captain, who broke the seal, opened the envelope, and removed the sheet of cream-colored paper with its frantic scrawl of black ink.

Conway smoothed the paper on the desk, leaned over it, and read aloud:

"'Captain Conway: You are hereby ordered to bring your entire command to provide aid and protection to my battalion during the construction of the Garderville Dam and Irrigation Project. Please be advised, I am contending with hostile elements both among the Indians and the local population. My men are harassed daily.

'This matter is to be given highest priority, superseding all existing orders. Failure to comply to the fullest will result in court-martial.

'Major Brian Sacke, Commanding.'"

Conway looked up, and there was a wry smile pulling at the corners of his mouth. "Sounds to me like what he's saying is, 'Help, or else.'"

Kincaid nodded. "Yes, sir. What galls me is that Major Sacke seems to think he has to threaten us in order to get help we've already been asked to provide."

Conway paused to relight his cigar and leaned back once more. "Those engineering types are a strange lot, Matt. The Corp of Engineers, as a whole, is the darling child of Congress and they pretty much get what they want. Many of their officers, especially those with engineering degrees from major universities, have risen to the top, and most of them are too young and inexperienced to go to the latrine by themselves, let alone command an entire battalion. Other officers, older and more seasoned, have been passed over in the process, and you often find a young officer giving orders to older men with more time in grade, which, as I'm sure you realize, leads to a lot of resentment.

"Generally speaking, engineering outfits are just about as tough as they come, and I've known a few front-line infantry outfits that have gotten their butts kicked royally when the two bunches happen to wander into the same saloon. There's not one of them who would come crying to a mounted infantry unit to pull their fat out of the fire, and that includes the officers who have risen through the ranks on merit for service in the field. Obviously that's not the case with our Major Brian Sacke, Commanding."

Cohen cracked his knuckles with a crunching pop before flexing his fingers in remembrance. "They're a tough bunch, sir, I can personally testify to that as a fact. This Major Sacke sounds more like a shavetail second lieutenant still pissin' West Point water than CO of a tough engineering battalion."

"That he does, Ben. I've found it to be true in the past that if a man has to hide behind rank, he's generally got a stomach problem."

Kincaid smiled. "No guts?"

"No guts."

"Wyoming Territory is a hell of a place for a man like that to be, Captain. Especially if you're one of the poor bastards serving under him."

"No doubt about it. Have either of you seen Windy?"

"Yes, I did, Captain," Kincaid replied, crossing to the window and looking out. "He wanted to pick up a chaw of cut-plug. He knows about the message. He should be here any minute. As a matter of fact, he's crossing the parade right now."

"Good. Maybe he can fill us in on a little bit of what to expect up there. According to what I can make out from the map, Garderville is about a day and a half's ride northeast of here. I'm not familiar with the exact location of this construction site, but—"

The captain stopped talking as the chief scout for Easy Company stepped through the doorway. Wearing fringed buckskins with a revolver sagging from one hip and a bowie knife from the other, Windy Mandalian was the embodiment of frontier strength and spirit. His rugged face was dominated by an aquiline nose, and his dark features, combined with his taciturn ways, gave him an unsettling, Indian-like appearance. Rumor had it that there was in fact some Cree blood in his veins. He was known by all in the High Plains country as a fearless, formidable force on the field of combat, while he was admired for his fairness of mind and desire to resolve issues without a fight. But when fighting was the final alternative, there were few, either Indian or white, who wished to cast their lot against him.

"Morning, gents," Windy said in an easy, laconic voice. "Matt said you'd probably be wantin' to jaw a mite with me, Captain."

"Yes, Windy. Thanks for coming." Conway made no offer of a seat, as he knew the scout generally preferred to stand. "Let's get right to the point. What do you know about the country up around Garderville?"

"More'n some, less'n others, I 'spect."

Conway read him the dispatch, then asked him what he made of it. Windy scratched his black whiskers vigorously and replied, "Well, Captain, accordin' to that telegram, it sounds to me like this Major Sacke is wearin' his brains where his asshole should be. The only place where they could build any kind of a dam up there would be in a place they call Ryan's Ravine. A pretty good-sized stream called Cole Creek runs through there. It was named for a man called Josh Cole, after the Sioux put an arrow through his back and lifted his scalp. His son John runs cattle on the homestead now, with a lot of government land leased to him besides."

"Do you know him?"

"Met him a time or two, right after his pa was killed. Matter of fact, I helped track down some of the killers. Never did find his wife, though."

"His wife?"

"Yup. His wife turned up missin' same time his pa was killed. Old John thinks the Sioux took her."

"Did they?"

"Like I said, Captain, we never did find her."

"Is he the kind of man who would harass an engineering battalion trying to build a dam?"

"I suppose he would, if he thought they were gonna take his water away, which, knowin' the government, they probably aim to do. Don't blame him a damned bit if he does. Worst place in the world for a damned dam anyway."

"I don't know any of the particulars, Windy. Why do you say that?"

"Well, if they're gonna build a dam, that must mean they want the water for irrigation to set up some farms in the area. Hell, if they want to do that, water's the last thing they need."

Kincaid had been listening to the conversation, and now he

said, "I'm afraid I don't understand, Windy."

"That's 'cause you ain't a farmer, Matt," the scout said, glancing at Kincaid with a sly grin.

"And you are?"

"Nope. But I do know somethin' about it. All that prairie land around Garderville is stone-hard pan. Ground looks just fine on top, but down about two feet it's harder'n sun-baked adobe. The water just lays there, and any seed some poor bastard plants will rot before it ever kicks up any crops. Summer wheat is about the only thing they could grow, and natural rain would take care of that. Ride across that country in the fall, winter, or spring, and it's like ridin' across a swamp."

"Then why the hell would the government want to build a dam there? If what you just said is accurate, that's absolutely stupid in the first place."

Windy's grin widened. "I think you just answered your own question, Matt."

"Major Sacke mentioned some Indian problem, Windy. Can you fill us in on that?" Conway asked.

"Some, I s'pose. Cole Creek separates Cole's property from the Oskalla Sioux reservation at one point. Now the Sioux were given that land after losing their rights to the Paha Sapa after going on the warpath, as all three of you know. The ones that didn't go north to Canada with Sitting Bull, that is. I've heard rumors that some of the young ones have slipped back down to Wyoming Territory, but I don't know it for a fact. One of them is supposed to be the son of Stalking Crow, a Lakota chief, and he's a young buck who goes by the name of Black Eagle. Supposed to be a real hothead. Anyway, the Sioux who turned themselves in were promised that they would never have to move again and that no more land would be taken from them. I don't 'spect they'd look real kindly on the government building a dam on their property, which Ryan's Ravine is. That section was given to them because it's an ancient burial ground, and the Sioux are mighty superstitious about the way their spirits are treated."

"Sounds like kind of a mess, doesn't it, sir?" Cohen asked. "Apparently Cole thinks he has a legitimate bitch, the Sioux think they have too, and without a doubt, Major Sacke thinks he is doing the right thing. Kind of sounds like Easy is caught in the middle again."

"Yes it does, Ben. And when everybody thinks they're right

21

and justified in their actions, it creates an especially dangerous situation. Have two platoons prepared to move out this afternoon. Which one is Greer in?"

"Third, sir."

"That's good. They're due for combat patrol anyway, according to the rotation. Make it the first and third. Have them outfitted for a long stay in the field."

"Yessir," Cohen replied, rising and moving toward the door.

"Ben?" Conway said as the sergeant passed through the doorway.

Cohen stopped and turned. "Yessir?"

"You've been pretty much confined to that desk for quite a while now. How would you like to go along with Matt and Windy?"

The sergeant's lips split into a wide grin. "I'd love it, sir."

"Fine. I can take care of things around here while you're gone. If those engineers are as tough as we both think they are, Easy might need a senior noncom along who knows the ropes in the back alleys himself."

"I was born there, sir. It'll be my pleasure."

"I thought that was the way you'd feel. Have the troops prepared to move out in two hours."

"Right, sir," Cohen replied, easing through the doorway again.

After Cohen had gone, Kincaid turned to the captain and offered a knowing grin. "If you're expecting that kind of trouble, sir, maybe we'd better send Maggie along as well."

Conway shook his head at Kincaid's reference to Cohen's fiery Irish wife. "No, we'd better give Sacke's boys a little break. I'm afraid Maggie would whip two squads of them all by herself."

Kincaid's face sobered now as he glanced at the dispatch again. "Those engineers aren't going to like being baby-sat by a mounted infantry outfit, Captain. There has never been any love lost between them and us. I doubt that they'd ask us to come if they had their way."

"I know. And we wouldn't go if we had ours." Conway looked at Kincaid with understanding, calculating eyes. "The same rules apply to this mission as they have to those in the past, Matt. Use your best judgment and do whatever has to be done. I'll back you up one hundred percent. You're going to be up against a major and, since it's a full battalion, three

22

captains as well. Not to mention an equal complement of officers of your own rank. Don't forget, you were given specific orders to go there and protect that engineering battalion." Conway hesitated and repeated the words again. "You were given specific *orders* by Major Sacke, and that gives you a free hand to do what must be done. Even though he outranks you, he can't interfere in your operation unless he rescinds that order. If he does that, you simply come back here. That is my direct order. We'll see what happens after that."

"I understand, sir, and thank you. I wouldn't be surprised if a little leverage might be necessary. From the way it looks at first blush, he's going to be some kind of character to deal with."

"Count on it," Conway replied as his gaze shifted to Mandalian. "Windy? See if you can't nose around and find out what those Sioux are up to. Let's try to settle this thing without a fight if possible."

"That's a tune that might be easier to hum than sing, Captain. If those engineers are already digging on Lakota ground, they're bound to be more than a little pissed off. Another army outfit came onto their tribal homeland in the Paha Sapa and started digging around. One of the military geniuses was named George Custer, as I'm sure you recall, and his troops found a little something called gold. I doubt the Lakota have forgotten what happened to them after that, and I'd bet my last nickel they won't go for it again."

"I know," Conway said with a helpless shrug, "but what the hell else can we do?"

Windy smiled crookedly. "We could just leave 'em alone, Captain. That's all they wanted in the first place."

His name was Charlie Simms, a diminutive man with a leprechaunish beard, pointed and gray with age. As Indian agent for the Oskalla reservation, he had been informed of the proposed dam on Cole Creek and had protested vehemently to the authorities back in Washington, with little or no success. He knew the Lakota—or Sioux, as the Bureau of Indian Affairs incorrectly referred to them—and found them to be among the fiercest, deadliest, and proudest of all the Plains Indians he had ever encountered in his long years of service to the government. His involvement with the Sioux had been a love-hate relationship, but there was always an underlying aura of mutual respect.

23

Simms knew of their problems, sympathized with their losses, and tried to get them to understand that no matter how badly they wished to turn back the clock, the life their ancestors had enjoyed for centuries would never be known again. The westward expansion of white civilization was a burgeoning reality, and the only chance the Lakota would have would be assimilation into the white American culture, if such a thing were possible.

The older ones seemed confused and bewildered, while those just coming of age had fallen into the trap of bitterness and resentment. It was in that atmosphere that Charlie Simms had broken with his old friend, Sitting Bull, and sadly watched him lead his people away from their homeland and into the vast wilderness of Canada. And now it was with the same heavy heart that he turned his horse away from the agency and in the direction of Ryan's Ravine, as he had done several times previously. On those occasions he had found Major Sacke to be totally closed-minded on the subject of the dam's feasibility. He had rested his entire case on the fact that the Sioux were not farmers, had no intention of becoming farmers, and would not tolerate the loss of any more of their land to those who would farm the region. Because of the major's intractable attitude and curt dismissal of any compromise, Simms had not gone into the subject of the burial ground, or the need to relocate the Sioux village once the project was completed. He had felt that common sense would eventually prevail, but now, with construction started, he was determined to impress on the major's mind the likely consequences of actions taken. Simms knew the Sioux would not relocate again peacefully, and with Black Eagle and Medicine Hawk in the territory once more, he was certain there would be reprisals for the flooding of an ancient Lakota burial ground.

As the agent rode leisurely in the warm morning sun across the plains he so dearly loved, Black Eagle was particularly plaguing to his mind. He knew of the warrior's background and thought he could understand the intense hatred burning in his heart. After all, Simms mentally observed as he negotiated a dry wash, it must be an exceptionally difficult thing to be the son of a proud Lakota chieftain who had been senselessly murdered by a white man. Through reports from other Indians who had fled to Canada with Sitting Bull, as had Stalking Crow with his family, and then returned, he'd learned of the chief's death at the hands of a white fur trapper along the banks of a river in the wilds. Stalking Crow had just shot an otter with his bow and arrow and was retrieving it from the stream when a .44-40 slug crashed into his back and slammed him to senseless death in the chill water. Young Black Eagle, armed only with a knife, had attacked the trapper and killed him, but not before the knife blade had been drawn across his own chest, leaving a scar that was both a badge of triumph and a constant reminder of his hatred for white people.

Angry, hurt, and bent on revenge, Black Eagle had returned to Wyoming Territory with a large band of other young warriors who shared his desire to reclaim their homeland or die in the attempt. But for all of Black Eagle's vengeful inclinations, Simms had a secret conviction deep in his heart that the young warrior's restless anger could be vented in a direction other than war, if it were not for one man: Medicine Hawk. Medicine Hawk was perhaps five years older than his young chief, and there was something about him that instantly prompted a feeling of uneasiness in Simms on the occasions when he had met him before the march to Canada. There was a cunning deceitfulness that permeated his being, the look of a coward and a bully who would only fight if he had a decided advantage. He reminded the agent of a skulking coyote as he thought about him now— a coyote biding its time and waiting for a weak calf to stray from the herd so that victory could be achieved quickly, mercilessly, with no chance for reprisal. And even though he had not seen Black Eagle since his return from the north, Simms had learned that Medicine Hawk was with him and had become the chief's inseparable companion and constant advisor.

Feeling the pleasant sensation of heat spreading across his shoulders and down his spine, Charlie Simms began to remove his jacket while the horse picked its leisurely way through a shallow draw breasted on either side by rolling, undulating hills. With the coat just down to his elbows and immobilizing either arm, he concentrated to get free of one sleeve and reached behind his back to grasp a cuff with his right hand.

"*Heya*, white devil!"

Simms glanced up in startled surprise and saw twenty warriors galloping toward him, ten on either side and appearing suddenly upon the crest of the swells. The agent struggled to pull the coat up over his shoulders again, but a hand grasped the material behind his back in the same instant that another snatched his reins up with a jerk.

Simms instantly recognized Medicine Hawk, holding the reins with a cruel, triumphant smile while Black Eagle silently watched the agent from off to one side.

Ignoring Medicine Hawk, Simms offered a cordial, generous smile toward the young chief. He had always liked Black Eagle in the early days before the Battle of the Little Big Horn, and he had known at that time that he would develop into a powerful leader of his people. He could see in the Indian's eyes that he felt none of the triumph over the agent's capture that Medicine Hawk enjoyed, but there was still that haughty pride and spirit.

"Hello, Black Eagle. It's a pleasure to see you again."

The Sioux nodded curtly toward the agent while waving a hand, and the Indian behind him released Simms' jacket.

The agent smiled again and shrugged into his coat. "Thank you, Black Eagle. These old arms don't take the bendin' like they used to."

Black Eagle continued to watch him in silence for several seconds before saying, "You have lied to my people, gray one."

"Lied? How have I lied to you?"

"The white man's crazy water. You knew of it and did nothing to stop it."

"I'm afraid you're wrong, my friend. I—"

"You are not my friend," Black Eagle interjected tartly.

"Perhaps not, but I was a friend of your father. Is it not the way of your people to honor friendships established by your elders?"

Simms thought he detected a hint of uncertainty in the warrior's eyes before it was corrected.

"Our old ones are dead. We, the young, make no friends with white men and wish only to see no more of you."

"And I wish it could be that way as well, Black Eagle. But I know differently. You have to accept the white man's way or die by it."

"We are not afraid to die, gray one. And we are not afraid to kill."

"We should start with him," Medicine Hawk said with a threatening shake of his Spencer toward the agent. "It would show the others that we do not play children's games."

Simms watched the Indian evenly, with no indication of fear. "I am not afraid to die, either, Medicine Hawk. And I would expect my death to come at the hands of a cowardly liar like you. It is worthless scum like you who make the white leaders think they are justified in the treatment of other people."

Instantly, Medicine Hawk swung his rifle and the tip of the weapon cracked along the side of the agent's jaw. The sight tore a deep gash in his cheek. The gray beard turned crimson with the sudden flow of blood, but Simms did not fall as he stared icily at the warrior. Enraged, Medicine Hawk slammed the barrel down, and the agent's hat fell off, exposing his balding head to the sun. The old man's shoulders drooped, he sagged sideways and toppled from the saddle.

"That is enough, Medicine Hawk. If it is time for the gray-beard to die, I will be the one to kill him."

"It is time," Medicine Hawk replied, excitement glinting brightly in his dark eyes. "Kill him now."

After struggling to a sitting position, Simms forced one leg beneath him, then rose to one knee. He found his hat and placed it gingerly on his head as he looked up at the Sioux chief. They watched each other in silence momentarily before Simms said, "I am ready when you are, Black Eagle. Prove to yourself and the others that you are just as great a coward as Medicine Hawk."

"Say no more, old one."

"Why not? Your father and all the great Lakota chiefs who have gone before him would be very proud to see you do the work of a crazy woman. And when Wakan Tonka calls for you, you will go to him not with the great bonnet of a brave warrior, but instead with the shaven head of a coward."

"I will hear no more from you. Your life will be spared this day, but you may not be so lucky next time," Black Eagle replied, staring down at the agent, who had managed to rise to his feet. "Where are you going?"

"To do my job. To try and talk the army major out of going ahead with his proposed dam. It is useless, I know, but I have to try one more time."

"It is useless, as you say. There is no more time for talk. Stay away from there."

"Why?"

"I have told you, stay away. That is enough. I have spoken."

27

With those words, the warrior lifted his hackamore and raced across the plains in the direction of Ryan's Ravine, with the others following close behind.

Charlie Simms watched until they had disappeared, then wearily lifted boot to stirrup, dragged his body upward, and settled unsteadily into the saddle. He could feel the burning lump beneath his hat, and the blood-encrusted beard was stiff along his jaw, but he stared straight ahead, giving no indication of pain. His eyes never wavered from their focus on the horizon, like a blind man's eyes as he moved forward through a lifetime of eternal night.

three _____

Sergeant Hatcher heard the tearing crash of another tree hitting the ground, and with a calculating glance at the lowering sun, he estimated at least an hour, maybe two hours of light left before his crews would have to withdraw for the day. The timber details had been working well, with nearly enough jack-pine felled and trimmed to begin setting the first layers of the dam. The diversion channel was proceeding equally well, and by the time they neared the water level, a sufficient amount of logs would be available to dam the stream and alter the creek's flow, thus making possible the completion of the re-mainder of the dam. Ground was now being cleared for the pipeline that would be required through the low prairie swell to bring water to a thirsty land, and he felt a sense of pride in the efforts of his battalion. These soldiers of his, who were not paid to engage in military campaigns—thick-armed, burly men—worked with a kind of silent dedication in a manner that would make one think they truly loved the back-breaking labor to which they were constantly subjected.

Hatcher was not known among his troops as a gentle man,

and few others labored under that misconception either. His nose, broken many times in various brawls, was slightly twisted to one side, and there was a thick flatness about it that gave his face a stepped-on appearance. A scar ran from the lower right-hand corner of his mouth to the point of his jaw, and his right ear was disfigured from an ancient wound never properly treated. In general, there was a threateningly sinister look about him, and the turned-down corners of his mouth did little to alter that appearance. Hatcher was proud of his reputation as a fighter, and passed up no opportunity to improve upon a record that contained no losses in recent memory.

On the other hand, Hatcher was thoroughly dedicated to the men who served under him, and those who did not meet his standards were soon whipped into line or pleading for transfers to another assignment. Originally a farm boy from Illinois, he took great delight in seeing anything grow as the result of hard labor, and he brought that same sense of commitment to his love for the Army Corps of Engineers. There was a fierce pride about him concerning his branch of the service, and God help the man who gave voice to a dissenting opinion.

Perhaps it was the mellowness of the coming evening, or the satisfaction of a day's work well done, but in either case, Hatcher felt a warmth well up within him as he watched two men loop chains around a pair of logs and expertly attach them to the trace lines of a pair of mules. He approached the soldiers and rested a hand on the rump of the mule nearest to him.

"Harris, you take this turn on back to the site while me and Arnie rig up one more round. That'll be about it for today. We're gonna be out of light pretty soon now."

"Sure, Sarge," Harris replied with a grin. "I got me a pass to go into town tonight and I ain't had my ashes hauled in better'n a month now. I'm horny as a tomcat, and this day can't end too fast for me."

"Aw, don't listen to that bullshit, Sarge," Arnie replied with a wink. "If he got laid last month, I'm a goddamned choirboy."

"You ain't been inside a church since Custer was a corporal, you old bastard," Harris snorted, taking up the lead rein. "And as far as gettin' laid goes, ever' time we go into town, I've gotta point out to ya which is the girls and which ain't. Someday maybe I'll teach—"

The rifle shot snapped like a bolt of prairie lightning, and Private Harris didn't live to finish his sentence. The bullet smacked into his chest and he spun in a drunken stagger to one

30

side before pitching facedown onto the grass with a hole torn through his left shoulder blade where the slug had exited.

Hatcher immediately dove for the cover of a tree stump, while several more rounds tore into sod and wood, like angry hornets seeking out their prey. Corporal Arnie Sorenson remained standing with horror-filled eyes fixed on his dead friend, and his body seemed immobilized by shock. Hearing more weapons open fire from the cover of the trees, Hatcher looked away for an instant to bellow an order to his stunned soldiers.

"Get to your weapons, men! Fall back and form a defensive firing line!"

The engineers bolted from their work stations to snatch rifles from where they had been stacked, and ran in crouched positions to throw themselves behind any barrier that might provide protection. Then the sergeant heard the mules bray in terror, and the trace chains rattled violently as the animals bucked and kicked in their panic. Miraculously, Sorenson had not been hit even though he had made no effort to seek cover. Finally the mules could take no more and they plunged toward the open prairie, snapping the drag chain tight.

"Look out, Arnie! Behind you!" Hatcher yelled frantically, but his warning came too late. The twin jackpine logs jerked forward, and the one to the left crashed into Sorenson's knees, throwing him to the ground and beneath the bouncing, thrashing logs trailing behind the panic-stricken mules. He was dragged under the load for nearly fifty yards before falling into a slight depression. One motionless, booted foot remained visible above the lip of the depression. Nausea swept through the sergeant's stomach and the urge to vomit rose in his throat.

The soldiers behind him were firing with sporadic, poorly aimed shots at ghostly targets filtering through the trees, and as suddenly as it had begun, the shooting from beyond the treeline stopped and an uneasy silence settled over the work site. Rising cautiously, Hatcher saw one lone Indian's mount burst through an opening in the timber, and then it too was gone.

"Hold your fire! The dirty bastards have quit!" the sergeant said as he rose to his knees, drew his feet beneath him, and sprinted toward the depression. Sorenson's uniform had been torn to shreds, he was bleeding profusely from several wounds, and one arm was twisted grotesquely beneath his back.

Hatcher gulped in several deep breaths as he knelt down

31

beside the wounded soldier and gently touched his hair.

"Arnie? Can you hear me?"

Sorenson's eyelids fluttered before opening slowly, and his eyes were blood-red from burst vessels. His mouth was swollen, bleeding, and bruised, but he managed to utter a few pained words.

"Sorry, Sarge. How's . . . how's Harris?"

"He's dead, Arnie. Killed by the first shot."

It seemed as though Sorenson tried to nod, but the pain was too great and Hatcher knew immediately that the man's neck was broken. "You're gonna be all right, Arnie," Hatcher said soothingly but without conviction. "You're banged up pretty bad, but you're too damned tough to let a couple of logs get the best of ya."

Sorenson smiled weakly, and as if they were too heavy to hold open, his eyelids slowly closed. The tensed muscles in his neck relaxed and his head lolled to one side to rest against his shoulder.

"Arnie?" Hatcher said urgently.

Silence.

"Arnie!" Hatcher said again. A rattle escaped Sorenson's throat and Hatcher said no more. He knew the soldier was dead.

Hatcher stared at the corpse for nearly a minute while his eyes gradually filled with tears. And when he finally rose and turned toward the forest, moisture glistened in twin trails down his cheeks, and his body trembled with rage. Hatcher's fist rose as a clenched hammer and he shook it toward the treeline.

"Come on, you dirty sonsabitches!" The sergeant's enraged voice rattled off the darkening timber. "Come on and fight, you filthy red bastards! You goddamned cowardly cocksuckers!"

Hatcher's men watched him in silence from a distance while their sergeant continued to scream his fury at an enemy long since gone. To a man, they felt an eerie sensation creep over them as a lone soldier stood there, his shadow stretched long in the setting sun, and screamed his pain into the gathering twilight.

Charlie Simms approached Major Sacke's tent ten minutes before the first shot would be fired and the futility of his mission would be proven true.

"You back here again?" Sacke asked, looking up from the plans spread across his desk as Simms entered the tent.

"Yes I am, Major. And I think you'd better listen to what I have to say."

"I have already given you an inordinate amount of my time, Mr. Simms. I am a very busy man and—what the hell happened to your face?"

Simms touched his jaw gingerly. "What happened to my face is exactly the same thing I am here to prevent happening to someone else's face."

"What the hell's that supposed to mean?"

"The Sioux are prepared to go on the warpath to prevent construction of this dam. They have already passed that threat on to me and I wouldn't be surprised if they're on their way here now."

"My dear Mr. Simms," Sacke replied superciliously, "I can't let a little threat from a few worthless renegades interfere with this project. Our work here has been sanctioned by the United States Congress, man. Can't you understand that? Now which comes first, the wishes of our government or the selfish demands of a handful of Indians who ought to feel damned lucky to have what we've given them?"

"What is the point of giving something with one hand and taking it away with the other?"

"We are taking nothing away from them. Hell, man, they'll benefit from this diversion as much as white people will! Christ, they can use the new stream bed for a swimming hole if they want to, for all I care."

"The Sioux don't swim."

"They can wade then, dammit!"

"Water to them has no reference to sport, Major."

Sacke's eyebrows arched disdainfully. "Mr. Simms, as I said before, I'm a very busy man. Now if you came all the way here to tell me this drivel, I'll have to say thanks but no thanks." He turned back toward the desk. "If you'll excuse me, sir?"

"I came here to tell you that you're not dealing with a handful of malcontents, nor are you dealing with a handful of renegades. Renegades, yes, but not a mere handful. Upon the strength of rumors I've heard, I would estimate the strength of Black Eagle's forces at somewhere near two hundred, and his right-hand man is a warrior named Medicine Hawk, who is bloodthirsty, ruthless, and bent upon the death of all whites on or near the Oskalla reservation."

Sacke turned slowly as a condescending smile spread across his face. "I don't derive statistical data on the strength of rumors, Mr. Simms. We in the engineers deal with precise facts and figures. Estimates are the fool's fodder of those who count buffalo for a living. And even if your rumors have the slightest hint of truth about them, there is an entire company of mounted infantry on the way here this very second to provide whatever security might be necessary to enable us to complete this project."

Simms shook his head in weary resignation. "You are inviting a bloodbath, Major Sacke. Have you no compassion for those who might die as a result of this useless project of yours?"

"Useless project! I'll have you know, sir, this is a high-priority matter with the people in power back in Washington!"

"People in power, did you say, Major?" Simms asked with a knowing smile. "And once this project is completed, those 'people in power' will know exactly whose was the guiding hand, won't they? That's very important to you, isn't it, Major? Even more important, perhaps, than preventing the loss of life?"

Sacke cleared his throat and adjusted his glasses. "Well, while I am only following orders and doing my duty, I would not be surprised if a promotion came my way for successful completion of a difficult assignment. There is even the possibility of reassignment to the general's staff, where I rightly belong. But let me assure you—"

The distant crack of a rifle silenced the major, and he listened in slack-jawed concentration at the popping sounds of several more weapons firing in rapid succession.

"What the hell is that?" Sacke asked, lurching to his feet and tearing at the flap covering the revolver in his holster. "Was that rifle fire?"

"Yes it was, Major," the agent replied with soft resignation. "I think the real price for your precious dam, the cost in human lives, is about to be exacted."

After he finally tore the reluctant flap free, he drew the revolver out clumsily and rushed toward the door of the tent, with Simms following behind.

As they stepped into the evening air, Captain Edgerton pounded up on his horse and pulled it to a plunging stop. His face was livid with anger and his eyes were filled with cold, hard contempt.

"The timber detail has come under fire, Major. Where the hell is that mounted infantry outfit?"

"Well, ah, they should be here any time now . . . Captain."

"'Any time now' isn't good enough. I told you to keep one of our companies back to provide a security guard, but you, in your all-fired, goddamned hurry to make a good showing here, said that wouldn't be necessary."

"I was told we would have security provided by other forces, Captain," Sacke replied weakly. "That just hasn't materialized as yet."

"And still you send that timber detail off by themselves? You can take that mounted infantry outfit and shove it up your ass, sir. There won't be another goddamned tree cut on this project until my men have adequate protection. Is that clear?"

"It isn't my fault if they haven't arrived on time, Captain."

"I'll take that up with the CO of those blue-legs, when and if he ever shows up."

"We have a schedule to meet here, Captain," Sacke said, mustering up an authoritative tone. "You can hear for yourself that the firing has stopped, and I'm sure our people have successfully beaten back any attackers they might have encountered. We will proceed as originally planned."

Edgerton cocked an ear and listened. It was true, the firing had stopped, and he glared down at Sacke while wheeling his mount. "Sounds like you can put that gun away now, Major. You couldn't have hit them from here with an artillery piece, anyway. Excuse me, I'm going out to check on my men."

Sacke ducked the rocks and gravel flying up from the horse's hooves, while glancing self-consciously at the big revolver in his hand. He reminded himself mentally to check and see if it was loaded as soon as he was alone again. He also remembered he hadn't fired a weapon since the early days of his army training, and even that brief exposure had been distasteful to him.

Sacke stabbed at the holster with the pistol barrel until he finally had the revolver successfully replaced, and then looked again at the agent, who had been silently watching him.

"It's been a while," Sacke offered with a weak grin.

"I can see that," Simms replied, stepping toward his horse. "It appears that your skill in the use of firearms is approximately

35

equal to your possession of common sense. Good day to you, sir. I have nothing more to say. There can be no stopping what you've started now."

Sacke watched the agent ride slowly away before turning to study the southern horizon. "Where the hell are you, god-dammit?" he muttered through clenched teeth. "If this project fails, it will be because of Easy Company, not me. But it can't fail, and no one is going to cause a failure. This son of a bitch is my ticket back to Washington, and nobody had better get in the way of that."

As he stalked toward his tent, he mentally envisioned the dressing-down that would fall on the CO of Easy Company the minute he arrived at the site. The mere thought made him feel better inwardly, and the thought of a shot of whiskey even brought a pleased smile to his lips.

The twin columns of Easy Company stretched across the plains like a blue snake slithering toward its den, and the gathering darkness brought out a deeper hue in their sweat-stained bay horses. At the head of the two platoons, Matt Kincaid and Windy Mandalian rode side by side, and Kincaid spoke while studying the vast expanse of nothingness unfolding before them.

"How much farther do you make it to be, Windy?"

The scout worked the cut-plug in his cheek and spat before offering a reply. "Half an hour. Maybe an hour at the most."

"Good. We've been pushing our horses pretty damned hard, and if we aren't there by then, we'll have to make camp for the night."

"We will be. We're about an hour and a half past Lost Hat Crossing, so we're in good shape." Windy paused to reflect, and wiped his mouth with the back of a hand. "Wish we'd had time to stop and talk with old John Cole. I'd like to hear his side of this little yarn."

"So would I, but our first priority is to back up that engineering battalion if necessary. Just as soon as we can make an assessment of the situation, I'll send you back to find out what the hell his people are doing."

"Good enough. I reckon it'll keep till then."

When Kincaid halted the columns at the edge of Ryan's Ravine, the sun resembled half an orange held at the edge of a table and illuminated by a powerful light, as it sank beneath the western horizon. Across the way they could see the sprawl of a miniature tent city, and the turned earth at the mouth of the ravine was a rich black against the field of green. A pile of logs was stacked to one side of a gaping trench that was the diversion channel, and they could see the treeline in the distance.

"Looks peaceful enough to me, Windy," Matt observed, noting the engineers standing in a grub line and awaiting their evening meal.

"So does a sleeping grizzly. Don't take long for her to change."

"Well, we're here. Let's go on over and find out what the hell we're up against. Where do we cross?"

"Just below where they've been diggin' there," Windy replied with a hint of disgust. "Can't understand how anybody could be damned fool enough to pick that as a place to dam the creek."

"You'll have your answer shortly. We're just about to meet the man who made that decision. Let's go on down."

The faces of the engineers were sullen as Easy Company rode slowly by the grub line, and their grumbling was clearly audible to the men of the two mounted platoons.

"Well, looky here! The blue-legs is lost again," one man said.

Another threw in, "There ain't a one of 'em what could pick an engineer's nose."

"We already done got our latrines dug, lads," a third man added. "Whyn't you go on back home where you're safe?"

The grizzled, battle-scarred veterans of Easy Company rode by in silence while looking down contemptuously from their mounts. But one man, Private Phelps, couldn't resist a retort.

"Oh, the engineers have hairy ears, the dirty sons of bitches," he sang in a low tone, but loud enough to be heard. "They jerk their cocks and rot their socks from diggin' all them ditches."

"Listen to that shit, would ya?" one burly engineer yelled to the others behind him. "Bet them boy's ain't that big once they get off them plow mules!"

Sergeant Ben Cohen had heard all he needed to hear, and turned in his saddle. "Shut up, Phelps. You heard the lieutenant's orders about silence in the ranks. Consider yourself on guard duty tonight."

The engineers laughed and banged their spoons on the bottoms of tin plates. "Now don't you be sassin' your sergeant there, blue-leg," a man toward the end of the line called. "He's the only one of you bastards what's got enough sense not to talk when he should be listenin'."

Instantly, Cohen wheeled his horse from the ranks and pulled to a stop before the last speaker. "Front and center, soldier!" he bellowed.

The engineers fell silent with expectant grins while their comrade glanced at them with a nervous, abandoned look.

"I said front and center."

The soldier stepped forward and lowered his utensils to his sides. "You're the sergeant. You do the talkin'," he said in a surly tone.

"You're damned right I'll do the talking. Who's your first sergeant?"

The soldier nodded toward a nearby tent, where a big man stood in the shadows. "Sergeant Hatcher."

Cohen glanced toward the silent man, who made no move to come forward. Cohen knew he could expect no help from the rival sergeant, but he also knew he had to take some action.

"What's your name, soldier?" Cohen asked, looking down again at the engineer.

"Locke. Private Harry T. Locke."

"I'm putting you on report, Private Locke. I'll take this matter up with your senior NCO later. Now fall back in line and keep your opinions to yourself." Cohen was speaking loudly enough so that there could be no chance of Hatcher's not hearing what he said. The firmness and authority in his voice, combined with his evident willingness to confront an entire company of engineers, silenced the men in the grub line. Cohen rode slowly down the line, as if challenging each man individually, before turning his mount and catching up with his own outfit.

"Thanks, Ben," Kincaid said, halting his platoons before the command tent while Cohen reined in by his side. "I don't think our boys could have taken a hell of a lot more of that."

"They'll get a lot more, sir. But they've had a long ride, and if push comes to shove, I'd like to see them get a little rest first."

"I agree," Matt replied, stepping down from his horse. "Bivouac our troops a considerable distance away until I've talked with the major. We might have a guard mount posted tonight, so keep that in mind."

"Yes, sir."

"Against who, Matt?" Windy asked with a chuckle, swinging down and ducking beneath his horse's neck. "The Indians or the engineers?"

"Our people will take care of themselves, Windy. You know that. Come on, let's go talk to the major."

Major Sacke was entirely aware of the arrival of Easy Company, but he purposely chose to remain seated at his desk while Captain Edgerton moved forward to stand beside the tent flap and peer outside. Edgerton knew full well that it was the major's way of asserting his authority, never meeting a junior officer halfway. When he saw Kincaid approaching, the captain moved back to stand a short distance away from Sacke's desk.

Kincaid stopped before the opening and called out, "Major Sacke? Lieutenant Matt Kincaid reporting for duty as ordered, sir."

Sacke said with exaggerated courtesy, "Captain, would you be so kind as to show the lieutenant in?"

Edgerton stepped forward and threw the tent flap to one side. "Come in Lieutenant. The major is waiting for you."

Followed by Windy Mandalian, Kincaid stepped inside and assumed the position of attention before the man who sat at the desk with his back still turned.

"Lieutenant Matt Kincaid reporting, sir," Kincaid said, feeling the first hint of irritation flit through his mind.

"I'll be with you in a moment, Lieutenant," the major replied as he feigned signing some important documents. After a lengthy pause, he turned, stood, and returned Matt's crisp salute. With the brief formality concluded, Sacke crossed his hands behind his back and paced across the tent like a man deeply engrossed in thought.

"Where is your CO, Lieutenant?"

"He's back at Outpost Number Nine, Major."

"I see," Sacke replied with a truculent nod. "And what, may I ask, is he doing there?"

"Pardon me, Major?"

"I sent specific orders for him to come here and bring his entire company with him. Your entire—what is it, Easy Company?—is here I presume?"

39

"No, sir."

"Explain, Lieutenant."

"There's nothing to explain, Major. On Captain Conway's orders, I am reporting to you with two full platoons of mounted infantry."

Sacke's eyebrows arched, and there was a smirk on his lips. "Two full platoons, eh, Lieutenant? Two full platoons an entire company does not make. Why weren't my direct orders followed to the letter?"

Now anger replaced irritation in Matt's mind. "Because your orders were illegal, Major, in terms of the War Department's directive regarding minimal strength at a frontier outpost."

"Come now, Lieutenant, are you inferring that you and Captain Conway are more familiar with military procedure than I?"

"I'm inferring nothing, sir," Kincaid replied evenly. "But with the major's permission, I would like to point out that it is the direct order of the commanding general, United States Army, that no outpost be left manned by less than one-third of its full complement of the personnel so assigned. Further, at no time shall the commanding officer and executive officer be removed from their assigned post during the same interval. Your order was in direct conflict with the general's. If I may be entirely candid, sir, Captain Conway didn't find it in the least difficult to determine which order superseded which."

Sacke cleared his throat, started to readjust his glasses, thought better of it, and clasped his hands behind his back once more. "Of course. Merely an oversight on my part," he said, his tone becoming more conciliatory. "Lieutenant Kincaid, I would like you to meet my executive officer, Captain Steven Edgerton."

Kincaid turned toward the captain and saluted. "It is a pleasure to meet you, Captain."

"I doubt it, Lieutenant, as I think will be borne out by future events," Edgerton replied, waving off the salute. "Tell me, why has it taken you so long to get here?"

"I don't consider a day and a half's ride a long time, Captain. We left two hours after the major's dispatch arrived."

"Did you now?" Edgerton said with a hard-eyed glance toward Sacke. "Were any other dispatches received previous to that one?"

"No, sir. There were none."

"I see."

"Dammit!" Sacke blurted, his voice sounding almost as flat as his slapping of fist into palm. "Why the hell can't anybody do anything right? I sent—"

Edgerton had heard enough. "That's precisely what I was wondering, Major. Good night."

The captain moved toward the door with the thick-muscled stride of a man used to heavy lifting, but he stopped as he passed by Kincaid. "I lost two damned good men today. My timber detail was ambushed by what we think were the Sioux. One man was killed outright and the other dragged to death. I don't like dead men, and I like excuses even less."

Kincaid leveled a steady gaze at the captain. "I'm here to prevent the former, and I have no inclination to offer the latter. Good night, Captain."

Edgerton's eyes swept over Kincaid and Sacke before he ducked out of the tent. Kincaid waited what he felt was a proper interval before he indicated Windy Mandalian with a motion of his hand.

"Major, I'd like for you to meet Windy Mandalian, chief scout for Easy Company."

Sacke eyed Mandalian's buckskins with a hint of disdain before nodding. "A pleasure to meet you, I'm sure, Mr. Mandalian. I was wondering what your function was. Tell me exactly, what is it that a scout is supposed to do?"

"Stay alive, mostly."

"Stay alive? Commendable objective, to say the least. Are you familiar with the Indians in this region?"

"Depends on what you mean by familiar. I know their ways as good as the next man."

"Would you say they're about to go on the warpath?"

"No I wouldn't, Major." Windy hesitated and scratched his chin. "If what your captain said is true, I'd say they already are."

"Surely, Mr. Mandalian, you can't call one little skirmish—"

"That was a testing raid, Major," Windy interrupted. "They want to know what your strengths and weaknesses are. How many Indians were killed today?"

Sacke shrugged his narrow shoulders. "None, at least to my knowledge. We were taken by surprise, as I understand it."

"And you lost two men?"

"Yes," Sacke replied, "but death in the line of duty is a thing all soldiers must be prepared for."

Kincaid had been watching the major, and he wondered if the man honestly didn't care about the deaths of two unarmed men engaged in the process of felling trees for a dam of dubious value. "Being prepared for death is one thing, Major," he said with slow emphasis, "but dying needlessly is another matter."

"I will decide what is needless around here, Lieutenant, and what is not. You will restrict yourself to the mission you have been ordered here to carry out. That being the defense of those engaged in this project. Any thoughts or conjecture regarding that mission, you will keep strictly to yourself."

"I don't think so, sir. When it comes to the safety and well-being of my men, I reserve final judgment. You build the dam and I'll worry about security."

Major Sacke smiled disarmingly. "Lieutenant, I hope it doesn't become necessary for me to remind you of rank, the chain of command, military protocol, and that sort of thing. You will do as ordered. And I will be the person to initiate those orders."

"Absolutely correct, Major," Kincaid said, pulling the gloves from beneath his belt and beginning to tug them on. "I will do as I was ordered. Those orders originated with *you.* I was ordered here to defend this engineering battalion in the construction of the Garderville Dam Project, which is precisely what I will do. I will take no orders from you in that regard, or from any of your subordinates for that matter, and will conduct my affairs to the letter of your orders as already stated."

"Why—why—this is preposterous, Lieutenant!" Sacke spluttered, his eyes widening in shock and disbelief. "I—I'm a major and you're nothing but—but a Lieutenant! You will abide by any orders exactly as issued, and right now I order you to hunt down those renegades and put a stop to this nonsense!"

"Sorry, Major," Matt responded, turning toward the tent flap. "The orders I received were issued by Captain Warner Conway on authority from the War Department. If you wish to argue the matter with him, you may do so. I am under direct orders from Captain Conway to return to Outpost Number Nine if you rescind your order charging Easy Company with full responsibility for protecting your engineering battalion." Kincaid stooped toward the tent flap, then stopped and turned with

42

his head near the opening. "It's your choice, Major. Why don't you take the night to think it over? Either my command stays under my full jurisdiction, or we leave under my full jurisdiction. It's really fairly simple when you think about it, sir. Good night."

Kincaid ducked out of the tent, and it was Windy's turn to pause and look back at the befuddled major. "Know what, Major?" he asked with a wink. "I think the lieutenant means it. If I were you—not tryin' to give you advice, you understand—I'd give 'er some hard thought before I tried to tell the lieutenant what to do. He's military right down to the toes of his boots, but that don't make him stupid. You might look into somethin' like that yourself."

Major Sacke watched the scout disappear before wilting into his chair like a flower exposed to extreme temperatures. "This is the worst goddamned thing I ever got involved in," he mumbled as his hand strayed toward the desk drawer containing the whiskey flask. "I need that lieutenant and his mounted infantry, he knows that. Without him, I know for a fact that Edgerton won't lift another finger to finish this dam, and I need a success here more than ever before."

The major sloshed some whiskey into a glass and spoke as he raised it to his lips. "Damn you, Jolene. If it weren't for you, I wouldn't be in the mess I'm in." He smiled as he remembered her warm thighs and caressing tongue. "Then again, if this works out, I'll be in your bed again, with my dress blues hanging on your doorknob, with the insignia of lieutenant colonel mounted on the shoulder boards. After that comes full colonel and then general. Surely your pappy would just love to see you married to a general."

Sacke's smile broadened even more as a thought materialized in his mind. He studied the plan for nearly ten minutes before turning toward the tent flap and raising his glass in salute. "Welcome to Ryan's Ravine, Lieutenant Kincaid. You're going to do the whole thing for me, just you wait and see." Then his face sobered and he slammed the glass onto the desktop with a wicked thud. "And when it's over, I'll see that you're busted back to private, and out digging latrines for thirteen dollars a month."

The thought of that eventuality seemed to please Major Sacke as he took up his glass again, leaned back in his chair, and propped his boots on the desk.

"Yes, sir, Lieutenant. You, Captain Edgerton, and that raggedy scout of yours are my ticket back to Washington," he mused as his tongue tickled the rim of the glass. "Like I said, welcome to Ryan's Ravine. I can't lose now. If anything goes wrong, it's on your head, not mine."

The major smiled again, then giggled, and finally threw his head back and roared with uncontrollable laughter. For the first time since coming to Garderville, he felt he was in charge at last—by not being in charge at all.

four

There were three blankets spread around a small fire from which wisps of smoke rose lazily into the breaking dawn. Two warriors sat side by side, facing the third Indian, who was seated alone as though he were an unwelcome guest. But they passed the traditional pipe around the fire, smoking silently and watching each other with eyes that revealed not the slightest hint of emotion. Finally, Medicine Hawk took one last puff, passed the pipe to Black Eagle, and folded his arms across his chest.

"Why have you come here, Hunting Fox?"

Hunting Fox was older than either of the men facing him, perhaps by as much as ten years, and there was a patient wisdom about his face that bespoke sadness and resignation to a fate wrested from his control. He wore a breastplate made of eagle bones and trade beads, tanned-leather clothing, and a single feather dangled from his braided, black hair.

"Why should I not come here, Medicine Hawk? This reservation belongs to all the Oskalla tribe."

"And that makes you proud?" Medicine Hawk snapped with a sweeping gesture across his chest to indicate the land surrounding them. "All of this once belonged to the Lakotas. Now we live on a small piece of land with a white agent telling us what only Wakan Tonka should place in our ears."

"It is true, we have lost much of what we once had. And we will lose more. But we could have survived at least, if you had not come back from Canada."

Black Eagle laid the pipe aside while his eyes held on his half-brother's face. "Is that why you have come here, my brother? To tell us we are not welcome on the land of our ancestors?"

Hunting Fox's gaze shifted from Medicine Hawk to Black Eagle, and there was something nearing tenderness and compassion in his voice when he spoke.

"I have not come to tell you that you are not welcome, my brother. I have come to tell you that what you do will bring much hardship to our people."

"Is taking what is rightfully ours considered to be hardship, Hunting Fox?"

A slight smile creased the older warrior's lips. "You live in the past, Black Eagle. In a past that died with our father, Stalking Crow. The white man will do what he wants, and we cannot stop him."

"Like they did in the Paha Sapa?" Medicine Hawk asked hotly. "They find the yellow metal and for that we are sent from our homeland. They dug there to find the yellow metal, and they are digging here now. It's bad enough that they anger the gods by stopping the Minni, but what happens if they again find that thing they treasure most?"

Hunting Fox shrugged. "As I have said, we cannot stop them."

"No, you and the other old women can't stop them, but warriors like Black Eagle and Medicine Hawk can."

"Only until more Americans come. And then you and those who follow you will be hunted down and killed. But it is not you that I am concerned about, Medicine Hawk. It is my brother and the others back at our village. The Americans do not always make certain who their enemies are, and many times kill all, in their desire for revenge against a few. Just like what happened to the Cheyenne at Sand Creek."

"*Kah!*" Medicine Hawk hissed in his high-pitched voice. "The Cheyenne were not prepared for them. We will be."

46

"We are prepared for peace, Medicine Hawk. That is the only preparedness we should be concerned with."

Black Eagle had been listening to the exchange, and now he said, "Is the covering of our ancestors with the Minni an indication of peace, my brother? Is digging on our land once more an indication of peace? No, they will take the Minni from us and use it for other white settlers and those who seek the metal that makes the Americans crazy."

"We were given this land with the promise that we would never have to move again," Hunting Fox said softly, "but that was before you killed the digger-soldier. Now more Americans come. Bird That Sees in the Night has told me of their arrival. They are the soldiers who kill, not dig. And they are the soldiers who will never let you rest until you are dead."

"Bird That Sees in the Night told you this?" Black Eagle asked, making no attempt to hide his surprise. "How many are there?"

"Many."

"As many as we have here?" Black Eagle asked, turning to indicate the warriors behind them.

Hunting Fox shook his head and drew the heel of his right palm across his left forearm to indicate the division of halves.

Medicine Hawk smiled triumphantly. "They are not enough to make war with the Lakota. And if more come, let them. We are here to fight, not to talk."

Hunting Fox looked at his brother. "Is that your opinion as well, Black Eagle?"

The young warrior remained silent as he watched the older brave across from him. Finally he nodded in indication that it was.

"So be it, then," Hunting Fox said, rising to a standing position. "You have heard my final counsel. From this day forth, we are enemies as well. You think only of your hatred for the Americans, some of which I can understand, but you do not think of the well-being of the Lakota. Your eyes are blinded by revenge, and it is Medicine Hawk who holds the blindfold in place. Peace be with you, my brother. I have spoken."

Hunting Fox started to turn away, took two steps, stopped, and turned back. "Your mother, Cloud of the Moon, has returned from Canada. She said to wish you well."

47

Trying to retain an impassive expression, Black Eagle nodded and glanced sharply away. Hunting Fox watched him a moment longer, then crossed to his pony and swung onto its back. Black Eagle turned to watch his brother leave, and felt Medicine Hawk's hand encircle his bicep.

"He is your brother only in name, Black Eagle. He is not your brother in spirit or pride. His heart is that of an old woman who will take only what is given. We are Lakota warriors. We will take what is ours."

"This thing of the horse soldiers is not good, Medicine Hawk," Black Eagle replied, watching the pinto pony lope across the plains. "They have come too quickly."

"*Kah!* They are few. They are here only to protect the digger-soldiers, not to hunt us." Medicine Hawk smiled, and there was a wild glint in his eyes. "But we will make them hunt us."

Slightly confused, Black Eagle glanced across at his companion. "Make them hunt us?"

"Yes, like the wolf digging at the hole of the prairie dog, while the little one escapes from another hole."

"Do not tell me children's stories," Black Eagle said sternly, regaining control with the departure of his brother.

"You are too quick to anger at one time, and too slow at another, Black Eagle. Now is the time to raid the white settler, John Cole."

"Why?"

"The Americans will have to come to help them, at least some. While they are searching for half of us, the other half will attack the digger-soldiers again. The horse soldiers will be like a dog chasing its tail."

The young chief contemplated Medicine Hawk's proposal in silence before a slow grin spread across his face. "It is good. We will raid with the rising of the sun tomorrow. Not all of our warriors, just enough to make the Americans think we no longer will attack the digger-soldiers. Then, when the horse soldiers leave to help Cole, we will strike against the digger-soldiers."

Medicine Hawk nodded and clapped Black Eagle across the shoulders, while watching him with a leering grin. "Have you seen the daughter of this John Cole?"

"No, I have not."

"I have. She is beautiful. An excellent prize for a Lakota

chief." He paused and studied Black Eagle intently. "You are the Lakota chief now."

The thought of taking a white woman for his pleasure seemed unsettling to Black Eagle as he glanced away. It was as though he were recalling something from his past, a memory that brought more pain than pleasure. He said nothing more to Medicine Hawk and, rising, he walked quickly away.

At seven o'clock that same morning, there was another group of men gathered together in conference. The weak, gray light of dawn had yielded to the spreading warmth of the rising sun, and six men stood before the headquarters tent from which emanated the gentle snoring of Major Sacke, immersed in blissful slumber.

With the exception of Windy Mandalian and Sergeant Ben Cohen, the group consisted entirely of officers: First Lieutenant Matt Kincaid, Captain Steven Edgerton, and Second Lieutenants Sheply and Ford, commanding Easy Company's first and third platoons respectively.

Kincaid glanced once at the angle of the sun, and then at Captain Edgerton. "Apparently Major Sacke isn't going to make our meeting this morning," he said with a nod of his head toward the tent. "Is that a correct assumption, Captain?"

"That's correct, Lieutenant. He came to my tent last night and told me I was in complete charge of construction on this project. He also said to tell you that security matters were entirely your responsibility." Edgerton shook his head. "Can't understand that, actually, because before you arrived he wanted to personally inspect every shovelful of dirt that came out of that goddamned hole over there."

Kincaid smiled and shrugged. "Well, Captain, I guess changing your mind is one of the prerogatives of rank. If you and I can cooperate, his latest decision could work for the benefit of all of us."

Edgerton's eyes hardened, as though any hint of familiarity were a sign of weakness. "I intend to cooperate with you bluelegs only to the extent necessary to get this dam built, Lieutenant. You might as well know out front, I haven't got a hell of a lot of time for you or your branch of the service."

"Knowing that one is welcome always gives one such a warm feeling, doesn't it, Captain?" Kincaid replied with an easy grin. "But since you're putting the facts on the line, I might as well do the same. I don't care whether you like me or not. Your rank means nothing to me, and I'm here for only one purpose: to fulfill the orders given me by my commanding officer. And I don't give a damn how tough you and your men think they are; just remember, we *are* supposed to be on the same side."

Edgerton shrugged his broad shoulders. "A formality at best."

"Fine, but we just might need each other more than you think before this thing's over. And while we're on the subject of formalities, you'll notice I've dispensed with the formality of calling you 'sir.' As far as I'm concerned, we're equals on this project, with you in command of your operation and me in command of mine. Is that acceptable to you?"

"Fine. I judge a man by what he does, not by what he says."

"I concur entirely. Now let's get on with the business at hand," Kincaid replied, turning to the two second lieutenants. "Mr. Sheply, your platoon is assigned the responsibility of protecting those working on the dam proper, as well as those working on the diversion canal. Your men will probably take a lot of heat because these engineers don't think they need us to protect them from Indian raids. But in reality, if they didn't, we wouldn't be here. Tell your men—"

"Just a damned minute, Lieutenant," Edgerton interrupted with a rising voice. "We didn't ask you here, the goddamned major did."

"I don't care who asked us here, Captain. The point is, we're here." Kincaid looked again at Sheply. "As I was saying, tell your men to keep their mouths shut and their eyes open."

"Yessir."

"Mr. Ford, two of your squads will be assigned to protect the timber-cutting detail. I want them mounted and in constant rotation around the perimeter of the area. Your third squad will go with Windy and myself to ascertain John Cole's objections to this project. Is that understood?"

"Yessir."

"Fine," Kincaid replied, turning toward Sergeant Cohen. "Ben, I might not be back until tomorrow morning. If I'm not, make out a duty roster and have guards posted at regular intervals. If anything happens to me, Lieutenant Sheply is in charge."

"I understand, sir."

"Did you have that conversation with Sergeant Hatcher that you mentioned you were going to have last evening?"

"Yes I did, Lieutenant. He said about the same thing Captain Edgerton said. We're about as welcome here as a turd in a punch bowl."

"Never did like punch anyway," Windy said while cutting off his first chew of cut-plug for the day.

Kincaid grinned. "With that stuff in your mouth, Windy, you couldn't tell the difference between the turd and the punch."

"Wrong, Matt. Cut-plug don't float."

Even Captain Edgerton allowed himself a smile at Windy's remark before sobering. "Are we finished here, Lieutenant? I've got men that need looking at."

"Yes we are, Captain. When the major awakens, I'd appreciate it if you would tell him where I've gone."

"If I see him," Edgerton replied with an unconcerned shrug as he sauntered away.

By seven-fifteen, Matt and Windy were mounted and leading the third squad away from the construction site. Kincaid felt a pleasant peacefulness come over him as they quit the undercurrent of hostility now falling behind them, and there was something strong, clean, and positive about being on the open plains with a sturdy horse between his legs. His mind wandered to Private Greer, riding third man behind him, and he knew it was because of Greer that he had selected this particular squad to accompany himself and Windy on the ride to Cole's homestead.

Greer's timid nature and reticent way would have made him a perfect target for the sharp-tongued engineers, and he wanted a little more time to study the young man before throwing him to the wolves, as it were. Personally, Kincaid found Greer an agreeable person, and he likened him to some of the artists he had read about. He had a withdrawn, shy nature, yet there was a look in his eyes that bespoke an inner depth, a need to express himself, though he seemed ill-equipped to voice the turmoil that surged through his brain. Kincaid wondered if it was the stutter that held the young man back, a thing he hadn't noticed until this patrol, and he determined to seek Greer out in a private moment to further analyze the working of his mind.

"Know what, Matt?" Windy asked, breaking Kincaid's reverie.

"Probably not, Windy. What?"

"Major Brian Sacke, Commanding, is one stupid son of a bitch."

"Now, that I did suspect. Do you have any particular reason for bringing the subject up?"

"Yeah. I got to snooping around a little bit last night, and I came across somethin' that I'd forgotten."

"Like what?"

"Like if the major's dam actually does get built, the reservoir behind it is going to flood one of the oldest Lakota burial grounds that I know of."

"You think that's what the Sioux are so pissed off about?"

"Part of it. That, plus the fact that they don't want anybody diggin' on their ground, especially since gold was found in the Paha Sapa. In addition to that, the major is planning to tunnel through that rise to the northwest and change the course of the stream to an old winter watershed that'll put the Lakota summer camp smack-dab in the middle of the river. Funny thing about Indians—they kind of like to go to the water instead of havin' it come to them."

"If the major didn't have his head up his ass, it seems like those things could be negotiated, with the exception of the burial ground."

"Not as far as some of the young bucks are concerned. Any negotiatin' that's been done in the past has cost them territory, not to mention pride."

"What do you know about this Black Eagle?"

"Not much. But I did know his father. He was a man to be reckoned with. He fought with Sitting Bull at the Little Big Horn and went with him to Canada, where I understand he was killed. At any rate, if the boy is tryin' to live up to the old man's reputation, he could be more'n a small problem. First chance I get, I'm goin' onto the reservation and talk with the Oskalla agent, a feller named Charlie Simms. Me and him are old partners, and he might be able to give us a little better idea of what's goin' on around here than anybody else I know."

"Yes, do that. Maybe tomorrow, after we've talked with Cole."

"Whenever. Sooner the better, I'm thinkin'."

It was just before noon that the main buildings of the Grace Land ranch came into view, a cluster of low-silhouetted dwellings, barns, and corrals situated beneath the shelter of a grove

52

of stately oak trees. Throughout the morning they had seen numerous cattle bearing the GL brand, and Kincaid was truly surprised by the size and apparent health of the herd. As they drew nearer he could see that the buildings were neatly kept and whitewashed, and their roofs covered with sod as a defense against fire arrows. The walls were obviously of jackpine mortared over with clay, and there was no doubt that the structures had been built with generations of usage in mind.

As they approached, they saw half a dozen horses tethered to a hitch rail in front of the main house, with double that many men gathered in the sprawling yard. Each held a Winchester loosely in his grasp, and Colt .44s were strapped to their lean hips.

John Cole broke off a conversation with his son and hired hands, and turned to stare at the approaching army patrol.

Windy leaned slightly toward Kincaid and said, "Let me talk to him first, Matt. If I remember rightly, old John ain't too much on government, no matter what form it comes in."

Kincaid nodded, appraising the stockmen before him and judging them to be as tough-looking a bunch of range hands as he had ever seen. When they reined their horses in, Windy adjusted the Sharps cradled in his arm, spat in a manner that was delicate for him, and inclined his head toward the large man with the gray mustache.

"You'd be John Cole, wouldn't you?"

"That I'd be," Cole replied, with neither welcome nor refusal in his voice. "What can I help you with?"

"Well now, John, it was us that kind of had the helpin' in mind."

"Don't need any help, mister, thanks just the same."

Windy cocked his hat forward to scratch the back of his head in thought. "Don't seem like that was the case 'bout twenty years back or so. Me and you tracked down some Sioux 'round that time. Would the name Windy Mandalian mean anything to you?"

Cole glanced away to search his mind, and when he looked back, there was a questioning, almost disbelieving look in his eyes. "A trapper, just come down from the Wind River country?"

"One and the same."

"Well, by goddamn!" Cole said, a grin breaking across his face as he stepped forward with hand extended. "Good to see you again, Windy. Never really gave me much of a chance to thank you after you helped me look for my wife, Grace. How you been?"

"Fair to poor skies, with a chance of rain," Windy replied with a grin as he leaned down to accept the offered handshake. "As far as waitin' around for your thanks, I'm not too long on that. Sorry we didn't have any more luck than we did."

"So am I," Cole said with a glance toward his son. "Guess that's in the past now." Then his eyes brightened again. "Remember my boy Jason? Step up here, son, and shake the hand of a real frontiersman."

The young man moved forward and grasped Windy's hand. "It's a pleasure to meet you, Mr. Mandalian."

"Pleasure to see you again, Jason. Last time we met, you didn't weigh much more'n two handfuls of dry hay."

Windy's eyes went to the older man again as he motioned toward Matt. "John, I'd like you to meet Lieutenant Matt Kincaid. Best damned soldier what ever shit behind a pair of boots. Matt, meet John Cole. Him and his people are the ones that helped make the territory what it is today."

Kincaid extended his hand toward the homesteader, and he could see by the look on the man's face that he was not overly fond of the military.

"Pleased to meet you, Mr. Cole," Matt said as his hand closed around the calloused, firm grip of the rancher. "Sorry we've intruded on you."

Cole shrugged with the withdrawal of his hand. "No trouble, really. Just talkin' with the hands about a problem that's come up." Now his eyes narrowed. "Like the government damming up Cole Creek."

Just then the door to the house opened, and a raven-haired young woman in her early twenties stepped onto the porch. She raised one hand to shield her eyes from the sun, and the apron tied tightly around her narrow waist accentuated the rounded flow of her hips and ample breasts, which were full and upright. Her face was pale-complexioned, with high cheekbones and full lips.

"Daddy!" she called. "Your sandwiches are ready!"

"Thank you, darlin'," Cole replied. "Come on out here a second. I want you to meet someone."

Kincaid watched her move down the steps with graceful strides, and he thought in that moment that she was one of the most beautiful young woman he had ever seen. She walked with authority, with confidence and poise, and when she stopped beside her father, Matt saw her tenderly slip her hand into his.

"Melinda, I'd like you to meet an old friend of ours," Cole said, looking down at his daughter with obvious pride before glancing up again at the scout. "This is Windy Mandalian. He helped me try to find your ma, back when you were a baby."

Melinda curtseyed and glanced down demurely. "It's a real pleasure to meet you, Mr. Mandalian."

Windy grinned. "The pleasure is mine, Miss Cole." The scout looked at Cole in mock surprise. "John, you sure this is the same little gal who was runnin' around here in pigtails, with dirt on her cheeks, twenty years back?"

Cole pulled his daughter tightly to his side. "That she is, Windy. That she is. It's amazing what a good hot bath, twenty years, and a few good swats on the behind with a razor strop will do. Melinda?" he said, indicating Kincaid with a sweep of his hand, "I'd like you to meet another guest. Lieutenant Matt Kincaid. Lieutenant? My daughter, Melinda."

Matt touched his hatbrim to her and thought he caught a faint blush in Melinda's cheeks as their eyes locked for a second. "It's an honor, Miss Cole."

Again, Melinda curtseyed, then glanced up at Kincaid with a shy but womanly smile. "Welcome to Grace Land, Lieutenant."

"Thank you, ma'am."

"Go get the bottle from the cupboard and set us up three glasses, will you, honey?" Cole said. "I'd like to have a drink with Windy and the lieutenant before I leave."

Melinda nodded, moving away, and Kincaid caught her sideways glance and brief smile as she walked toward the house, while Cole turned his attention to Windy.

"Windy, seems like the only time you cross my path is when I've got problems. There's hay in the barn, grain in the bucket, and water in the trough for your horses. Why don't you and the lieutenant light for a spell and we'll go on into the house for a short drink."

"I thank you, John," Windy replied, swinging down.

Kincaid turned in the saddle and said, "Corporal Wojensky, have the squad dismount and care for their horses. Stand at ease and wait for further instructions."

"Yessir."

Kincaid stepped down while Cole looked across at his son. "Jason, we'll be leaving here in half an hour. Make sure everybody has extra rounds, and bring along a sack of grain for the horses. Meanwhile, show the corporal where the feed is. When you're finished, come on into the house and have a drink with us."

The three men walked toward the house, and Kincaid could sense the strength of John Cole, the close-knit unity of his family, and it was obvious why their homestead had flourished while others had failed miserably. It was a fortress against the world, and Matt could see gun slits cut into the walls, heavily shuttered windows, fire buckets stationed at strategic locations, and a well, connected to the house by an enclosed runway, that would provide water during times of seige.

He wondered, as he often had, where homesteaders like John Cole got their strength, the innate courage that enabled them to build and sustain under the most arduous of conditions. Obviously survival was the first thought in their minds as they rose in the morning and the last thought in their minds when they went to sleep at night.

"This is a nice place you have here, Mr. Cole," Matt said as they neared the porch.

"Thank you, Lieutenant. Things haven't been easy and they haven't always been good, but we've managed. I've lived my life with my own pa always lookin' over my shoulder, judging everything I did, right or wrong. This was his place, and it will always belong to him." He hesitated and looked down at the ground. "Him and Grace, that is."

When they stepped inside, Kincaid was surprised by the spaciousness and utilitarian design of the house. With its low, crossbeamed ceiling, massive fireplace situated against the east wall, and rich leather couches complemented by lightly colored rugs of reds and yellows on the polished pine floor, the living room was luxurious and cozy at the same time. The adjoining kitchen, which they now entered, was spotlessly clean and well-appointed for the preparation of sumptuous meals.

Three glasses were placed on the table, and Kincaid noticed Melinda standing on her tiptoes with her arm outstretched in an attempt to grasp the bottle just beyond her reach. "Here, let me get that for you," he said, stepping forward quickly.

Melinda replied with a warm smile as she moved aside.

56

"When Daddy puts the bottle away, he forgets that some of us aren't quite as tall as he is."

"Keep you honest and sober at the same time, honey," Cole said, grinning. He pulled a chair out and touched Windy's elbow with the other hand. "Here, Windy, have a seat."

Kincaid handed the bottle across, while Cole pulled out a second chair. "Thanks, Matt. Have a seat and I'll pour. Would you gentlemen care for something to eat?"

"No thanks, John," Matt replied. "We've brought rations with us."

"Melinda's one hell of a cook," Cole said as he passed the glasses around and took a seat himself.

Kincaid smiled with a glance at the comely young woman. "I'm sure she is."

Melinda returned the smile as their eyes locked for an instant before she glanced toward her father. "Will there be anything else, Daddy? If not, I've got some mending to do."

"No, you go right ahead with whatever you have to do." Cole raised his glass and looked at the two men across from him while his daughter left the room. "Here's to you. Welcome to Grace Land."

"Thanks for the hospitality," Kincaid said, touching his glass to the other two.

When the glasses were lowered, Cole folded his hands one over the other and looked at the scout. "What brings you here, Windy?"

"Well, John, it's about that dam those engineers are building. I hear you have some objections to it, which I can well understand, and we'd like to hear your side of the story."

Cole's eyes hardened. "You're damned right I have some objections." He recounted his conversation with Major Sacke, and concluded, "That damned fool major doesn't know what kind of can of worms he's opening up around here."

"He doesn't know a hell of a lot about much of anything, it seems to me," Windy said with an agreeing nod. "But he does seem to have the solid support of the people back in Washington."

"They're just as bad as he is, if not worse. They haven't got the slightest idea what we're up against out here, and don't really give a shit, either. These past few years have been mighty dry, and this one is even worse. Cole Creek is the only reliable source of water we have, and with the falling water table, who

57

knows how long we can count on that? With that in mind, the dam itself isn't such a bad idea, but changing the course of the stream sure as hell is."

Kincaid turned his glass in thought, while shaking his head. "I wish there were some way I could intercede on your behalf, John, but there's not a damned thing I can do. Have you tried a complaint to the Department of the Interior?"

"Yes. I've sent three wires, as a matter of fact. Same reply every time. 'This project is part of an overall government plan that has congressional approval. It is vital to the interests of the United States, and there will be no alterations in the plans for construction.'" Cole drained his glass and poured angrily again. "Pure horseshit, that's all. I'm not the only one affected, and there's a hell of a lot of people pissed off downstream. That's where I'm heading right now, soon as we finish this drink. We're having a meeting over at Slim Barkley's place, and I can tell you this—everybody, including me, is fighting mad."

"I don't blame you at all, John," Kincaid said, watching his host closely. "My detachment was sent here to protect the engineering battalion against any outside interference. I certainly hope those orders don't lead to a confrontation between the army and the local ranchers like yourself. Personally, I think the dam is a stupid idea, and I'm in total sympathy with you and the others. But unfortunately, in my line of work I'm not asked to make judgments as to who is right and who is wrong. I am given orders to follow, and I have to carry them out."

Cole nodded as he raised his glass to his lips. "I understand that, Lieutenant, and whatever happens, I don't hold any grudge toward you. You've got your job to do and I've got mine."

"Did you know that the Sioux raided the dam site yesterday and killed two soldiers, John?" Windy asked.

"Yeah, I heard about it. That's why I'm leaving half my men behind to protect the place. I'd like to take them all with me, but I can't leave Melinda here unprotected."

"Well, maybe there is one thing I can do for you, John," Kincaid said, finishing his drink and shoving the glass to the center of the table. "How long are you going to be gone?"

"Should be back tomorrow morning."

"If it would be of any help to you, I can stay here with that squad of soldiers out there and keep an eye on the place. That's

58

kind of putting me in league with you, since you're planning to take countermeasures against the construction, but nobody has to know that besides ourselves."

Cole smiled and offered Kincaid a look of genuine respect. "I'd sure appreciate that, Lieutenant. Damned sure would. You and your troops can make yourselves at home out in the bunkhouse. Besides, that'd give you a chance to try out Melinda's cooking. If you've got a guilty conscience about helping me out, that should soothe things a mite."

"My conscience is clear, John. But a home-cooked meal does sound mighty appetizing."

Jason Cole stepped into the kitchen and poured a quick drink. "We're ready to go, Pa."

"Good. When you finish that drink, tell the other boys to saddle up. The lieutenant is going to stay here and keep an eye on things for us." Cole glanced at Windy as his son downed the drink in one gulp and headed for the door. "Would you like to ride along with us, Windy? Maybe you can help me keep some of the hotheads in line."

Windy looked at Kincaid. "Matt?"

"Sure, go ahead. And you don't have to tell me anything you might overhear. As a matter of fact, I don't want to know."

"Come on, John," Windy said, pushing away from the table. "Let's ride."

"Thanks again, Matt," Cole offered as they passed through the living room. "Won't forget your help if it comes to a showdown."

"You're welcome. Let's hope it doesn't. If it does, we'll deal with it at that time. Good luck. I'll be here when you get back."

five _____

There was a lazy tranquillity about the Grace Land homestead as the afternoon sun bore down with full intensity. Chickens wandered here and there, pecking and scratching in a seemingly purposeless manner, while a pair of dogs lay sleeping in the shade. Horses stood motionless in the corral, dozing in the warmth, while a sow with several piglets lay burrowed in the mud beside a water trough in their pen. The occasional call of a cow demanding the attention of her calf drifted on the stilled air, and an owl was perched in an oak tree high above the land, like an off-duty sentinel with eyes hooded over.

Matt Kincaid leaned against the barn door, one boot propped behind him, and surveyed the surroundings with appraising eyes. A blade of grass hung from the corner of his mouth, and he worked it periodically between pursed lips while he weighed the merits of military life against the obvious benefits of a domestic existence.

His was a homeless life, with food, a bunk, and a roof over his head provided by the government. He owned nothing, built nothing, and the future for him did not go beyond the next

60

day's patrol. That thought was a mildly troubling one. Did the satisfactions of serving well and honorably in the military offset the lack of permanence, the feeling of possession? When John Cole returned home in the evening after a day on the range, he came back to something. Something he had built with his own hands, something that was ever extending and growing, with generations of roots sinking deeper into the ground. His principal responsibilities were to himself and his family, with the only life-and-death decisions demanded of him being those that directly affected him and his livelihood. There was no call for him to go far afield, settling uprisings, disputes, and lawlessness that had no bearing on his own personal existence. He was not asked to protect people and projects he found distasteful to himself. If John Cole and the Grace Land homestead were not directly affected, he could simply hang his hat on a peg, tug off his boots, and plan for another day of improving on what he already had.

But a first lieutenant in the mounted infantry was another matter. Especially one assigned to a frontier outpost far from the glitter of Washington and those choice Eastern posts where rank was often achieved through servitude rather than service. And rank, aside from the nebulous satisfaction of a job well done, was the only yardstick by which success could be measured for the career army officer. Kincaid knew his having been passed over that last time had nothing to do with his performance. If performance of duties were the criterion for promotion, he had no doubt that a captaincy would be his immediately, as he rightly deserved. The promotions board, without doubt, adhered tightly to the old adage, "the squeaky wheel gets the grease," and neither he nor Captain Conway was prone to complaint or grumbling except when it directly affected the men of their command.

Kincaid wondered about those men as he shifted his weight to the other foot. They were his family, to be trained, cajoled, praised, and punished just as John Cole had doubtless done with his children. Of course they were, in the main, grown men and hardened combat veterans; yet, in a way, they were children who respected strength, fairness, and wisdom. And they looked to their lieutenant to provide that example and thus help them endure the rigors of army existence.

Still, Kincaid thought, tossing the blade of grass aside and crossing his arms over his chest, was the price he was paying

61

worth the rewards received? His only possessions in life were his uniforms, which he was required to purchase from his meager pay, which, when it came at all, was late, ending each month and another cycle in his life. Other than that, he lived in the bachelor officers' quarters, owned no furniture, and when the time came to transfer to another assignment, his entire stock of worldly possessions could be carried in a single bag over one shoulder.

The owl suddenly lifted from its perch, and Kincaid watched it sail effortlessly away, before his eyes lowered to sweep over the homestead once more. He had never really questioned his choice of a military career before, but somehow the beauty of Grace Land was troubling to him, and—

"Lieutenant Kincaid?"

Matt heard the soft voice behind him, and he turned to see Melinda standing there holding an outsized tray in her hands.

"Yes, Miss Cole?" he asked politely while rising to his full height.

A tiny blush crept onto her cheeks as she said, "I hope I didn't interrupt something."

"No, nothing at all. I was just daydreaming a little bit. This is a very beautiful place you have here."

"Thank you." A shy smile crossed her lips and she arched one eyebrow. "Daydreaming? Do you mean to tell me that a vigilant, courageous, and dashing army officer indulges in the same weaknesses that we mortals do?"

Kincaid returned the grin. "I'm afraid so, ma'am. But only when all the dragons have been slain, the villains crucified, and the cat put out for the night."

Melinda's light chuckle had a musical quality about it. "And have all those deeds been done?"

"They have, ma'am. For now at least. May I help you with something?"

"Yes, two things. First, this tray"—she hefted it in demonstration—"is getting a little heavy. And second, my friends call me Mindy, not 'ma'am,' 'Miss Cole,' or 'Melinda.'" She watched him closely now. "I would like to think that you're my friend, however temporary that might be."

Matt stepped forward quickly; taking the tray from her hands, he could smell the tantalizing aroma of hot oatmeal cookies combined with the rich smell of coffee emanating from the porcelain serving set on the tray. Several cups were stacked

62

there as well, and Matt noted that the tray was indeed heavy as he glanced up at Melinda's face.

"You're right, ma'am. This is heavy."

"Then we're not friends?" she asked with the tiniest of pouts.

"Of course we are," Kincaid corrected himself hurriedly. "Let me try again; you're right . . . Mindy. This is heavy."

"Thank you, Lieutenant. I—"

"Correction. 'Thank you, *Matt.*'"

Again, the pert smile. "Thank you, Matt. I thought you and your men might enjoy an afternoon snack. I hope that's not breaking some military rule?"

"No it's not," Kincaid replied with a grin. "Then again, it might be. Our cooks seem to avoid any show of courtesy as though it would bring on the plague. My men will be delighted with your thoughtfulness."

"And you?"

"Even more so. Will you join us?"

"No, I can't, thank you. Would you be so kind as to return the tray to the house when you've finished? That serving set belonged to my mother, and Daddy is quite jealous about those things."

"Maybe we shouldn't use them, Mindy. I'd hate to have something—"

"Nonsense, Lieutenant. I—I mean, Matt. You're all grown men. I'm sure you won't throw them at each other. I'll see you when you've finished," she said, turning and starting toward the house before looking back with a radiant smile and saying, "I hope they're good."

"I'm sure they are, and I thank you on behalf of my men." He watched her cross the yard, and he couldn't help but marvel again at her beauty and feminine charm. He waited until she had moved inside, with a final glance in his direction, before stepping into the bunkhouse.

"We've got a benefactor, boys," he said, placing the tray on the table in the center of the room. "Miss Cole seems to think we look a little underfed and was kind enough to take steps to correct that."

The aroma of freshly baked cookies was immediately discernible, and one private looked at the tray with a hint of disbelief. "Are those real cookies, sir?" he asked, unable to tear his eyes away.

"The genuine article," Matt replied, taking one and biting

into it with undisguised greed. "God, but those are good! Here, help yourselves. There's coffee there too, and I'm sure it won't taste like Dutch's. Be damned careful you don't break or chip those cups, though. They have some value to Miss Cole and her family."

One by one, the soldiers stepped up and took a handful of cookies. They carried the delicate cups as if they were so fragile that any sudden movement would cause them to shatter instantly. As they returned to their places, only one soldier hadn't moved, and Kincaid watched him closely.

"What's the matter, Private? Don't you like oatmeal cookies?"

Private Greer's eyes drifted from the tray to hold on Kincaid's face. "They're my f-favorite."

"Then help yourself."

"N-n-no thanks, sir."

"How long has it been since you've had homemade cookies?"

"A long t-time, sir."

"Then have one," Kincaid replied in a tone that wasn't quite an order but yet was more than a mere invitation.

Greer hesitated, then, almost timidly, he rose and walked to the table, gingerly selected two cookies, and half filled a coffee cup. All eyes were on him as he took a bite, and there could be no mistaking the nostalgic look crossing his face as he savored the flavor.

The young soldier nodded his thanks to Kincaid and returned to his place to slowly nibble the cookies in an attempt to make them last as long as possible. Kincaid continued to watch him a moment longer before turning to Corporal Wojensky.

"May I speak with you outside a moment, Corporal?"

"Certainly, sir," Wojensky said, rising and moving forward to follow Kincaid out the door.

"What do you make of Greer?" Kincaid asked when they were a safe distance away from the bunkhouse. "Does he stutter like that all the time?"

"No, sir. Only when he's nervous or around the other men in close quarters. I've talked with him in the stables and he seems to be able to speak normally most of the time."

"I see. Have the men been needling him again?"

"No more than they do each other. It just affects Greer differently, I guess."

"How old would you make him to be? His record lists him as being eighteen."

"Even though he's a big young feller, sir, I think that's stretching it a mite. I'd put him somewhere around sixteen or seventeen."

"Does he seem slow to you? Mentally, I mean?"

"He's different, that's all I can tell you, Lieutenant. It seems like he just wants to do what he's told and stay as far away as possible when he can. Kind of like a dog that's been whipped real bad; it'll do what it's told to do, but it won't trust anybody or anything."

Kincaid pursed his lips in thought. "Well, we can't give him any preferential treatment, but then I don't want him abused, either. Let's just bide our time and see if we can't pull him out of it."

"Yessir," Wojensky replied, falling in behind Kincaid when the officer stepped toward the bunkhouse. The tray, by this time, had only empty cups on it, so Kincaid took up the tray and glanced at Greer at the same time.

"Private, I'd like for you to see to the mounts. They're your responsibility until we leave here."

Matt thought he could see relief sweep over the young private. "Yes, s-sir."

"Good." Kincaid took up the tray and walked out into the sunlight again.

When he stepped onto the porch of the house, he banged his boots loudly to free them of dust, hoping also that the sound would alert Melinda to his presence. The door stood open, but no sounds came from within, and he hesitated in the doorway to peer cautiously inside.

"Mindy?"

The room was silent, and Kincaid entered a prudent distance before speaking again.

"Mindy? Are you here?"

Still no response, and Kincaid moved toward the kitchen. At the same instant he caught a flash of movement in the hallway. He stopped and waited while Mindy entered the living room; her concentration was given to adjusting the gathered-up hair at the back of her head. She wore tightly fitted jeans, a checkered blouse on which the top two buttons were free, riding boots, and a razor-brimmed black hat.

"Oh!" she gasped, startled. "I didn't hear you come in."

"I didn't mean to intrude. I just wanted to return your tray," Kincaid replied, somewhat embarrassed. It was the first time he had seen the outline of her full figure, and he could feel a flush creep into his cheeks as he looked at her perhaps a bit longer than necessary. "Pardon me for staring," he apologized, "but you are an incredibly beautiful woman."

"In this?" she laughed, taking the tray from his hands and setting it down on the kitchen counter. She turned to look at Matt and rested a hip against the counter's edge. "I know it's not ladylike, but I don't really care. Horses were intended to be ridden with a leg on either side."

"Horses?"

"Yes, horses. I'm going for a ride. It's my one form of recreation."

"I'm sorry, Mindy, but I really don't think you should be riding alone just now. Threats have been made against the settlers in this area, and I'm afraid it might be dangerous."

"Then what do you suggest, Matt?" she asked. "Perhaps you could join me?"

"Well, I—I promised your father that—"

"That you would take care of me. Fine. Then take care of me by joining me for a ride. Just on the chance that you might, I've packed a picnic lunch, fried chicken and things like that, and I know the perfect spot." She could read the hesitation on Kincaid's face and added, "I really would like to get away from the place for a couple of hours, Matt. Besides," she added with a twinkle in her eyes, "I'm going with you or without you. I'd rather it be with you."

"Mindy, I'd love to, but—"

"But nothing, Matt," Melinda said, taking up a wicker basket covered with a checkered cloth. "We'll be back before nightfall and we'll be on my father's property all the time. Now don't be a stuffed shirt. Join me. I'll get a blanket for us to sit on."

Resignedly, Matt took the basket from her and ushered her toward the door. "I'm against it, but I don't seem to have much say in the matter. The blanket won't be necessary. I've got a bedroll tied behind my saddle and we can use that. When we get to the barn, I'll have one of my men saddle your horse. Which one is it?"

"The roan gelding with a white blaze," Melinda replied as

66

they descended the steps. "His name is Rico, and I've raised him from a colt."

The earlier disturbing thought touched the corners of Kincaid's mind. "I've always wanted to do that myself," he said, crossing the yard with steps measured to match Melinda's. "But army life doesn't lend itself to such pursuits."

"I can understand that," Melinda replied. "Why do you stay in the military?"

"I don't really know," Kincaid answered honestly, while reaching for the latch on the barn door. "When I figure that out," he said with a smile, "I'll let you know."

They had ridden for nearly an hour, and their conversation had been one of relaxed cordiality, each of them exploring the other's past. They had started out with their horses well spaced, but the farther they rode, the closer the two mounts drew together. Finally, Melinda guided them through a draw that had been worn deep into the earth by spring rains, and she reined in at a place where bluffs loomed above them.

"Are we there?" Kincaid asked, watching Melinda slip from her saddle and reach up for the basket.

"Not quite yet. We'll leave the horses here, though, and go on foot the rest of the way. Come on, you're going to love it."

Kincaid stepped down, tethered the mounts to clumps of brush, retrieved the bedroll from behind his saddle, and followed Melinda upward along a short, narrow trail. When she stopped, her cheeks were bright from the mild exertion of the climb, and she motioned toward a dark hole in the side of the bluff.

"This is my secret cave," she said, touching Matt's forearm almost impulsively. "I come here when I want to be alone. I'm sure my father, my brother, and some of the hands know about it, but they've never bothered me when I'm here."

Kincaid glanced toward the opening, which was possibly twenty feet in width and an equal distance in depth. There was an inviting quality about the darkness inside, as though it were a cool oasis in the shimmering heat of a featureless land.

"I'll be damned," Matt said without thinking, and then added, "Excuse me. Sometimes I forget."

"No need to apologize, I've heard that and worse before. You spread the blankets and I'll arrange the food. Are you hungry, Matt?"

He nodded.

Melinda opened the basket and drew out a flask of brandy. "Good. A man is supposed to have an appetite, as I understand it. Do you like brandy?"

"Very much, on occasion."

"Is this one of those occasions?" Melinda asked.

"Yes, I suppose it is. Here, let me spread the blanket. You are about to dine on the universal tablecloth of the United States Army."

Melinda smiled as she began spreading out the picnic lunch. "Is that what the letters 'U.S.' stand for? I was thinking it stood for 'us.'"

Matt hesitated, then continued to smooth out the wrinkles.

The picnic lunch consisted of chicken, freshly baked bread, large pieces of pumpkin pie, and more cookies. It was more than Matt could eat, and he finally begged off.

"I'm sorry, Mindy," he said, dabbing the corners of his mouth with a napkin and laying it aside, "you must have had someone else in mind when you packed that lunch. I couldn't eat all that on three picnics, let alone one, but the food was excellent. Why didn't you have any?"

"I had a drumstick."

"One drumstick." he said disbelievingly. "How can you survive on that?"

Melinda laughed happily. "I enjoyed watching you eat, Matt." Her arms were hooked about her knees, and her head was lowered, the pink tip of her tongue absently caressing the rim of her glass. "There's something special about preparing food for a man and then watching him enjoy it. It makes you feel like you've done something he can't do, for all his manliness and desire to protect."

"You're right there. I doubt that I could boil water," Matt lied gently, while taking up his glass and resting on one side with his head propped up on his hand. "This is an exquisite spot you've found, Mindy. I can see why you enjoy coming here."

Melinda fell silent. Her eyes were locked on the prairie floor below, and she might have been sealed off from the world, so detached was her mien. Kincaid studied her for several long moments before speaking again.

"Did I say something wrong?"

"No," she replied in a distant voice. "I was in love with a man one time, or at least I thought I was. Did you know that?"

"No, I didn't."

"That was a silly question; there's no reason in the world why you should. At any rate, I loved him and would have done anything for him. He was the foreman over at the neighbor's place, where my father is now, and since my father didn't think I should ever go alone anywhere with a man until I was married, we met here secretly."

Kincaid stared into the amber brandy and swirled it in thought. "Is there some reason why you're telling me this, Mindy?"

"Yes. Excuse me for being brazen, but when I first saw you this morning, a feeling came over me that only Doyle had caused in the past. Right then, I wanted to bring you here to see if my initial feeling was true."

"And?"

"It was."

Feeling a trifle embarrassed and equally uncomfortable, Kincaid sipped his brandy and held the warm, biting liquor in his mouth for several seconds before swallowing. "What ever happened to this friend of yours, this Doyle?"

"He just left one day," she said, while her chin lowered to her forearm. "No goodbyes, no thank-you's, just gone. I've never heard from him since."

"I'm sorry, Mindy. I really am. Perhaps he had a reason and maybe he'll come back someday."

"Perhaps. I don't think I'm waiting for him, but maybe I am. I had never seen anyone like him until you came to our place today."

"Did your father like him?"

"No."

Kincaid allowed an easy smile to crease his face. "Well, at least your friend Doyle and myself do have one thing in common: your father didn't have much good to say about me, either, when we first met."

"He's that way, Matt. Maybe it's the life he's had, being without my mother all these years and continuing to love her and thinking she'll come back to him. He works constantly, as if exhaustion were his only release. I don't want to live like that, Matt," she concluded, turning toward him with a deep, searching look in her dark eyes. "I don't want to waste my entire life waiting for something that might never happen."

"What have you got in mind to do?"

"In exactly two weeks I'm catching a train to Chicago. I

69

have an aunt who lives there and I'll stay with her until I get settled."

"What are your plans then? To get a job?"

"No, not until I have to, at least. You might think this sounds scandalous, but I'd like to be an actress."

"Well, Mindy, I don't know much about the theater, but if beauty is a prerequisite, you should be a smashing success."

He thought he saw a faint blush creep onto her cheeks while she lowered her eyes and looked away. "Do you really think so?"

"I know so. You are the most beautiful woman I have ever met."

Their eyes met and held for a moment. Suddenly, Mindy smiled and reached for the brandy flask.

"That's enough of that," she said, tilting the bottle toward Kincaid's glass and pouring. She was kneeling above him, and he could see the rise and fall of her breasts as she breathed. Her lips were slightly parted and her eyes were on Matt's face while the liquor trickled into the glass. Matt could feel the warmth of a thigh pressing against his leg, and could smell the rich fragrance of her as she hovered above him with the two freed buttons of her blouse exposing a hint of cleavage. His hand slowly went to the back of her neck, and he pulled her mouth gently toward his. Their lips touched in a hesitant, testing kiss, and then pressed tightly together as she lowered herself onto his chest. His fingers found the tortoiseshell comb that held her hair drawn back, and he deftly pulled it free and her ebony hair fell about his face. Somehow, the brandy flask was placed to one side and her fingers went to the back of his head, while his arms encircled her narrow waist. Their kiss was somehow tense, as though both held themselves in check to the extent of their will. After a brief parting and then another long kiss, which sent a shiver tickling down Matt's spine, he placed his hands against her cheeks and tenderly pushed her face away.

"Mindy, I want you more than you could imagine, but I don't want to take advantage of a situation. Your father entrusted his homestead to me while he is gone, and I don't want to violate that trust by taking something even more valuable to him than his home."

Mindy smiled affectionately and kissed his lips lightly. "You're taking nothing of his, Matt. And you are taking nothing of mine. If anything, you're giving. I brought you here, you didn't bring me."

Kincaid closed his eyes hesitantly. "I don't want to—"

"To what, Matt? Make love to me? I'm a grown woman and I know what I'm doing. As I said, I was in love once before."

Matt looked deeply into her eyes and he could feel the warmth of her body on his taut stomach, the pressure of her breasts on his chest, and taste the lingering flavor of her kiss. His hand went to the back of her head again, and they rolled to lie on their sides, tongues probing and hands searching out the delicate parts of each other's bodies. Unnoticed, the brandy flask tipped over, and from the prairie rose the distant lowing of cattle as the sun settled toward the horizon.

It was nearly dark when they galloped their horses into the main yard of the Grace Land homestead. Melinda had seemed thoroughly ecstatic upon leaving the cave, and when they had neared the homestead, she'd challenged Matt to a horse race. They had held hands nearly all the way back, and when Matt accepted her challenge with a good-natured grin while releasing his grip, Melinda had spurred her mount and jumped to an early twenty-yard lead. Now she reined her horse in, half a length in front of him, and there was the joyous look of youthful freedom on her face.

"I told you I'd win."

"Sorry, young lady," Kincaid replied, stepping down and holding Melinda's mount for her, "but I'd have to say you cheated back there."

"Where?" Melinda asked with a mischievous smile. "The cave or the race?"

"Both. Now let me help you down and I'll put our horses away."

"You're such a gentleman, Matt," Melinda replied, slipping from the saddle. "Are you always this courteous to the ladies you take advantage of?"

Matt caught the hint of playful challenge in her voice. "Only future stars of the theater who have greatness in their minds and courage in their hearts." Then he added, as he led the horses toward the barn, "Not to mention various widows and orphans along the way."

"Matt?"

Hearing his name softly spoken in the gathering twilight, he stopped and turned. "Yes, Mindy?"

"Will you spend the night with me? And hold me close, tenderly and gently like back there? It's so lonely in that big old house."

"Mindy, I—" Kincaid said, feeling an extreme sense of guilt.

"For me? It will be our only night together."

"Are you sure it'll be all right?"

"I'm sure. No one will know but you and me. Please, Matt. I don't want to be alone tonight."

Matt hesitated, but he knew the answer he would give. Just the thought of holding her naked body next to his sent a familiar shiver through his loins. "All right, Mindy. Let me put the horses away and check on my men. It shouldn't take more than half an hour."

"That'll be perfect. I'll have time to freshen up." With that, she blew him a kiss, turned, and walked away.

Kincaid watched her depart through the deepening shadows. He wanted to reach out to her, to grab her and tell her of the loneliness he also felt, but instead, he led the two horses toward the barn. There would be this night, he knew, and then there would be no more. He quickly stripped the saddles away, curried the mounts, and poured a ration of grain into separate troughs before blowing out the lamp and quitting the barn.

As he crossed the yard in the direction of the bunkhouse, he glanced once toward the main building and saw a single lantern burning in what he assumed was a bedroom window toward the rear of the building. His pace quickened as he angled toward the dull yellow light spilling from the windows of the crew's quarters.

six _____

A swath of pale moonlight filtered through the window and splashed across the foot of the bed in a room so totally silent that even the measured breathing of one peacefully asleep seemed overly loud. Melinda lay curled up next to Matt's side, with one leg carelessly draped across his thigh, while her tousled hair spread across the white pillow on which her head rested, cuddled against his shoulder. With one arm encircling her shoulders and the other crooked beneath his head, Matt continued to stare at the ceiling above the bed as he had for nearly an hour; contrary to what one might expect, his mind was not totally given to the delicious ecstasy of the lovemaking they had so recently shared.

Instead, he thought of the alien comfort and warmth of the generously appointed bedroom, the silken sheets, the down-filled comforter with matching pillows, and the delicate body pressed closely to his. The contrast between his present surroundings and those he had known for so long in his room at the BOQ back at Outpost Number Nine weighed heavily upon his mind. Coarse linen, scratchy blankets, a pillow seemingly filled more with lead than feathers, and a cold sod floor swept clean daily in a cloud of dust. And he wondered again if he had made the right choice in life. A home like this, a woman like Melinda, could be his, he thought. There would be delectable meals each evening, the weary satisfaction of working one's own land throughout the day, and children asleep in the adjoining rooms, snuggled up in the safety and warmth of their father's home. There would be church on Sundays, followed by a family picnic, with corn on the cob dripping with freshly churned butter.

But, he wondered almost in the same thought, what would the sacrifices be? The camaraderie of his fellow officers, the respect of men who trusted and needed him, the satisfaction and inherent thrill of danger that came with combat patrols. Yes, he concluded, those things he would miss, but what he would miss most of all was the feeling of commitment to something larger than himself, to something that was for the universal good and not merely for personal gain and comfort. The freedom that came with riding at the head of a column of mounted infantry, and into never-ending, challenging situations, with life or death the ultimate outcome.

Kincaid felt Melinda stir by his side, and he became aware of the change in her breathing. He could feel her eyes upon him in the darkness.

"Have you been sleeping, Matt?" she asked in a husky voice.

"No. Not much."

"Why?"

He shrugged one shoulder. "I've got too much on my mind, I guess."

"Army business?"

"No, not really. The business of life would be more accurate."

Melinda tossed her head to clear the hair from her eyes, while her right hand went down to close over Kincaid's. "Why do you do it, Matt?"

"Do what?"

"Stay in the army. A man like you could have anything he wanted in civilian life."

Kincaid hesitated before responding. "If I knew the answer to that, Mindy, I'd tell it to myself."

"Doesn't it get lonely?" she asked, pressing her cheek against his chest. "I mean, never really having anything? Going from post to post, solving everybody's problems but your own?"

"Yes, I suppose it does. But it has its rewards as well."

"Do you have . . . any women friends? By that I mean, are you seriously involved with someone?" she added quickly, as though embarrassed, "Don't answer that if you don't want to. I didn't mean to pry."

Kincaid pulled her toward him with a gentle tug. "You're not prying, and my answer to that is, if I did have, I wouldn't be here with you right now."

"I'm glad. Do you meet many women? In your job, I mean?"

"A few. Not too many."

"Are they like me? Willing, even wanting, to go to bed with you?"

"What are you getting at, Mindy?" Kincaid asked, turning his head slightly to look down at her.

"I just don't want to think what we've had is . . . cheap . . . or that you think badly of me because I seduced you, more or less."

"I was as anxious to sleep with you as you were with me. There was no seduction involved. To answer your question, yes, I've met some very nice ladies, and some not so nice. But since I can't offer them anything in the way of home comforts, it never goes beyond that."

"Have you ever thought that maybe one of them, even myself perhaps, would be perfectly happy with what you do have?"

"Mindy," Matt said with a slight plea in his tone, "I'd rather not talk about it, and please don't be offended. That thought's been on my mind since we left the cave, but what I do is too dangerous, too insecure to build anything positive on."

"Will you ever marry?"

"I don't know. Maybe when I'm CO of some outfit and not on combat patrol all the time. For right now, though, about the only thing I could offer a woman is widow's benefits."

He could feel her shudder and press more tightly against him. "I don't want to think about that. Let's talk about something else."

"That's fine with me," Kincaid replied, stifling a slight yawn.

"What time is it?"

"Just before dawn."

Suddenly, Matt's body stiffened and his ears strained to

75

pick up something as yet undefinable. He lay still, staring upward and not risking a single breath.

"What is it, Matt?" Melinda asked in a whisper.

"I'm not sure. I just have the feeling someone's out there," Kincaid replied, freeing himself from her embrace and slipping out of bed. He crept to the window on bare feet and scanned the yard, now pale gray with the coming dawn, then closed the shutters softly and turned to pull his pants and boots on. After he tucked his shirt in and was strapping on his gunbelt, he turned to look at the woman who was staring at him in wide-eyed silence from the bed.

"Do you have a gun in your room, Mindy?"

"Yes, there's a shotgun in the closet."

"Good." Kincaid stepped to the closet, found the double-barreled weapon, checked it for rounds, and laid it on the bed. "I've got to get to the bunkhouse and alert my men," he said, speaking rapidly now. "I think we're about to be attacked, maybe by the Sioux. I'll bring half the squad back to protect this main building, leaving the other half to protect the out-buildings. Do you know how to fire this thing?"

Melinda nodded. "Yes, I hate it, but I do know how."

"Good. If anyone gets in here before I get back, you won't have time to reload." He looked down at her with a mixture of seriousness and tenderness in his eyes. "And even more importantly, if my men and I are killed, do you know what to do?"

There was a strange evenness and lack of fright in Melinda's voice when she replied. "Yes I do, Matt. I have been taught that, since I was a little girl. The last round is for myself."

Even for a battle-hardened veteran like Matt Kincaid, the thought of that beautiful head blown away by the violent blast of a shotgun was something he'd rather not think about. He squeezed her firmly before propping her up against the headboard with the shotgun across her lap. "If that door opens and it's not me . . ."

Their eyes locked on each other's, and there was no further need for words. Kincaid kissed her quickly on the lips, then turned and was gone.

He hesitated by the living room door, opened it just a crack, and estimated the distance from the main building to the bunkhouse. It was a good fifty yards. He knew he would be a totally exposed target in the spreading light of dawn, and he wondered briefly if his imagination might be playing tricks on him. Perhaps his senses had been too acutely tuned to danger, and there was no real threat at all. But then something born of years of combat tugged at the corners of his mind—that nagging feeling of danger, the overpowering awareness that something was not as it should be. Then he realized what it was. The roosters were not crowing, and the common sounds of barn yard animals at the break of day were not there. Pulling his Scoff from its holster, Kincaid took one last deep breath and sprang through the door, clearing the porch steps in a single leap and hitting the ground in a tumbling roll. Two shots instantly rang out, tearing up chunks of dirt and rock behind him, but Matt was on his feet and running in a zigzag dodge toward the bunkhouse. Three more shots were fired, and he could hear the unmistakable war chant of the Sioux, rising from somewhere near the corrals, as he dove beneath the hitch rail in front of the bunkhouse and slammed his way inside.

The soldiers were already in their positions at the gun slits in the walls. The crashing roar of exploding shells filled the confined room, and the acrid smell of gun powder stung his nostrils.

"Corporal Wojensky!" Kincaid shouted at the senior noncom.

"Yessir!" replied the corporal, his unshaven face flushed with the thrill of combat.

"I'm taking half of your squad with me to the main house! You cover us, then keep the others here!"

"Right, sir!" He called out the names of five men, and they sprang toward the door to await Kincaid's instructions while the others continued to fire.

Kincaid looked out a window. Ghostly figures were slipping stealthily toward the house through the litter of wagons and equipment. He ran toward the door.

"Follow me! We'll have to fight our way in!"

Bounding through the doorway, he squeezed off two quick shots at the lithe figures running in crouched positions, and he saw one of them fall as he heard the soldiers behind him, clattering onto the small porch of the bunkhouse.

"Spread out and cover each other! We've got to get inside the house."

They advanced across the yard in a "run, drop, and fire" progression, repeating the process every ten yards or so. The

Sioux were now returning fire, and there was a constant rattle of weapons blasting away to the rear. Seeing one warrior with a pitch torch in hand rush forward and draw back his arm to throw the missile against the facing wall, Kincaid snapped off a hastily aimed shot and watched only long enough to see the Indian lurch forward, then sprawl upon his face in the dust, the torch falling by his side.

A soldier next to Kincaid took a shot in the stomach and pitched to the ground in a twisting arc, his Springfield dropping unnoticed to the ground.

Matt hesitated, knowing the mounted warriors would not be long in joining the attack, then he leaped to the wounded man's aid, while watching three braves dart through the front door of the house. He took aim with his Scoff at the dark doorway, but the three braves had already disappeared inside. With the exception of the three who had gained entry into the house, the other Sioux were falling back to shoot from behind whatever protection they could find. Calling out to another soldier to aid the wounded man, Kincaid bolted, zigzagging, toward the house.

His boot hit the porch step and he struggled upward, covered to the rear by the others, who had turned to fire as they backed toward the relative safety of the house.

Kincaid dove through the doorway in a tumbling roll and came up with a blazing weapon. His first shot caught one Indian squarely in the solar plexus and sent him staggering backward to tumble over an ottoman, while Matt instantly whirled and fired again, and the second warrior banged against the wall with a bullet through his chest.

Kincaid was panting heavily as he lurched to his feet, and his mind screamed to him: *That's only two! Three made it through the door! The bedroom! Melinda!*

Matt lurched forward, seeing the hallway as nothing more than a blur through sweat-drenched eyes. His thumb closed over the hammer again, and drew it back with a dull metallic click that was muted by the crashing weapons firing behind him. Then he rushed forward. There seemed to be an awful space of distance and silence between him and the darkened passageway. His legs felt heavy and sluggish, and it seemed as though he were moving in some ethereal world, bounding forward but gaining no headway.

Then the booming crash of a shotgun shattered the stillness

before him, and he saw a body reel across the hallway to slam against the far wall and slump to the floor. Kincaid pumped two rounds into the apparently lifeless form, and hesitated for an instant beside the bedroom doorway before lunging inside.

"Melinda! Don't!" he screamed, seeing the young woman, her eyes rolled back in terror, with the huge twin barrels of the gun inside her mouth and a finger pressed against the trigger.

"It's me, Mindy," he soothed in a gentle voice. "They're all dead. You're safe now." Then he spoke slowly but firmly. "Just take your finger away from that trigger."

The girl made no movement, except for a curious twitching of her head from side to side. Kincaid inched forward, speaking in comforting tones as he moved, his eyes locked on the white-knuckled finger pressed against the trigger.

"You're all right now, honey. Don't do anything. You're safe and I'm here to protect you. Remember the cave?" he asked, passing the corner of the bed now. "You and me in the cave, remember?"

Her eyes watched him, giving no sign of recognition. The finger remained locked where it was, just half a foot-pound's pressure from instant oblivion.

"Now I'll tell you what I'm going to do," Matt said, laying the Scoff gently on the bed while the battle that was still raging outside registered in his mind. "I'm going to take that gun from your hand"—he reached forward as he spoke—"and put it away. You won't need it anymore."

Suddenly, like a snake striking, his hand shot forward and the heel of his palm closed between the hammer and the firing pin just as she pulled the trigger. Sharp metal dug into his flesh. Without reacting to the pain, Kincaid took hold of the weapon and gently pulled it from her mouth before easing the hammer back and freeing his hand from the searing bite of spring-loaded metal. He laid the shotgun on the bed and reached up to touch Melinda's face tenderly.

"It's all right now, honey. It's over. All over."

Her face trembled beneath his hands, and her lips moved in an attempt to speak while her eyes searched his face with the first hint of recognition.

"Matt? Is it—is it—you?"

"Yes, it's me. You're all right now."

"I killed—I killed him."

"I know, Mindy. You did what you had to do."

"Oh God!" she cried, sobbing now, her hands darting up to cover her face in anguish. "I killed him!"

"You did what you had to do, Mindy. Remember that. He would have killed you. Or worse."

"I thought—I thought you were one of them," she sobbed, "and I was going to—to kill myself."

"I know you were, honey," Matt said, stroking her hair and pulling her head to his chest. "You were only doing what you were told to do," he concluded, but his words sounded flat and empty.

Her arms shot out and pulled him to her, and there was frantic desperation in her tone as she rubbed her cheek against his. "I want to go away from here, Matt. I have to go away from here! I can't take it anymore. The constant fear, the memory of my mother living in the house like she was still alive! I have to get away! I'm not brave like they are, Matt! I have to get away!"

Kincaid could feel her warm tears on his own face, and he hugged her tightly while listening to the continuing rifle fire outside. He pushed her away and looked directly into her eyes. "Mindy? Listen to me." His voice was stern but not demanding. "It's not over yet. My men need my help, and one of them is wounded. He needs your help. Can you pull yourself together?"

Melinda watched him, biting her lip and trying to squeeze back the tears. Her reluctant nod was almost imperceptible.

"Good," he said, releasing his grip and kissing her lightly. "Pull some clothes on while I go out and see what things look like. Everybody has to pitch in if we're going to get out of this mess. We're badly outnumbered and we're going to need all the help we can get."

Melinda nodded and Matt withdrew, pausing to look at her one more time before turning and striding through the door and back to the battle. He knelt beside the wounded soldier, whose eyes were closed. The only sign of life was the painful grimace on his face and the weak rising and falling of his chest.

"I think he's done for, sir," one soldier said, squeezing off a quick shot before glancing over his shoulder.

Kincaid stripped the blood-soaked cloth away to examine the wound, and replied as he concentrated on his work, "Let's not count him out before we've done everything we can, Private. How many do you think we're up against?"

"A whole goddamned bunch of 'em, sir. Looks like thirty

or forty at least. But we've beaten them back so far."

"What's it look like down at the bunkhouse?"

"The boys seem to be holdin' their own pretty good. Whoever built this place knew somethin' about fightin' Indians."

"Yes, he does," Kincaid said almost absently, as he studied the torn flesh in the wounded man's lower chest. He could see the flecks of pink mixed with blood seeping from the hole, and he knew a lung had been punctured. He also knew that Private William Phillips would never see the setting of that day's sun.

Hearing the rustle of skirts beside him, he turned to watch Melinda drop to her knees and gingerly touch the dying soldier's forehead. If she was afraid now, Matt could not detect it in her face, which was composed and concerned only with the needs of the moment.

"How bad is it, Matt?" she asked, studying his face intently.

The look in his eyes would have been enough, but he shook his head to indicate that there was little or no hope.

Mindy rose quickly to rush toward the bedroom, mindful of the shots slamming into the heavily shuttered windows. "I'll get pillows and blankets. Let's make him as comfortable as we can. There are clean cloths and a bucket of water in the kitchen. Get them for me, please, and I'll clean that wound."

Kincaid smiled inwardly and watched her depart before retrieving the requested items from the kitchen and placing them beside the trooper. Then he went to a gun slit and peered out. "There should be an equal number of them waiting just over that swell," he said in the direction of the private nearest to him, while continuing to scrutinize the corrals and outbuildings. "They'll attack on horseback soon, and try to get close enough to put the torch to these walls. Shoot their mounts out from under them, concentrating on the ones who get the closest."

"Yessir." The private hesitated. "Shouldn't we send someone back to the main command for reinforcements, sir?"

"No. They'd be dead before they got a half-mile. And if they did make it, they'd be leading the others into an ambush. We'll have to fight it out ourselves."

"Right, sir, whatever you say," the private replied, squinting down his gunbarrel once more and firing. "They might take us, but they're sure as hell gonna have to work for it."

Kincaid moved from man to man, checking extra rounds and assessing their situation from a defensive standpoint. If

81

there was any fear in their hearts, none was shown, and each man fired with the calm concentration of troops practicing on a firing range. These were good men, Kincaid thought, good men who deserved good leadership. The last thought in their minds was to back away from a fight, to give up and quit when the going got tough. They were totally committed to the purpose they served, and aside from the expected grumblings, not a single veteran in his command had ever expressed the desire to quit the service and make an easier life for himself on the outside.

That last revelation disturbed him, and Kincaid felt a sense of personal disgust pass through his mind, the kind of disgust a man feels when he realizes he has placed individual gain above the welfare of others. The muscles were tensed along his jaw when he quit his inspection, reloaded the Scoff, and turned to add his weapon to the firepower of the defenders. No one had ever questioned his ability to command, Kincaid thought, firing and seeing a warrior sprawl onto his back; did he have the right to question his own desire to command and be the leader of men committed to a higher cause?

It was a rhetorical question, he knew, and his eyes were drawn to Melinda as if by a magnet. She was kneeling over Private Phillips with her hands pressed deeply into her lap, and tears streamed down her cheeks. Kincaid could tell at a glance that the soldier was dead, and he felt a sudden impulse to ignore the battle raging around them, rush to her, and take her into his arms. She seemed so alone, so defenseless, staring down, wide-eyed, at the dead man lying before her.

"Here they come, sir," said Private Richardson, off to his left.

Kincaid's head snapped back toward the gun slit, and he could see the large, mounted war party split into two groups as it raced toward the homestead. The first section veered toward the bunkhouse, while the second bore directly down on the main house. Perhaps as many as ten warriors held burning, pitch-laden sticks above their heads, with black smoke trailing behind them. The bunkhouse was already coming under increasingly heavy fire, but Kincaid could see that the main thrust of the assault would be toward their own positions.

"Take your time and aim well," he said in a calm voice. "Go for the ones with the torches first. Let them come another thirty yards or so, then fire when I do."

Kincaid was watching the leading Indian over the barrel of the Scoff, and he could see the warrior's red and yellow warpaint as the Indian rode in, crouched low on his pony's withers. Then he squeezed the trigger and the horse fell, while the Springfields around him opened fire once again. Other mounts went down, but the warrior at the head of the group recovered from his tumbling roll and sprinted toward the house. Kincaid fired a second time, and the Indian straightened from his crouch as though jerked upward by an invisible wire, to hang there for an instant before toppling onto his back with a bullet through his throat. The torch fell to the ground, where it continued to burn harmlessly until another brave beside the corral leaped forward, snatched the flaming stick, and threw it toward the porch with a mighty heave. A shot from one of the Springfields smashed into the Indian, and Kincaid watched him fall while hearing a solid clunk as the stick hit the wall and fell onto the tinder-dry flooring of the porch.

Kincaid sprang toward the door. "Cover me!" he yelled, reaching for the bar that sealed the door shut and shoving it to one side. "I've got to put that damned thing out!"

"*Matt!*" Melinda screamed. "Don't go out there!"

"Haven't any choice," Kincaid replied, opening the door just a crack and peering out while he braced his legs for a sudden lunge. "We've already got a fire started."

With those words he was gone, running in a hunched-over position and firing the revolver in his hand as he raced toward the snapping crackle of burning wood. Several shots slammed into the chinked logs beside him, but miraculously he was not hit. He holstered the now-empty pistol in one swift motion while reaching down to snatch the torch burning fiercely on the cut timber of the porch. He could feel the heat on his face, and knew that in a matter of minutes the entire porch would be engulfed in flame. Tossing the stick onto the ground, he dove toward a nearby water barrel and hit flat on his stomach in the same instant that a round thudded into the oaken staves, sending a gush of water over him. After taking a second to catch his breath, Matt lurched upward, grabbed the bucket hanging next to the barrel, plunged it into the water, and sloshed water onto the flames in one motion. He was engulfed by smoke now, and he shielded his eyes while dipping and throwing again. With the third repetition, he could see that the flames were out, but he decided to try a fourth toss. Then, when a bullet ripped the bucket from his hand, he ducked down again and raced for the door. One shot tore stingingly across his upper thigh, and another nipped the brim of his hat just as he dove into the opening, which was immediately sealed behind him.

Kincaid rolled onto his back and raised his leg to examine the wound. It was beginning to hurt, and his trouser leg had started to turn crimson with the flow of blood.

"Matt! You've been hit!" Melinda yelled, leaping up and rushing toward him.

"It'll be all right, Mindy! Stay back and stay down!" Kincaid was on his feet again now, jamming fresh cartridges into the Scoff and hobbling toward the wall. "We'll take a look at it later."

As suddenly as they had attacked, the Sioux withdrew, and Kincaid emptied his revolver at the warriors fleeing on foot. The soldiers with rifles concentrated on the mounted Indians, who were rapidly riding out of range.

The room was filled with the odor of burned gunpowder, and a pall of heavy gray smoke hung from the low ceiling. A crushing quiet settled over the house, while Kincaid leaned his back against the wall to tear his trouser leg away and gingerly touch the mutilated skin.

"Here, Matt, let me take a look at it," Mindy said, moving forward with a basin of water and some clean cloths. "I'm not much good when it comes to fighting, but I do know how to doctor a wound."

Kincaid smiled down at her as she began to dab the blood away. "You're pretty good with a shotgun too, as I recall."

"Don't remind me," Melinda replied with a shudder, while wringing out the cloth and pressing it to the wound again. She glanced up at him with worried eyes and continued to work. "How long will this go on, Matt? I'm not sure I can stand a whole lot more."

"Sure you can. You'll be here when it's over," Kincaid said in an attempt to console her before glancing toward Private Richardson. "How much ammunition have we got left?"

"Not much, sir. Our extra rounds are on the supply horse down in the barn."

"Yes, I know. I imagine Wojensky's people are running low themselves. I'll need a volunteer to go down there and

84

bring back more ammunition, and some for Wojensky's men as well."

"I'll go, sir," Richardson said without hesitation.

"Fine. Thank you, Private." Kincaid turned to look out the gun slit and over the yard, which was littered with fallen horses and dead Indians. "You'll have to be quick, but be careful. I think they all withdrew, but you never know. We'll cover you from here."

"How long have I got, sir?"

"I'm not sure. But I do know they'll attack again."

"Will they, Matt?" Melinda asked, wrapping a bandage around Kincaid's thigh and concentrating on her work. "How much more can we take?"

"I'd say we're good for one more assault. If they come at us a third time, we may be out of luck and ammunition both. I don't want you to worry about that, but I do want you to know what to expect." He watched her closely while she knotted the bandage. "If worse comes to worst, Mindy, you know what to do."

"Yes, I know," she replied with a slight tremor in her voice. "Could you have one of your men load the shotgun for me? I couldn't stand to walk by that Indian lying back there again. In the meantime, I'll try to find something for your soldiers to eat."

"Watkins? There's a shotgun in the bedroom and some extra shells in the closet. Get them, load the gun, and bring it out here."

"Yessir."

Kincaid looked at Melinda again. "Is there food in the bunkhouse, Mindy?"

"Yes, there's plenty."

"Good." He reached out and touched her cheek gently. "Mindy?"

The young woman looked up at him tenderly. "Yes, Matt?"

"No matter what happens, I want you to know that you're one of the finest people I've ever met."

Melinda lowered her eyes and pressed his hand to her cheek. "I feel the same way about you, Matt. If—if it happens, what you're talking about with the shotgun I mean, would you do it for me?"

"Let's not talk about it. We'll do what has to be done when

85

the time comes, if it does. Until then, it's my job to make sure that you, my men, and myself get out of this thing alive. Remember when you asked me why I stay in the service?"

"Yes, I remember, and I don't need an answer anymore. Just seeing the relationship you have with your soldiers is all the answer I need. I wish it could be different, but I know it can't."

The tears had begun to flow again, and Melinda turned away. Kincaid watched her until she disappeared into the kitchen, before looking at Richardson again.

"All right, Private. We'd better get on with it. We've got two chances, slim and none, you know that as well as I do. Let's make damned sure we don't wind up empty-handed with the second chance."

"I'm on my way, sir. We ain't never been beat yet, and it ain't gonna happen today, either." Richardson moved to the doorway, stopped, and turned with a wink. "Me and the boys ain't gonna let Easy Company lose the best damned officer we've got. Be back in a minute with enough goddamned shells to blow every damned featherhead in the territory back to the Happy Hunting Ground."

When Richardson was gone, Kincaid barred the door again and leaned against it for a moment with his eyes closed. When he opened them again, Watkins was stepping over the dead warrior and approaching him with the heavy shotgun in his hands. The sight of the weapon made Kincaid suddenly tired, and he ran a hand through his hair with a weary sigh.

"Just lean it against the table over there, Private. I don't want to see that damned thing again unless I have to use it."

seven

Major Brian Sacke pulled his boots on with a leisurely tug, yawned, ran a hand across the back of his neck, and scratched his crotch as he crossed the tent to the water basin situated under a modest mirror. Leaning close to the mirror, he curled his lips back and ran his tongue over his teeth, before yawning again while a gurgle rumbled through his stomach. The sound, in combination with the gnawing pangs of hunger, reminded him that he had missed breakfast for the second day in a row and caused the determined thought to pass through his mind that he wouldn't miss lunch by sleeping through it, as he had the day before.

It was a contented man who took up lather and brush to begin daubing his face for a much-needed shave, a man who had known nothing but joy since the decision had been made to leave the defense of the battalion up to Lieutenant Kincaid, and the construction of the dam to Captain Edgerton. Gone were the worries about failure, ridicule, and contemptuous glances from men who had yet to learn the meaning of respect for their commanding officer. To Sacke, it felt good to be in command without having to bear the responsibilities that went with being the sole decision-making personage on the project. Now he felt securely in command through his most recent decision—to make no decisions at all—which would leave him in the perfect position of taking credit for whatever accomplishments might be achieved and totally absolved of any blame for things that might go awry. If the dam was completed successfully and on schedule, he would certainly give a modicum of credit to the pair of junior officers, once he was safely ensconced in a comfortable office in Washington.

The major ceased lathering his chin just long enough to examine his bloodshot eyes and resolve not to have a drink before two in the afternoon at the earliest. Then his thoughts returned to the military situation at hand. If the dam was a failure, he would condemn and censure those same two men with a vengeance, and press for their immediate resignation from the service. It was a secure situation, as Sacke saw it, and the only way to be in command of a project of this nature; he could use the ambitions and talents of those below him in rank to fuel the fires of his own advancement, while always having them there as a cushion against failure.

Sacke was humming softly as he began to draw the razor down along his lean jaw, after having stropped the blade carefully and meticulously. He could hear the men chattering in the grub line now forming for the noon meal, and he knew his orderly would be arriving shortly with a tray of lunch. He visualized the lines of men with tin plates and utensils in hand, in comparison with the elegantly served meals in the officer's mess back at division headquarters. His musings were interrupted when he accidently nicked the skin just above his Adam's apple.

"Damn," he muttered, dabbing at the spot of blood with a towel while thinking that a drink would surely ease the pain. *Yes, that's it,* he decided. *In the future I'll not have a drink before noon. That hour should be well past already.*

Forgetting the shave momentarily, and turning to pour a generous ration of whiskey, he thought about the one decision he had been forced to make during Lieutenant Kincaid's absence. It had involved the first sergeant of Easy Company, Ben Cohen, and had centered around this very hour of day, the noon meal. A commotion of sorts had arisen regarding rotation through the grub line, and the engineers had squawked that the mounted infantry was getting a better deal.

Since the men of Easy Company were being fed in the common mess of his regiment, Major Sacke had concluded that there was no reason for them to be treated differently from the engineers at mealtime. They would stand in line just like everyone else and eat during the same hours.

Cohen's argument had been that his men should eat in shifts, before and after the engineers, enabling them to take their repast quickly and resume patrolling the area. To support his viewpoint, Cohen had pointed out the growing resentment between the two military factions. Any means of preventing their mingling together should be seized upon to avoid pointless fights and bickering.

Sacke raised the glass to his lips, careful to skirt the lather around his mouth, and remembered how wonderful it had felt to give a direct order to someone and have it obeyed. He had pooh-poohed the need for constant vigilance in broad daylight, and remembered having said something like, "Sergeant, if your men aren't tough enough to mingle with engineers, then perhaps *we* should be protecting *you*, instead of the other way around." After that came the direct order stating that all men from both outfits would fall in for grub at the same time. At the time of the decision, Sacke had not been mindless of the fact that his siding with the engineers might shore up his failing image with the soldiers of his regiment.

It was good, Sacke reminded himself as he placed the glass on the table and took up his razor again, to keep underlings in line and never allow them too much authority. Especially a lowly sergeant who had nothing better to do than ride around on a horse and pretend to be coordinating defenses. Those infantrymen were too damned arrogant anyway, when they were mounted, and it served them right from time to time to have to walk on the ground and stand in grub lines like the common soldiers they were. Secretly, Sacke had been pleased by Captain Edgerton's absence during the discussion of the previous day and only slightly disturbed by Cohen's truculent acceptance of the direct order with the reminder that the matter would be put directly before Lieutenant Kincaid, upon his return from the Cole homestead. Sacke had been equally firm with Kincaid's two second lieutenants when they came to appeal the sergeant's case, and he knew that his task would not be so simple with the first lieutenant. But what the hell, he had concluded as the two men left the headquarters tent, rank and respect for rank were the cornerstone of the military establishment, and first lieutenants were no exception to that rule.

With half his face shaved, being extremely careful not to damage a single hair of his mustache, Sacke turned his attention to the other side, drawing the sideburn up and poising the razor for a downward stroke. Had he drawn the razor a half-inch farther, he may well have cut his ear off in frightened response to the violence that erupted outside.

It began with the pounding of hooves, shouted commands, startled questions, and then the resounding blasts of dozens of rifles firing simultaneously, combined with the rolling thunder of more running horses. Tin plates clattered to the ground and wounded men screamed, while other soldiers shouted back and forth. Boiling pots of stew were knocked over in the mad scramble to quit the grub line and get to weapons. Several stray bullets ripped through Sacke's tent, and he ducked instinctively with a cautious glance at the flap, which was still hanging open.

The crescendo of rifle fire increased to a deafening roar, and the major, forgetting his half-lathered face, rushed toward the entrance with towel in hand. He poked his head through the canvas and saw warpainted Indians mounted on ponies, racing back and forth, firing at the fleeing soldiers and throwing fire sticks on top of dry canvas tents. Fully one-third of the camp was ablaze by now, with blue-uniformed soldiers running toward weapons stacked with military precision well away from where the grub line had been. One squad of mounted infantry wheeled and surged in the center of the fray, firing when weapons were loaded and swinging rifles like clubs when they were not. Off to the right, Sacke saw half a dozen braves throw their firebrands onto the pile of logs stacked near the dam site, and watched in horror as his precious materials burst into flames to send a towering pall of gray smoke into the sky.

The soldiers, mounted infantry as well as engineers, had managed to get to their weapons by this time, and were returning fire, but Sacke did not notice, so awestruck and immobilized was he by the scene unfolding before him. Another bullet ripped through canvas, hitting the center pole of his tent. The pole cracked with a resounding pop, and the roof of the headquarters tent slowly settled around Major Sacke, like an air-filled sheet settling in the water.

Sacke struggled out from beneath the shroud of suffocating canvas, and shook a fist at the Sioux still racing their horses across the center square of the makeshift compound.

"You dirty bastards!" he screamed in a high-pitched voice. "You dirty bastards!"

Another shot kicked up dirt at Sacke's feet, and the major jumped back, shrinking toward the safety of his fallen tent. Dropping to his hands and knees, Sacke crawled inside, groping in the darkness for his revolver, which he finally found lying in a puddle of water formed by his overturned shaving basin. Weapon in hand, the major retraced his crawl until he was free of the canvas again. Shaving lather entirely covered one eye when he staggered to his feet, and his face was contorted into a mask of hatred, like a young boy who had just witnessed the smashing of his favorite toy.

There was a warrior not twenty yards from him when Sacke raised his revolver, drew back the hammer, and pulled the trigger, squeezing his eyes shut in expectation of a resounding blast. Nothing happened, and the major cocked the weapon again and pulled the trigger with a similar result. The warrior was watching him now, totally disdainful, while Sacke pulled the hammer back a third time and released it upon an empty chamber. Then the Sioux, with a blood-curdling scream, wheeled his pony to charge, and the hatred on the Indian's face registered momentarily in Sacke's mind just before he dove beneath the canvas again to burrow his way inward like a mole searching out the tender roots of a spring plant. And there he stayed until the battle was over, not knowing that his life had been saved by one carefully aimed shot from a lowly private of Easy Company, who had taken a bullet in the shoulder himself.

The entire siege lasted no more than ten minutes, and the Sioux were gone almost as quickly as they had arrived. The success of the surprise raid could easily be measured in terms of the very few dead they left behind. The encampment was a shambles, with tents destroyed, logs burning, cooking kettles strewn about, and wounded or dying men lying where they had fallen.

It was an enraged Sergeant Ben Cohen who lifted up the rumpled canvas and dug his way toward the motionless figure

91

curled in a fetal position with his hands covering his head. Contemptuously, he nudged the major's leg with a toe of his boot.

"You can come out now, sir," he said mildly. "The boog-eymen have all left."

Sacke struggled to his feet, adjusting both his uniform and his composure during a brief pause, then tried to look Cohen directly in the eyes. "I was reloading my weapon, Sergeant, when the tent collapsed. I was trapped and couldn't—"

"Spare me the bullshit, sir," Cohen replied, stooping to pick up the Schofield that was lying near where the doorway had been, and handing it to the officer. "I've seen worse things happen when untested men come under fire."

"Worse things, Sergeant?"

"Yes, worse. Cowardice is one thing, sir, sometimes it's uncontrollable. But flagrant ignorance? That's another matter."

"I'm afraid—afraid I don't follow you, Sergeant."

"You follow me, Major. I told you my men should be kept separated and on constant patrol. On your orders, that didn't happen, and the result is fourteen dead, eleven of yours and three of mine."

"Fourteen?"

"Yes, Major. Fourteen. You'll have Lieutenant Kincaid to answer to for this when he gets back."

Now Sacke's chest puffed out, and he gripped the barrel of the pistol held by his right side. "Need I remind you, Sergeant, that I am a major in the United States Army. Lieutenants, as I recall, salute majors, not the other way around."

"That might be the case with most lieutenants, Major. But not with Lieutenant Kincaid," Cohen said evenly. "With him, rank is one thing, but blind ignorance is another matter."

"I am not concerned about your Lieutenant Kincaid in *any* manner, Sergeant," Sacke said superciliously. "And I would advise you to keep your rank in mind as well."

"Sorry, sir, but I'm in complete agreement with Lieutenant Kincaid."

"Then you will go down with him," Sacke said impulsively, with a threatening glare. "Now find Sergeant Hatcher and send him to me. I want this tent repaired immediately."

"Before the wounded are taken care of, sir?" Cohen asked with an arched eyebrow.

"Yes, dammit," Sacke snapped. "This command is only as

good as the headquarters by which it lives."

Cohen shrugged with a wry smile. "That's what I'm afraid of, sir. These are the same headquarters by which it dies."

Cohen turned and walked away without saluting, and Major Sacke watched him leave, rage burning in his guts.

"How is your leg, Matt?" Mindy asked, handing a ladle of water up to the tall lieutenant.

"It's all right, Mindy, thanks," Matt replied, sipping the water and hobbling on one leg to peer out through the gun slit again. The second attack had just ended, and he wondered when the third, which he knew was inevitable, would begin. The total destruction of the Cole homestead seemed to be of paramount importance in the mind of the young warrior chieftain of the Sioux, a man whom Kincaid had seen briefly during both raids, but upon whom he could never gain a clear field of fire. He had no idea why the Indian was so determined, but he had no doubt that he was, and he dismissed the questioning thoughts from his mind while turning to Private Richardson.

"You got back just in time with that ammunition, Private. Good work. How much have we got left?"

"Damned little, sir, and the boys down in the bunkhouse can't be in much better shape. I'd say maybe ten rounds to a man."

"That's not going to get it, Richardson. We need help and we need it bad."

"My offer is still good, sir. I'm willing to try and make it back to the dam site for reinforcements."

"Thanks, but I imagine they're under attack themselves. Besides, I need you here. Remind me to put you in for corporal when we get back home."

"Thank you, sir. But I'd rather die a fighting private, if it comes to that, than be a living corporal."

Kincaid smiled tiredly. "I hope it doesn't turn out that way. But we've got some fight left in us, and they're pretty well shot up themselves. Maybe the cards will fall our way before this is over."

"I hope so, Lieutenant," Richardson said. Then he smiled and relaxed slightly from the rigid position behind his gun. "Do you know who Private Greer is, sir?"

"Of course. As I understand it, he takes quite a lot of heat from you fellows."

"Yes he does, Lieutenant, but not from me. I'm not trying to put the others down and build myself up, but I don't go along with that 'Queer Greer' shit. He's different, and that's his right far as I'm concerned. Anyway, guess who I found in the barn when I went down for that ammunition."

Kincaid puzzled for a moment. "Greer?"

"Yessir. He was keeping the horses calm, and you'd have thought he was back on his pappy's farm, if he's got a pappy and his pappy does have a farm, instead of right in the middle of a battle."

"Well, I'll be damned," Kincaid said in genuine surprise.

"And he was ready to fight to protect those horses, too, sir. He leveled that old Scoff at me when I came through the door, and would've blowed by head clean off if I hadn't yelled at him first."

"That's good to hear. Maybe he's got the makings of a soldier in him after all."

"Don't think so, sir, if you don't mind my offerin' an opinion. He's good in some ways, but as a fightin' man he just ain't got it. If this war was all about protecting horses, he'd be a she-wolf with cubs behind her. But when it comes to killin' men, he just don't have a stomach for it. Know what the other boys said when I took that ammunition into the bunk-house, Lieutenant?"

"No, what?"

"They said he cut and run. He was just plain yellow when the shootin' started, and he cut and run. Ain't none of us go for that kind of thing."

"No, and neither do I." Kincaid hesitated a moment before speaking again. "Tell me, did you talk to Greer in the barn?"

"Yes, sir, I did. First I told him not to kill me, and then we shot the shit a little bit while I was gettin' them extra rounds."

"Did he stutter? I mean, when you were talking normally, did he stutter?"

It was Richardson's turn to pause, and he scratched the back of his head. "No, come to think of it, he didn't. Talked normal, just like you and me are doing. What do you make of that, sir?"

"I don't know yet. But it is something to think about."

"Damned strange, if you ask me. Normally it takes him five minutes just to say hello, but now, with his ass hangin' over the fence, he—"

"Here they come again!" a soldier farther down the wall yelled. "Looks like they're coming straight at us and don't give a damn about the bunkhouse!"

Kincaid turned and looked again through the gun slit. The battle had raged for nearly three hours, and the house, with windows shuttered and doors barred, had become increasingly hot and the putrid air was stifling.

Matt's eyes fell on the shotgun leaning against the table, then drifted to Melinda's face. He could feel her intense gaze upon him, and he smiled with a resigned shrug of his shoulders.

She returned the smile, as though accepting the final outcome without question or regret, and held up the Bible in her hands for him to clearly see.

Kincaid nodded, turned back to his position, and leveled the barrel of the Scoff once again. *This is it,* he thought. *Ten minutes more and it will be all over. There will be one less passenger on that train to Chicago, and a simple handful of medals to be handed out posthumously to any living relatives.*

It was with a sense of bitterness and determination that Kincaid leveled his sights on a warrior in the front rank, and tightened his finger on the trigger while saying loudly enough for all to hear, "Choose your targets carefully, men. Don't waste any ammunition and make every shot count. Let's take as many of these bastards with us as we can."

With that, he squeezed the trigger and the battle was on again. But not for long. After no more than five minutes, the rifles along the wall fell silent and, one by one, the shots from the bunkhouse were lessening at a proportionate rate.

"We're out of ammunition, Lieutenant," Richardson raged, jerking his empty weapon from the gun port. "Request permission to take them on hand to hand, sir."

"Permission denied, Private," Kincaid replied, squeezing off what he knew to be his last round. "For the moment anyway," he added.

Noticing the diminishing fire from the defenders, the Indians threw caution to the winds and charged their ponies onto the porch with a resounding clatter of hooves. It was apparent that they had exhausted their supply of torches, and with the thrill of victory welling in their minds, they fired indiscriminately through the gun slits, sending bullets thudding into the living room.

Melinda had moved to a corner of the room, and Matt

95

backed away from the wall, taking the shotgun with him and cocking its hammer while listening to the crash of rifle butts on the door.

"When they break it down, club as many of them as you can before they take us," he said calmly to his men. "We might be out of ammunition, but we're not out of fight."

The soldiers gathered by the door with weapons raised, while Matt placed an arm around Melinda's waist and drew her to him.

"It looks like we're out of aces," he said, calculating one final shot before the end. "When they break through, I'll—"

The distant sound of rifle fire—obviously repeating Winchesters, interspersed with the booming roar of a throaty Spencer—reached his ears, and Kincaid stopped midsentence. The banging of rifle butts on the door ceased and the clatter of hooves on the porch died, while the noise of the incoming rounds increased as those firing the weapons neared.

"Well, I'll be damned," Matt said, grinning now and pulling Mindy even more tightly to his side. "That old son of a bitch made it after all!"

"What?"

"It's Windy and your father," Matt replied, releasing his grip and rushing to the gun slit once more. "They've come back!" He shoved the twin barrels through the port and triggered a blast at the Indian nearest him, and the warrior slammed forward against his horse's neck and tumbled to the ground. Kincaid took aim again and fired a second shot while Private Richardson threw the bolt aside and rushed out to club an Indian with the stock of his rifle.

John Cole, his son Jason, and Windy Mandalian were in the lead, with twenty other riders spread out behind them. Rifles blazed as they pounded toward the homestead with their horses at a dead run. The Sioux were speeding away to the right, and some ponies were double-mounted, with warriors on foot swinging up behind their comrades. The stockmen veered in that direction and pursued the fleeing Indians halfway to a distant rolling swell on the prairie floor; then, mindful of the possibility of an ambush on the other side, they pulled in their mounts and turned for home.

During the time of the chase, Kincaid had hobbled to the bunkhouse to learn gratefully that none of his men had been killed or wounded, then returned to the porch to stand beside

Melinda with his arm around her waist as the stockmen rode into the yard. Their horses were sweat-lathered and breathing hard through flared nostrils, and it was obvious they had been ridden nearly to the limits of their physical endurance.

Kincaid saw Cole's eyes narrow as he saw the lieutenant's arm around his daughter's waist, and Matt smiled cordially without attempting to remove his hand.

"Glad to see you made it back, John. You couldn't have come at a better time."

"Yeah, looks like we did, at that. Windy here heard the shooting about half an hour ago," Cole said, swinging down and dropping his reins to the ground. "Might've wind-broke a couple of horses getting here, but they can be replaced." He looked into Melinda's eyes and took her outstretched hands as he approached. "But my daughter can't be. Are you all right, honey?"

"Yes, daddy. I'm a little shaken, but Matt and his men saved my life and your property."

"*Our* property, honey," Cole corrected.

Melinda smiled tiredly. "Our property."

As father and daughter were speaking, Kincaid withdrew and stepped toward Mandalian, who had dismounted and was reloading his Spencer nonchalantly.

"Looks like I owe you one, huh, you old renegade?"

Windy worked the chaw bulging in his cheek, and spat before answering, "I'd say we're pretty close to even over the long haul, Matt. Looks like they took a bite out of your leg. Bad?"

"No. Little trouble walking, but I'll be fine once I'm on horseback again. Could you make out who the leader of those Sioux was?"

"Nope. Too busy shootin' to look at faces."

Cole moved down to join them. "I did. And I'll bet a side of beef it's Black Eagle, the young buck I talked with at Lost Hat Crossing a few days back. At the time he said that if the dam went in, me and mine would be the first ones to die."

"Looks like he meant it," Windy said laconically, glancing around at the dead horses and fallen warriors, and the charred side of the building. "I'd say he wound up with the short end of the stick this time, though."

"He wouldn't have, Windy, if you hadn't come back. We were out of ammunition. That was their third raid this morning, and they paid a pretty heavy price. Must want to take John's homestead real bad for some reason."

"The Sioux don't need a reason," Cole threw in heatedly. "Just the fact of us bein' white seems to be reason enough."

Windy opened the breech on his Sharps to make sure a fresh round had slid home, then cradled the rifle in the crook of his arm and looked at Cole with an even stare.

"I know you've had it tough in the past, John, and I don't rightly blame you for the way you feel about the Lakota. But I can't bring myself to put all the blame on them. They haven't exactly had a fair shake in this mess themselves."

It was obvious from the manner in which Cole looked at the frontiersman that he held him in high regard, and he restrained a show of anger.

"Did we attack them, Windy, or did they attack us?"

"They attacked us this time, John. A few years back it was the other way around," Windy replied. "They don't think like we do and don't understand our ways most of the time."

Cole opened his mouth to speak, but Windy waved his protestation away. "I know about your wife and pappy, John, and I know the grief you bear and I feel plumb awful about that myself. But what happened then is history now. We've got to think about the present and leave the past to memory. However wrong they are, I believe the Lakota think they have a good reason for making war again, and the nearest white settler is the logical target."

"Meaning me."

"Meanin' you. Like I said, they don't think like we do. That dam is being built by white men under orders from the white man's government, and the Lakota, especially these young hotheads, are convinced that it's for the benefit of other white men, not Indians. Which, by the way, is probably a hell of a lot more right then wrong. Add to that the fact that an ancient burial ground of theirs is about to go underwater, and you get the same sort of reaction you'd expect from swattin' a hornet's nest with a stick."

A relatively short, wide-bodied man wearing soiled clothing and a three days' growth of beard on his ruddy face shifted in the saddle and spat contemptuously. His beady eyes were on Mandalian's face, but he spoke to Cole.

"John, I didn't ride all this way to listen to a bunch more Injun-lovin' bullshit from this army tagalong here. I heard enough of that back at Slim's place."

"I don't care what you want to hear, Tate," Windy said evenly, "but I'll damned sure bet the truth would scorch your virgin ears."

Tate's gaze shifted to Kincaid. "You the head soldier of the dam-buildin' project?"

"No, I'm not. I'm in command of the escort detachment sent here to protect those who are building the dam."

Cole stepped forward. "I'm sorry, Lieutenant. I haven't made the proper introductions." His hand indicated each of the mounted riders as he spoke. "This is Orin Tate, Slim Barkley, Jed Owens, and Larry Britton. Gents, this here is Lieutenant Matt Kincaid." Cole looked at Kincaid. "These fellows are all neighbors of mine, and they've got just as much need for Cole Creek water as I have. In some cases, like Orin and Larry, they stand to lose more than I do if the creek is diverted. They came back here to talk with you about what in hell we can do to stop this damn fool project before it gets out of hand."

"I'd say it already has, John," Kincaid replied before glancing up at the riders. "Pleased to meet you gentlemen."

The homesteaders nodded, but there was no hint of welcome or greeting on their faces. Sensing the tension, Cole glanced at his son, saying, "Jason, get some of the boys and drag those dead horses and Indians out on the prairie someplace. They'll come back for their dead, if they can get to 'em. Meantime, we'll hunker down in the shade with a good bottle of whiskey. I think a stiff belt would do all of us a world of good."

Cole turned toward his daughter. "Mindy? Would you mind getting a couple of bottles from the cupboard and bringing 'em out here?"

"Yes, daddy, I would," Melinda said flatly, her lips trembling. "One of them is still—"

"There's a dead warrior inside," Kincaid interjected. "Your daughter killed him with a shotgun."

Disbelief filled Cole's eyes. "You mean they got that close?"

"That close. One of my men is dead in there, as well. Private Richardson!" Kincaid called over his shoulder toward the group of soldiers standing nearby.

"Yessir?"

"Get a detail and remove that Indian. Then load Private Phillips on his horse. We'll bury him when we get back to the dam site."

"Yessir!"

The sound of four pairs of boots clomping up the porch steps filled the silent void between Kincaid and Cole until the older man finally spoke with profound sincerity.

"I owe you a lot, Lieutenant. More than I could ever repay."

The memory of that afternoon in the cave flitted through Matt's mind and he shifted uncomfortably. "You owe me nothing, John. If either one of us is in the other's debt, it is I to you."

"How do you mean that? Hell, man, you saved my daughter and my homestead both!"

Kincaid could feel Mindy's eyes upon him, and he shook his head, saying, "Never mind. I'd rather not try to explain."

Cole shook his head and walked toward his house. "Guess I'll get the whiskey myself," he mumbled, shuffling away like a tired old man. "You boys find a cool spot under one of the oaks back there. I'll be right out." He paused by his daughter and placed a hand on her arm gently. "Come on, Mindy. I'd like to talk to you alone for a minute."

eight ————————————

It was nearly fifteen minutes later when John Cole descended the steps with a whiskey bottle in either hand. There was a troubled look on his face and he walked like a man concentrating deeply on something other than the direction of his footsteps.

"Hey, John! Over here!" Tate called when it appeared that Cole had not seen them. "What the hell took ya so long? Have to make the damned stuff?"

Cole's head jerked up in surprise and he veered toward the group beneath the oak tree with a pained, shuffling gait. Kincaid and Mandalian had been talking off to one side by themselves; breaking off their conversation, they joined the others. With his eyes locked on Matt's, the old homesteader stopped and watched Kincaid in momentary silence, and his expression revealed neither animosity nor friendship. The sun bore down on the two men just beyond the shade-darkened ring upon the ground, and Kincaid's facial features remained equally as impassive as those of Cole. The others watched the two men, shifting positions impatiently while they waited until Tate spoke again.

"Come on, John, dammit! You've seen soldiers afore. Pass one of them bottles over here."

Cole nodded, breaking off the stare, and stepped forward to hand one of the bottles to Tate and the other to Britton. "Drink up, boys," he said in a dispirited voice. "I'll have a little pull when you've all had one."

The bottles were passed around, and eager, parched lips drank thirstily before the bottle was handed on. After Windy had taken a drink, he offered the bottle to Kincaid, but Matt's eyes were on Cole again, as were the homesteader's on him.

"Sure you want me to drink your liquor, John?" Kincaid asked softly, ignoring the extended bottle.

Again there was a silent hesitation while the second bottle was pressed into Cole's hand. Finally the stockman slowly raised the whiskey and inclined the neck of the bottle slightly toward Kincaid.

"Sure, son, go ahead and drink," he replied, as if a decision had somehow been arrived at. "Might help ease the pain of that wound of yours. Here's to you."

Kincaid returned the salute and drank deeply, then passed the jug along.

As if the whiskey had fueled the fires of his resentment, Tate glared at Kincaid, "All right, soldier boy, what you gonna do about it?"

"About what, Mr. Tate?"

"About that consarned dam! What the hell else?"

Kincaid watched the stocky man with an even stare. "No more than I've done already, sir. I was sent here to protect the engineering battalion. That's what I plan to do."

"And that's all?" Tate asked incredulously.

"'Pears to me that's a purty good-sized chore in itself," Windy said, watching the homesteader closely.

"I ain't talkin' to you, Mandalian. I'm talkin' to the blue-leg there." Tate's eyes narrowed while he raised the bottle to his lips. "That dam ain't goin' in, soldier boy. You might just as well get used to that fact."

Ignoring the implied threat, Kincaid said, "If you think you have a legitimate complaint, as I believe you do, take it up with the proper authorities back in Washington. Until my orders are changed, I'll carry them out as given."

"Take it up with Washington! That's all you army types ever say—take it up with Washington! Can't you get it through your thick skull that we, all of us here"—Tate's hand described a broad, angry swath—"pay your goddamned wages, not Washington?"

"If you pay my wages, Mr. Tate, I'd like to point out that you're doing a damned poor job of it," Kincaid replied coolly, tiring of having to endure the homesteader's wrath.

The other stockmen chuckled, and Tate's face reddened.

"Well, if you want to be a government lackey all your life, that's your problem," Tate blurted. "Probably couldn't make it on the outside anyway."

"I don't think my future, either military or civilian, is the subject in question here, Mr. Tate. John Cole said you had come here to talk with me. I would suggest you get on with it. I've got to get back to my command."

Cole had been watching the exchange in silence, and now he said, "About the raid this morning, Lieutenant—what's your position on that?"

"The guilty ones will be caught and brought to trial, John. If they resist, they will be killed."

"When?"

"At the first opportunity. As I've said, I have specific orders to protect that engineering battalion as a first priority. When I was sent here, my superior officer had no idea of the extent to which the situation had deteriorated. As a result, I haven't enough soldiers to provide protection for all the homesteads in the area and still maintain sufficient strength to carry out my primary mission. At the first opportunity, I will go in pursuit of Black Eagle and see him brought to justice personally."

"Brought to justice!" Tate scoffed. "The only justice Indians understand comes under the hooves of a white man's horse!"

"I can understand that interpretation of justice coming from you, Mr. Tate. However, I don't happen to agree." Knowing some action should be taken, and desiring the information himself, Kincaid turned to his scout. "Windy, you said the agent at the Oskalla reservation was an old friend of yours, didn't you?"

"Yup, he is."

"Would it be too dangerous for you to ride over there alone, after we leave here, and have a talk with him? I'd like to find out for certain who are the main Indians behind this rebellion."

103

"Dangerous, Matt?" Windy asked with a wry grin. "What's that?"

Kincaid returned the smile. "I knew the answer before I asked the question." Matt looked back at the silent, sullen faces surrounding him. "That's the best I can offer you at this point, gentlemen. Until I can capture the ringleaders, we'll just have to fight this battle one skirmish at a time."

Tate had been drinking more heavily than the others, and each mouthful seemed to intensify his anger. "You ain't said nothin' about stoppin' work on that dam."

"You're absolutely correct, Mr. Tate, I haven't. I have no authority to do that, even though I am convinced of its foolishness, just as you are."

"Let me tell you one thing, soldier boy," Tate snarled. "Maybe us and them Injuns is on the same side in this one, and just don't know it. They don't want the dam, we don't want the dam, and the only people who do are you government assholes. Now I—"

"Hold on, Orin," Cole said, "you don't need to insult—"

Tate brushed the attempt at courtesy aside with a wave of the bottle. "Let me say my peace, John. If you ain't got no stomach for it, then you can get out. Like I was tellin' you, Kincaid, your dam ain't goin' in, an' that's final. You'll have us to fight as well as the featherheads, if you don't back off now."

"The law applies equally to all, Mr. Tate, white men as well as Indians. Break the law and you will be punished. Now, if none of you has anything more of substance to say, I've got to be going."

Kincaid waited, his eyes going from man to man, and nothing was said, so he turned to John Cole. "John, I'd like to talk with Mindy before I leave. Do you object?"

Cole's gaze dropped to the ground and he nudged a pebble with the toe of his boot. "No, I don't object," he said in a lowered voice. "She wants to talk with you as well."

"Thank you. Windy? Would you tell Wojensky to have the squad mounted and prepared to move out in ten minutes?"

"Good as done, Matt."

"Thanks," Kincaid said, already moving toward the house with long, limping strides. He stopped beside the door and rapped softly on the jamb. "Mindy?"

"Yes?" a distant voice called.

"It's me, Matt."

"Come in, please."

When Kincaid entered, he saw her rising from the sofa and taking a damp cloth from her forehead in the same motion.

"Are you all right?"

"Yes, I'm fine. Just a little headache, that's all. I'm not used to getting shot at for three hours at a time. Won't you have a seat, please, Matt?"

Shaking his head, Kincaid wondered if he detected an air of detachment in her voice. "No thanks. I haven't got time. I just wanted to come and say goodbye."

"Goodbye," she echoed with a wistful smile. "Will there ever be another hello?"

"Mindy, you know my situation."

"I know. I just wish—wish it could be different, that's all."

"And so do I, but it can't."

There was a strained silence between them while Mindy worked the cloth in her hands and then looked up at Matt again. "My father knows about us," she said quietly.

"I thought he did."

"I didn't tell him everything, just that I cared for you very much. I imagine he suspects the rest."

"What happened between us was a beautiful thing, however wrong it was. I'll never forget our time together."

Melinda smiled bravely through moistened lashes. "Yes, you will. You'll forget me, just like I'll forget you. Happiness in life seems to be that way."

"Mindy, I—I really don't know what to say," Kincaid managed with an uncharacteristic stammer. "Except that there'll be plenty of times when I'm feeling lonely that I'll think of you and how beautiful you are."

The short distance between them seemed like eons of time, light-years of space. They looked deeply into each other's eyes, and there was a communication that no spoken words could have matched. Finally, Kincaid shrugged and held his hands outward in a helpless gesture.

"Well, Mindy, I guess I'd better do what I came here to do." He hesitated, watching her nibble her lower lip. "Goodbye, Mindy."

"Goodbye, Matt." Her voice grew distant again, trailing off. "Thanks for—for everything."

Matt made an impulsive move toward her, but she stopped him with a hand placed lightly on his chest. "No, Matt. Please.

105

I'd love to have you kiss me, but my emotions just won't take it."

"I understand," Matt said. "Mine aren't exactly rock-hard at this moment either. Good luck in Chicago, all right?"

Melinda nodded, unable to say any more, and Kincaid touched her cheek lightly before turning away. She spoke again just as he passed through the doorway.

"Matt?"

He stopped and turned to look back. "Yes?"

"I think I was a little hasty just a minute ago. I'm sure I won't ever forget you."

He smiled, then shut the door gently.

It was nearing dusk when Windy Mandalian reined his horse in before the agency building on the Oskalla reservation, and he wondered, as he often had before, why the government persisted in painting their buildings white. Painted wood, as he thought everyone knew, was in violation of an ancient Indian belief; they preferred to see it turn a weathered silver gray with age. The door stood open and the sounds of gentle snoring came from inside, and Windy grinned in the twilight as he stepped down from his horse and looped the reins over the hitching rail.

"Hey, Charlie!" Windy called, dragging the saddlebags from his horse and stepping onto the porch. "This ain't exactly a red-hot welcome for an old drinkin' pardner, you know!"

Still no answer from inside, and Windy stood framed in the doorway while waiting for his eyes to adjust to the interior gloom.

"Charlie, dammit! It's me, Windy Mandalian. Now get your ass up and pour me a drink, or I'll lift what little scalp you've got left!"

"Huh? What? Who's there?" the little agent spluttered, bending forward at the waist while scrubbing the sleep from his eyes with the knuckles of both hands. "What in tarnation—"

Then he focused on Mandalian while struggling to throw the blanket from his legs and stand at the same time. When he finally managed to free himself of the bed, he padded on stocking feet to greet the tall man walking through the doorway. Without his boots, he looked even more diminutive than he actually was, as he reached up to grasp the scout's hand.

"Windy Mandalian," he said almost mystically. "Is it really you?"

"Last time I checked, it was. How you been, you old bastard?"

"Not good. Not good at all. Got a touch of the grippe, I 'spect, and can't sleep much at all."

Windy grinned. "You sleep all day and then expect to sleep at night too? You haven't done an honest day's work in—" Then Mandalian saw Simms' battered face, and his expression went blank instantly. "Who did that to you?"

"Never mind," Simms replied with an angry wave. "Come on over here to the table and let's have a drink. I haven't seen company worth drinkin' with in so long I almost forgot my manners."

Windy draped his saddlebags over one chair, then pulled another out and turned it backwards while Simms splashed whiskey into two tin cups and shoved one toward the scout.

"I suppose there's better whiskey, then again, I suppose there's worse," the agent said, sinking wearily into another chair. "Here's lookin' at you, Windy," Simms concluded, raising his cup before drinking.

"And here's to you, Charlie. How the hell have you been?"

Simms gazed into his cup and shrugged weakly. "'Bout like the whiskey. I guess. Sometimes better, sometimes worse. Funny thing, Windy," he said, leaning back in his chair, "the older you get, the more things seem to wear you down."

"You're just about ready to give up this agent business, aren't you Charlie?" Windy asked, looking around at the barren dwelling. "Comes a time in every man's life when he's done about everything he can do for other people."

"I suppose so. But I kinda wanted to hang on for a while, to see things work out right for these people. I knew it would be a long time in coming, but I'd hoped to see it before my time was up."

"You sound like you've got one foot in the grave and the other in a mud waller."

"Maybe I have, Windy, maybe I have. Could be it's time to turn this job over to younger fellers."

Windy studied the frail little agent. "Sometimes bein' younger ain't all it takes, Charlie. You know these people, their way of life, the way they think. It takes years to learn that, as you and me both know, and most of the young ones

107

I've met don't know their ass from a corn cob when it comes to Indian matters."

"That's true," Simms agreed sadly, "but that applies to the young bucks as well, when it comes to understanding the white man and the inevitability of his eventual takeover of traditional ground." The agent appeared to be warming to his subject and continued, "Take the Oskalla here on this reservation, for example. The old ones know the fight is over and lost, but the young ones feel betrayed by their leaders and no longer will listen to wise counsel, either from me or them."

"Are you speaking of any one brave in particular?"

Simms touched his face gingerly. "Yes I am. The one who did this to me."

"Black Eagle?"

"No."

"Who, then?"

"His name's Medicine Hawk. Completely crazy, just down from Canada, and he's a snake-oil salesman if I ever seen one. The problem is, the oil he's selling is white man's blood."

"I've seen that happen before, as well. Even though one man is supposed to be the leader, somebody with a louder voice gets listened to." Windy studied the whiskey cup. "What do you make of this Black Eagle? Isn't he the son of Stalking Crow?"

Simms seemed reluctant to respond. "Yes he is. Stalking Crow is dead now, killed by a white trapper up in Canada, as I understand it."

"What do you make of the boy? Is that the reason why he's taken such a hatred for white people?"

"Who can say?"

Mendalian pondered the agent's response, thinking he detected a hint of reluctance, and decided to press on, forcing the agent to tell all he knew.

"You know, Charlie, I have some reason to suspect that Black Eagle led a raid against a white homesteader today. And I also think he led a raid against the construction site at Ryan's Ravine."

"Really?" Simms asked with feigned interest. "What line of work are you in these days, Windy?"

Windy knew his suspicions had been accurate and the change of subject was merely a ploy to alter the direction of the conversation. "Still scoutin' for the army. Outfit called

Easy Company, from down south a ways." The piercing look in Windy's eyes caused Simms to look away. "Those two raids netted three dead soldiers, Charlie. There will be army action taken now, you know."

"I suppose so," the old man responded with a sigh. "Will it ever end, my friend? The bloodshed and hatred in the name of a cause that is not entirely just but which, just the same, will triumph in the end?"

"Some smart feller with a pen and paper might figure it out someday, but right now all we've got to go on is our instincts." Windy's eyes narrowed and studied the agent closely. "And Charlie, my old friend, my instincts right now tell me you're not tellin' all you know about this Black Eagle."

Simms fidgeted with his cup, turning it in circles before rising to get the bottle and pour another ration. "You're right, Windy, I'm not. But I've got my reasons."

"What would those be, Charlie?"

"I knew that Indian boy's daddy real well. Good man. Noble, proud, a fine leader of his people. When he went north with Sitting Bull, it wasn't because he wanted to, it was because he had to."

"How do you mean?"

"I'll get to that in a minute. But first, the reason why I'm tryin' to protect the boy. Couldn't be more'n twenty, if that. Fine-looking young man, just like his daddy was. He's going to be killed if he keeps on with what he's doing, and with him will go some of the finest blood of the Oskalla tribe."

"Well, raidin' a homestead like John Cole's in broad daylight ain't gonna keep him on this old earth too long, let me tell you that," Windy said matter-of-factly as he raised the cup for another drink.

The agent blinked and leaned forward with a start. "Did you say John Cole's homestead?"

"Yup. He hit there this mornin', determined to burn the place down and kill every white man he could lay his hands on, as I hear it. And one white woman, too. John Cole's daughter."

"So," Simms said in a subdued voice. "He's started already."

"What was that, Charlie? The bark of that old Sharps seems to be gettin' to my ears. Don't hear so good anymore. What'd you say?"

The agent's gaze drifted slowly toward the scout. "It's not

your hearing, Windy. What I said I didn't mean for you to hear."

Windy slammed his cup down on the table, and whiskey sloshed over the side. "Dammit, Charlie, you'd better start meanin' what you say for me to hear. Sure, I like your company and your whiskey, but I didn't ride over here tonight to swap stories about old times. We've got the makin's of a full-scale war on our hands, and I think you're one of the men who could help me prevent that."

"I know, Windy, I know. And please pardon me if I'm being evasive. Like I said, I've got the boy's best interests at heart. Do you know of a Lokota chieftain named Hunting Fox?"

"Yes, I've heard of him."

Simms nodded. "He too is the son of Stalking Crow. He was the only member of his father's family who didn't go to Canada, and now he is the only voice of reason that the Oskalla have."

"What about him?"

"He came to see me today, and what we talked of, I was pledged never to reveal to another living man."

"Well, Charlie, I ain't all the way alive, but I'm not dead yet, either. If what he had to say can help straighten this mess out before more lives are lost, including Black Eagle's, I'd like to hear it."

"Yes, I suppose you should. He told me something that no other white man knows and no other Indian talks about."

"I'm listenin', Charlie."

The old man hesitated before speaking again. "Do you know why Black Eagle has such a hatred for white men? Aside from the fact that his father was killed by one?"

"If I did, I probably wouldn't be here talkin' to you right now."

"Probably not, and that's a pity. Shame we can only get together in times of trouble. Anyway, be that as it may," Simms said with a weary, almost foredoomed shrug. "Let me ask you something, Windy."

"Shoot."

"If you were the son of a fierce, famous Oskalla chief, what would be the one thing you would be the most proud of?"

Windy shrugged. "My heritage, I guess. My bloodline, as they call it."

"Exactly," Simms said with an agreeing nod. "And what

110

would be the thing that would bring out the most hatred in you?"

"I don't know what you're gettin' at, but there's nothing I hate more than being lied to."

"And you're in good company. Black Eagle doesn't like being lied to either."

"I don't understand, Charlie. What are you trying to say?"

Simms smiled wearily. "Let me answer your question by asking you another. Given what you just said, wouldn't you be pretty hurt and damned mad to think you were a full-blooded Lakota, the son of one of the mightiest chiefs the tribe has ever known, and then, after he is dead, to learn the truth?"

"About what?"

"Black Eagle is a half-breed, Windy. His mother is one hundred percent white."

"And Black Eagle knows that now?"

"Yes he does. Let me backtrack a bit. Stalking Crow fled to Canada with Sitting Bull because he knew that if he turned himself in with the others, they would be counted, and it would be revealed that his wife was white, and she would be taken away from him. According to Hunting Fox, who is full-blooded Oskalla, by the way—"

"That means Stalking Crow had an earlier wife?"

"Yes he did. She died a few years after Hunting Fox was born, and that's why Stalking Crow took the white woman." Simms paused, then continued his story. "Anyway, like I was saying, Stalking Crow valued his new wife more than anything, and would stop at nothing to prevent having her taken away. In the course of things, she bore him a child, Black Eagle, and after the Battle of the Little Big Horn, the three of them went to Canada.

"Now, the white woman was black-haired and dark-featured, much like yourself, and over the years she adopted Indian ways, wore their clothing, and picked up the language. I'm sure it was done as a matter of survival, because she had no choice, really. She came to be known as Cloud of the Moon, and by the time Black Eagle was old enough to concern himself about such matters, she was indistinguishable from the other women except that she continued to act like a white woman in her dealings with men. She was no squaw, in other words, and expected and demanded to be treated like a wife."

When the agent hesitated to reach for his cup, Windy asked,

"Why did Hunting Fox tell you all this?"

"Because he is concerned about the fate of his people. He hasn't forgotten what happened to the South Cheyenne at Sand Creek, and he's concerned that the actions of his half-brother will bring on another massacre of the same kind."

"I see. When did Black Eagle find out he was a half-breed?"

"After his father was killed, Cloud of the Moon—who, according to Hunting Fox, has returned from Canada as well— told Black Eagle of his heritage, thinking it might help ease his hatred for white people. Unfortunately, the end result was the exact opposite."

Simms fell silent again, brooding perhaps over the fact that he had revealed a secret that had been told him in deepest confidence.

Windy honored the older man's silence for a while. He freshened their cups with another splash of whiskey, then looked directly at the agent.

"Charlie, I know this is tough on you, revealing a secret like this, and it would be tough for me as well. But I have to ask you one more question."

Simms smiled wearily. "I expected as much."

"Do you know the name of the white woman? Her real name?"

"Yes I do."

"There's an awful lot at stake here, Charlie. You know that as well as I do. We both want to see this thing end with as few people killed as possible, and this revolt put down before another Sand Creek does happen." Windy paused, then asked, "What's her name?"

The agent's trembling hand slowly went to his cup. His eyes were blank again as the whiskey moved toward his lips and he whispered softly, "Her name is Grace Cole. She's John Cole's wife."

nine ⸻⸻⸻⸻⸻⸻⸻

At approximately the same time that Windy Mandalian arrived at the Oskalla agency, Matt Kincaid and the third squad of the second platoon returned to Ryan's Ravine. The sun was sinking beneath the horizon, and there was a calm peacefulness about the setting as Kincaid halted the detail and looked at the encampment across the draw. But there was none of the normal, after-work bustle of grub lines, soldiers washing in the creek, and tools being mended for the next day's labor. Then something odd caught his eye, and Kincaid studied the tents in the closing darkness. Fully a third of them were of a different color—the color of new canvas, as opposed to the faded green of the others. One-third of the camp resembled new spring grass, while the remainder might have been the sun-bleached, beaten grass of fall. The first unsettling hint of concern touched the corners of his mind while his eyes drifted to the dam site. The logs were in the stream bed, with the dam nearly halfway completed, and water continued to flow over them. The diversion channel had obviously not been completed. He could see that little if any progress had been made. Then he noticed something missing, and he squinted to make sure that what he was seeing was not a trick of faulty vision.

Where once there had been a great pile of logs, now there were none. In their place was a scorched patch of earth. A short distance away he could discern what appeared to be crosses planted in the ground, and he tried to count them, but couldn't do so accurately from this distance. He thought about the dead soldier strapped to a horse behind him, and a silent rage burned in his brain as he urged his horse forward and down toward the crossing. He could see a lamp burning in the headquarters tent as he reined in and stepped down. His first impulse was to tear the tent flap aside and burst inside to confront Major Sacke, but he restrained himself and turned toward Wojensky.

"Corporal, have Phillips' body taken care of, and see that our horses are fed and watered. Then rustle up some grub for your men." He glanced around the silent camp. "If you can find a cook around this goddamned place."

"Yessir."

Kincaid did not reply and was already crossing the space between himself and the headquarters tent with long, angry strides. He threw the flap back, and ducked inside. Major Sacke, clad in a bathrobe and slippers, lay on his bunk with a whiskey glass in one hand and an old newspaper in the other. He looked up with a hint of fright before offering a weak smile.

"Thank you for asking permission to enter, Lieutenant," he said acidly.

"To hell with your permission to enter! What the hell's going on around here?"

"Going on?" Sacke asked innocently, while offering the paper for Kincaid to see. "I, for one, am catching up on some month-old news. It seems that the new administration back in Washington—"

"Fuck that! I mean here, right here and right now. Where the hell are the logs for your precious dam?"

"Unfortunately we've suffered a slight setback. Nothing permanent, mind you, just a fire."

"Were you attacked by the Lakota?"

"A minor skirmish at best," Sacke replied with a dismissing shrug.

"Minor skirmish! If even one man is killed or wounded, any

114

fight is major combat, not a minor skirmish. How many men did you lose?"

Sacke adjusted his glasses nervously and cleared his throat. "Well, actually only fourteen were killed outright. The fifteenth died several hours later."

"*Only* fourteen!" Kincaid yelled, barely able to control the urge to jerk the major off his bunk and smash his face to a bloody pulp. "Were any of them my men?"

"Yes, I'm afraid so. The fortunes of war, or misfortunes, as it were."

"How many?" Kincaid asked, advancing toward the bed.

Sacke drew his knees up instinctively and raised the paper as a shield. "Now just a moment, Lieutenant. You know striking a senior officer is a hanging offense."

"How many?"

"Soldiers have to expect—"

Lashing out with a violent sweep of his hand, Kincaid knocked the paper aside and Sacke curled up into a ball against the head of his bunk, with the whiskey glass carefully poised to prevent spillage.

"How goddamned many, Major?" Each word was spoken with deadly emphasis while Kincaid loomed above the bed, his fists clenched in white-knuckled hatred.

"Ahem, if I remember correctly, I think the total was three. Hardly any, actually, when you consider my losses," Sacke observed tentatively.

Kincaid glared down at him. "I've got one dead man outside, and that makes four. Four, Major. Four good men killed because of your own stupid project, which will serve no useful purpose other than providing a footstool for your own personal aggrandizement back in Washington, which is goddamned well where you belong."

"If I must remind you, Lieutenant, this project was authorized by the United States Congress, with approval of the President himself." Sacke risked a slight, deprecating smile. "Pretty long odds for a first lieutenant to go up against, wouldn't you say?"

Kincaid turned abruptly, stalked to the desk, snatched up a glass, and filled it with whiskey. He realized he had no desire for a drink, but he also knew he had to do something with his hands to prevent himself from strangling the major where he lay. After taking a big swallow, he drew in several breaths, straining for control, before he turned toward the major again.

"How did it happen?"

"What?"

It was building again, and Matt took another drink. "The attack. How did it happen?"

"In the usual way, I suppose. I'm really not all that experienced in these things. We were taken by surprise and—"

"Taken by surprise? Where were my patrols? The way things were organized, there was no possibility of your being taken by surprise if everyone was doing his job properly."

In response to the major's hesitancy, Kincaid repeated the question. "Where were my patrols?"

"They were having lunch, Lieutenant," Sacke said cautiously.

"Lunch? They were having lunch?" Kincaid said incredulously. "You make it sound like everybody had their little picnic blankets spread out, playing cards and telling jokes while the cooks stirred the stew with their rifle barrels. I left specific instructions with Sergeant Cohen that my troops were to eat in shifts, before and after yours, with never less than three-fourths of my men on patrol at all times."

"Then that will have to be taken up with your sergeant, won't it, Lieutenant?" Sacke said, building up to a lie but knowing it was his only immediate means of escaping Kincaid's wrath. Lies had worked well to buy time in the past, and a means to smooth them over was always preferable, to the major's way of thinking, when concocted away from the heat of confrontation.

"What do you mean by that? Ben would never disobey a direct order from me."

"'Never' is tantamount to infinity, Lieutenant, and none of us knows exactly what that is, now do we? When you departed two days ago, I left the coordination of defenses entirely up to your people. It appears they failed to live up to my high expectations."

Even though he was confused, Kincaid was convinced that Sacke was lying, and the only way to prove that was to talk to Sergeant Cohen himself.

"Where is Cohen right now? I'll get him in here and he'll defend himself in front of both of us."

Sacke drained his glass, rose with a groan from his bunk, and crossed the tent for a refill. "I'm afraid that is impossible

116

at present, Lieutenant. Sergeant Cohen isn't here."

"He's not here? Then where the hell is he?"

Sacke spoke with his back turned, and concentrated on his pouring. "He and one of your platoons are in town on leave. Along with one of my companies."

"What?" Kincaid snapped, not believing what he had heard. "There's no way that Ben would leave a defensive assignment, or any other assignment for that matter, without specific permission from me, unless he was ordered by a superior officer to do so."

Sacke turned slowly and offered a weak smile. "In a manner of speaking, Lieutenant, you might say that's what happened."

"Major, I am sick and fucking tired of your doubletalk and runaround horseshit. Now I want an explanation, straight and clear, and I want it now! No more of this 'in a manner of speaking' shit. Lay it out now and lay it out fast, or I'm going to shove my fist so far down your goddamned throat you'll have to ask me to open my hand to scratch your ass."

"Please make an effort to control yourself," Sacke said, wilting into a chair in the profound hope that Kincaid wouldn't hit a seated man, especially one wearing glasses. "It's really very simple. Today is the end of the month, as you might recall, and the end of the month is payday in this man's army. I have been authorized to honor the pay vouchers for your men, due to the length of their assignment here, which will be reimbursed to my paymaster through Captain Conway."

"I know all that. Get on with it."

"In light of that arrangement, your men were paid today as well as mine. Our troops have worked hard, Lieutenant, damned hard, and they deserved a break." Sacke gazed across the tent with a self-sacrificing look. "We senior officers never seem to get a chance to rest, but that's one of the accepted hardships of command responsibility, I suppose."

"Major, damn you—" Kincaid growled threateningly.

"I'm getting there, Lieutenant, I'm getting there. As a consequence of the recent attack, several of the men, including your Sergeant Cohen, seem to be under an increased strain. Cohen, while I have no doubts that he's a good soldier, has been acting irrationally of late, and I felt that a few drinks in town might restore him to his normally jovial self."

"Ben has never been jovial in his life."

"Be that as it may. At any rate, he and his men were given a pass into Garderville, where, I would assume, they are having

117

a whooping good time with the men of my command."

Kincaid shook his head in disgust. "Do you know what happens when engineers and infantry wind up in the same saloon at the same time, Lieutenant? Do you have any idea?"

"Well, while I do have the occasional drink, I don't normally visit saloons frequented by enlisted men."

"They damned near kill each other, Major, and sometimes do!"

"A pity."

"Did Ben object to going?"

"You might say he was a little reluctant."

"Was he directly ordered to go?"

"Yes. I found that a little strange, having to order a man to go out and have a good time."

"You, Major are one stupid son of a bitch and not qualified to judge a sack race, let alone command an entire battalion." Kincaid slammed his half-full glass down on the desk, causing Sacke to flinch. "Where was Captain Edgerton when all this was going on?"

"All what?"

"The attack."

"He was gone with an escort detail of your men to pick up the payroll at the train station. The westbound was late—a locomotive had broken down or something—so he didn't return until this afternoon."

"Jesus Christ," Kincaid muttered, turning toward the tent flap. "Is Edgerton here now?"

"He's in his tent, I presume."

Kincaid stopped in the doorway and looked back at Sacke. "I'm going to get to the bottom of this, Major, right to the bottom. And when it's over, I'll personally ride to Washington if I have to, to make sure that you never have command over anything again. Not even a latrine detail."

After waiting a few minutes to make sure that Kincaid had actually gone, Sacke smiled, freshened his glass, and turned to the desk to take up pencil and paper to prepare a telegram to the Department of the Army. Forgetting the address and other formalities for now, he began to work on the body of his message.

Dear General Wittenburg:
    Sir, It is with great reluctance that I contact you and

118

ask for the immediate removal of one First Lieutenant Matt Kincaid as commander of the escort forces sent here to provide surveillance during the construction of the Garderville Dam Project. While the project is going smoothly and on schedule, the lieutenant referred to is totally incompetent, rude, unobservant of proper military protocol, and completely devoid of a grasp of the situation at hand. I strongly recommend an investigation into his character and moral conduct as an officer.

On to other matters: We have established an excellent rapport with the settlers in the area, as well as with the local Indian population, and your confidence in my judgment shall be borne out in full measure. Your honorable servant, I remain,

Major Brian Sacke, Commanding.

Sacke reread the message with delight, then signed his name with a flourish, returned the pen to its holder, and took up his drink once more. As he returned to his bunk, he yawned, stretched luxuriously, and snapped the creases out of the paper to resume his reading.

Night had fallen when Kincaid stepped from the tent, and the evening breeze sweeping across the campsite was cooling on his heated face. He was glad to be away from the major, but even more glad that he had been able to control his anger. Five minutes alone with him, he thought, stopping to snatch a twig from the ground and worry it in his hands as he walked, and it would have been all over. He would have hit him for sure, and once started, there would have been no stopping. He visualized the smashed glasses, broken teeth protruding through mutilated lips, and a nose twisted and splayed across one of the major's cheeks. So great was his rage that he did not doubt for a second that he would have done those things. Sacke's careless dismissal—*Well, actually only fourteen were killed outright. The fifteenth died several hours later*—kept surging through his mind in a constant orbit, like a ball swung on the end of a string.

"Dammit," he muttered, walking slowly and trying to regain his composure before reaching Edgerton's tent. "How could the army ever send a man like that out here with a full battalion under his command?"

Kincaid stopped just short of the captain's quarters, snapping the twig violently and casting it aside. He didn't anticipate a much more pleasant encounter with Edgerton, but he knew he had to talk to the man and try to salvage something, to understand why it had happened, and thereby assuage his own feelings of guilt for ever having left the construction site in the first place.

There was a quiet serenity about the evening, as though the engineers had completely forgotten their ill-conceived project and were merely biding their time until orders to return back East were received. The occasional laugh or loudly spoken phrase drifted out to Kincaid from the various tents around him, but the sense of death, of loss, was absent, and that realization was greatly disturbing to him. Is this nothing but a game? he wondered, seeing the dark shadows of one of his patrols pass by in ghostly silence. A politician's game in which we are all pawns to be sacrificed at the will and whimsy of a man who aspires to the political life himself? There could be no other reason for this project, so poorly had it been planned and executed, than to feather the nest of someone now comfortably asleep on a down-filled mattress back in Washington.

At the call of his name, Edgerton looked up from the engineer's plan he held in his broad hands, and turned away from his cramped desk with its single lamp burning on one corner.

"Yes?"

"Lieutenant Kincaid. I'd like to speak with you for a few moments if possible."

"Certainly, Lieutenant. Come on in."

When Kincaid stepped inside and straightened, he saw the captain rise from his chair and offered his hand. "Good evening, Lieutenant," he said with a cordial smile. "This is the first opportunity we've had to meet informally."

Somewhat surprised and more than a little shocked, Matt returned the handshake. "To be honest with you, Captain, I hadn't anticipated such a warm greeting."

"An entirely justified opinion, Lieutenant. May I offer you a drink?"

"Yes, please. I'd like to have one that I could drink for enjoyment rather than to hold down my anger."

Edgerton withdrew a bottle and two glasses from a desk drawer, and poured while he spoke. "I assume you've just spoken with Major Sacke?"

"Yes I have."

"We're dealing with a madman here, Lieutenant." Edgerton ceased his concentrated pouring and looked over his shoulder. "Would it be all right with you if we forget this business of formal titles? We're here to do a job, not kiss each other's asses."

"Fine with me, uh, Steven, is it?"

The captain nodded. "Good. As I was saying, Matt, we're dealing with a madman here. An egomaniac who will stop at nothing to achieve his own personal goal, which, by the way, is first to be a general and then a senator." Edgerton turned and handed a glass to Kincaid, then offered a chair, which Matt accepted, while the captain seated himself in another and crossed his long legs comfortably. Edgerton studied Kincaid closely before speaking again. "I think I owe you an explanation, and perhaps an apology as well."

"In what way?" Kincaid asked, offering his drink forward in toast. "Here's to you. Thanks for the drink."

"My pleasure. I'll make the explanation and the apology at the same time. The reason I've been so rude to you, as I am to everyone when in the major's presence, and particularly to him when we're alone, is that that's the only weapon I have to keep him under some semblance of control. He is entirely dependant upon military propriety; it's his only means of hiding his ineptitude. He respects no one of lesser rank than himself, but he does fear strength. By keeping Sacke in constant fear of me, I can manipulate him to some degree, and thereby keep this command together."

"Can nothing be done through channels? That man is not only a menace to himself, he also has a very good chance of screwing up all we've done out here in the past few years."

"That he has, and in response to your question about channels, the answer is no. In Major Sacke's case, the channels you speak of end at General Wittenburg's desk, back in Washington. Wittenburg is a senile old fart who coincidentally turns out to be Sacke's uncle. 'Lyin' Brian,' as he was known back East, is the apple of his uncle's cataract-clouded eye."

"I see," Matt responded, pursing his lips and nodding in thought. "Then that's how he achieved command in the first place."

"Precisely. I am, as they say, between a rock and a hard place. There's no way I can have Sacke removed from command, but I can't allow my men to become sacrificial lambs to whet the political appetites of others—particularly the major, whom I despise with a passion so great that no other living human being could match it."

Kincaid chuckled around the rim of his glass. "I'm working on it, Steven. Given time, I'm sure I can catch you." Then his face turned serious once again. "What happened yesterday? Why weren't my troops on patrol?"

"Sacke, of course, told you it was Sergeant Cohen's doing?"

"In so many words."

"Well, let me set you straight on that, first of all. When I got back from securing the payroll—again, the major's idea—your sergeant approached me to explain what had happened and ask for help. During my absence, Sacke ordered him to take his men off patrol and put them in the grub line with mine. He said he nearly begged the major to change his mind, but old Brian must have felt he'd finally made a decision and was going to stick with it. Besides, he's made so few that he couldn't tell a good decision from a bad one. I admire your sergeant, Matt. If he weren't so damned tough, I think he would have cried over the loss of those three men of his. Serving under Major Sacke, I have learned to accept the loss of my men. Correction: I have learned to *expect* it—tunnels improperly shored up and collapsing, dams breaking with men working downstream—but with Sacke commanding, there is little I can do about it."

"Can't we do anything? Wire Washington and have him removed from command? Anything?" Kincaid asked with desperation. "This can't go on much longer."

"I know," Edgerton replied, nodding. "But let's just bide our time. I think, in this case, that Sacke has reeled out just about enough rope to hang himself. There's no doubt that he has you and me in mind as scapegoats if this project fails, which it will. Before that happens, though, let's give old Brian a chance to hang himself."

"You mentioned the imminent failure of this project. What are your personal views on the feasibility of this dam?"

"Stupid beyond compare, and I've built a lot of stupid dams at the behest of the Corp of Engineers. The way Sacke has this designed, it will wash out with the first heavy rains of winter. So if we can hold out that long, my plan is to build the dam, leave, and let nature take care of the rest. Unfortunately, it appears we can't hold out that long without the loss of more

122

men, which I want to prevent, if at all possible. May I get you another drink?"

"Yes, please."

Edgerton rose to fill their glasses again, and Kincaid thought about his apprehensions upon approaching the captain's tent. He had been absolutely confident of his dislike for the man, and now he found him to be a warm, intelligent, and compassionate human being. He marveled at the captain's mastery of this charade, and praised him mentally for his ability to be on top of a situation that seemed to be helplessly out of control.

When Edgerton pressed the glass into his hand once again, Kincaid said, "Thank you, both for the drink and what you've told me here tonight. In response to your earlier statement, however, you are correct. We can't wait for winter and nature's demolition of this project. We've got a full-scale Indian war on our hands, the stockmen in the area are about to form their own militia, and if we can keep the lid on this thing for another week I'll be surprised. Thanks to Major Sacke, a treaty has been broken, and even if we can pull this thing off, there will have to be reprisals against the offending parties."

"I'm fully aware of that, Matt. And that's where we've got Sacke by the balls. He often sends telegrams to town by courier, to be forwarded over Western Union wires to Washington, which are always read by me first, unbeknownst to the Major. In each of those telegrams he mentions how things are going swimmingly around here, the dam is on schedule, everybody loves us, that sort of shit. Well, I've kept a diary of those telegrams, plus a diary of what has actually happened out here, and there isn't a congressional committee on Capitol Hill that wouldn't throw Sacke out of the army in an instant once the truth is revealed. But we need more time, more evidence. If we can just hang on and bide our time, we'll have him right where we want him." Edgerton paused to sip his drink and study Kincaid. "Speaking of telegrams, I wouldn't be surprised if one were sent out about you tomorrow."

"About me?"

"Yes. It's happened in the past. Sacke wires his uncle about an officer who, according to the major's interpretation, is a misfit. Two days later that officer is gone, drummed out of the service, and asking for a job as a plowhand."

"That's bullshit, Steve. I mean what he intends to write, if he intends to write it."

Edgerton smiled. "Trust me, he does. But not to worry. As

I said, I see all the telegrams sent by the major, and yours will go out painting you as the best damned officer ever produced by the United States Military Academy, not to mention one who has been decorated for bravery in the campaign against the Cheyenne."

"You know about that?" Kincaid asked in surprise.

"Of course," Edgerton responded with a twinkle in his eye. "I know my way around a telegraph office myself."

"Well, I'll be damned," Kincaid said, admiring and respecting the captain even more. "You engineers certainly work in strange ways."

"How else could one survive around a man like Major Sacke?"

Kincaid nodded with a chuckle. "I see what you mean. But we've got another problem on our hands that none of your telegrams can help us with. We've got one platoon of mounted infantry and one company of engineers both in the same town on the same payday night. I'm sure we're both aware of the end result of that combination."

"Yes we are. Do you know why your men are in town with mine?"

"Sacke ordered them to go."

"Correct, but do you know why he did that?"

Puzzled, Kincaid shook his head, "I guess not. Why?"

"Because he wanted to keep you separated from Sergeant Cohen as long as possible, so you wouldn't learn the truth about the change in the eating schedule. He put the blame on Cohen to buy time to build up a legitimate lie. I'll have to commend your sergeant, Matt. He wouldn't have gone if not directly ordered to go."

"I didn't think so."

Edgerton finished his drink, as did Kincaid, and the captain placed both glasses on the desk and reached for his pistol belt. "Well, I suppose we should ride in there and see if we can't cool this thing down a little bit, you with your men and me with mine. Have you ever been to Garderville?"

"No I haven't."

"There are two places to drink there, the Frontier Saloon and the Last Ace. My men prefer the Frontier, so I imagine you'll find yours at the Ace. If neither group has crossed the other's ground so to speak, we may be able to prevent a fight before it starts."

Kincaid stood and adjusted his hat. "Let's hope so. I know the reputation you engineers have, but my men are pretty good scrappers themselves."

The captain smiled as if reliving a pleasant memory. "Yes, I suppose they might be quite evenly matched. Want a little side wager?"

"My men are outnumbered three to one," Matt protested.

"There's pride among the engineers, Matt. If they do get into a fight, the sides will be even. A bottle of whiskey, perhaps?"

"You're on, Steve," Matt replied, grinning. "And let's hope neither one of us collects."

"One more thing, Matt," Edgerton said, placing a hand on Kincaid's shoulder as they stepped from the tent. "Let's keep this little meeting of ours between ourselves. Sacke knows we've talked, but he doesn't know what we've talked about. When we're around other people, let's maintain the same level of animosity we've demonstrated in the past. If the major thinks we hate each other, he'll be less likely to suspect we're in league against him."

"Sounds like a good idea to me, Steve," Kincaid said, stopping and turning to face Edgerton. "Let's see if it still works." He frowned and snarled, "Captain, you and every other engineer I've ever met are the epitome of the perfect asshole."

"Thank you, Lieutenant. Perfection is a thing of beauty. Perhaps that's why mounted infantrymen are so insistent on kissing them."

"Excellent, Steve," Kincaid said with a grin. "Obviously we don't need much rehearsal."

"No, Matt, we don't. We know our lines pretty well," Edgerton replied, matching the grin. "Get your horse and meet me back here while I get mine."

Kincaid walked toward Easy Company's bivouac area, and when he passed by Major Sacke's tent, he heard the familiar, contented snoring. He smiled to himself in the darkness.

ten

Garderville's only reason for existing rested with the twin water towers situated alongside the Union Pacific railroad tracks. All trains, traveling east or west, stopped there to refill their tanks and deposit and collect mail. Then they were gone again with a clatter of wheels on splice-joints, cars swaying behind their hitches and enveloped in a cloud of smoke emanating from the puffing, straining engines.

With its small complement of railroad personnel, merchants, local homesteaders, and stockmen, Garderville was normally a peaceful frontier community that boasted a church for each of its two saloons, which provided the principal elements of respectability. In the beginning there had been great excitement at the possibility of a dam being built nearby and the eventual arrival of new settlers. The merchants in particular had rubbed their hands in glee at the thought of fat army payrolls being spent in their town during the construction, but the mood changed quickly once they met those engineers face to face on a payday. The drunkenness, the fights, and the rowdy behavior had driven most of them to the shelter of their homes on payday nights, or any other night when the soldiers were on pass.

The townspeople were now surly and resentful of the military, and they wished the soldiers would merely pack their picks and shovels and leave. They saw them only as seducers of women, drunken thugs, and a threat to their community. That viewpoint was totally in contrast with the cheering, bustling welcome they had given Major Brian Sacke when he had announced to the gathered residents that he had selected Cole Creek over several other prospective sites partially because of its proximity to Garderville. What they hadn't known was that Sacke had chosen the site in large measure because it was near the railroad line and he could travel back and forth to the East Coast in the relative comfort of a railroad car as opposed to the miseries of riding on horseback. He had also hoped that Garderville might avail him, in part at least, of some of the amenities he had enjoyed back East, such as the occasional fine meal with a good selection of wines, but such was not the case.

Now the major rarely ventured into town, if at all, and made no attempt to address the outcries of rage directed at him regarding the conduct of his soldiers. He simply ignored them, hoping, as he did with most unpleasant things, that they would somehow go away or rectify themselves through the natural course of events. They hadn't, and Sacke continued to shrink further back, making himself entirely unavailable for comment by directing all complaints to a junior officer who had absolutely no authority to institute change.

There were four people in Garderville on this particular night who had no doubt that the payday wrath of the army had fallen upon them again, like a plague of locusts. Those four were the harried bartenders at the local saloons, two to each establishment. Especially afflicted were those manning the plank in the Frontier, where thirsty, raucous engineers were lined up four deep, shouting insults and commands for more drinks and faster service.

Across the street and at the other end of town, the situation was slightly more tolerable in the Last Ace; the mounted infantrymen were fewer in number and less inclined to demand the impossible.

Inside the Frontier, Sergeant Fred Hatcher stood with elbows hooked on the bar, a huge cigar clamped between his teeth and a full glass of whiskey turning aimlessly in his hands. The

127

room was smoke-filled, its rafters rattling above the harsh voices of burly men, but Hatcher seemed not to notice, as though his mind had drifted far away from the din. He was thinking about a decision that was his to make, but which the whiskey and the men surrounding him would eventually make for him. He could hear it building now, with ominous threats and rumbling complaints growing louder in response to a bunch of "blue-legs" drinking in what the engineers assumed to be their town.

Hatcher smiled softly, clutched the cigar in the thick fingers of his left hand, and inhaled a deep gulp of whiskey. He had been there before, and even though age and many fights had robbed him of some of his speed and endurance, the thought of a good brawl was pleasing to his mind.

"How many blue-legs did you make out when I sent you down the street, Private?" he asked the young soldier next to him.

"Thirty-five, Sarge. I snuck up to the window and counted 'em, like ya tol' me to."

"Thirty-five, huh? That's about what I figured it'd be."

"When we gonna take 'em?"

The cigar moved toward Hatcher's full lips again. "When the time is right, son. When the time is right."

In a similar position of prominence, Sergeant Ben Cohen stood at the bar inside the Last Ace. His broad, scarred hand closed around the whiskey bottle and he poured generously before sliding the bottle along the bar to the next man. Although he gave no indication of concern, he too was contemplative, nursing a cigar and squinting through the smoke at the back wall. Snatches of conversations going on around him registered in his mind.

". . . we'll kill the bastards . . ."

". . . one of us to three of them ain't bad . . ."

". . . I want that ugly son of a bitch with the tooth missing . . ."

A slight smile crossed his lips. He had seen numerous cases where the soldiers of two rival outfits had fought it out toe to toe, then drunk together when it was over and gone into combat side by side in a big battle. Cohen anticipated a major confrontation with the Sioux before many more days had passed, and it was obvious that his mounted infantrymen were outnumbered. If they were to win, his men and the engineers would have to join forces against a common enemy.

He had watched and mentally calculated Sergeant Hatcher since their arrival at the dam site, and while there was no doubt that he was as tough a man as Cohen had ever seen, there was also a quality of fairness and justice about the man. He knew that when the fight with the engineers came, which he knew was inevitable, it would be equal numbers to a side.

"What say we just kind of mosey on down there and get this over with, Sarge?" one soldier asked, helping himself to a drink. "Can't let 'em get too drunk or it'll be too damned easy."

Cohen smiled again. "No, let them come to us. If there's going to be a fight, let them be the ones to start it. We'll save ourselves for the finishin' part."

"Think they got any women down there we could take away from 'em?" another soldier asked with a baleful glance around at the all-male crowd.

"No, and if they did, they wouldn't be worth takin'. Engineers are pretty blind when it comes to pickin' out a purty women from a mule's ass," another man threw in, saving Cohen the need for response.

The remark sparked a round of laughter, and Cohen felt good about the relaxed confidence of his men. As seasoned combat veterans, they didn't scare easily, and when the chips were down, they always came through.

Back in the Frontier, Sergeant Hatcher took another drink, then studied the amber liquid in the bottom of the glass. "I need thirty-five volunteers," he said just loudly enough to be heard.

There was instantaneous silence when the sergeant spoke, then excited jabbering filled the room as hands shot up and men pressed forward to be chosen. Hatcher continued the deep surveillance of his drink and spoke again without looking up.

"Corporal Riley, you pick out thirty-five. I want 'em out in the street when I finish this whiskey."

Names were called out and boots scuffled across the floor as the chosen ones made their way toward the door. When Riley finished counting, he called his own name as the thirty-fifth man, then turned to Hatcher.

"Thirty-five of the best, Sarge. What about the rest of 'em?"

"They can watch, cheer, do whatever in hell they want to, but I don't want a one of 'em liftin' a finger to help. Is that understood?"

"They heard ya, Sarge."

"Good." Hatcher downed the remainder of his drink in a single gulp, drew a massive forearm across his mouth, and turned toward the door. "Let's go take a crack at 'em."

The thirty-five combatants formed a group behind Hatcher, with many of them rolling up their sleeves and spitting on their knuckles, while the remainder formed a loose mob to the rear. The sound of brags and challenges rolled down the street before them as they marched toward the Last Ace.

Hearing the sounds outside, one man of Easy Company sprang to the window, chanced a peek outside, then turned back toward the others. "Here they come, boys," he said with a trace of excitement and anticipation, while turning the cuffs up on his sleeves. "Sounds like the party's about to begin."

Cohen casually relit his cigar before taking another drink. He made no effort to move from the bar, and his silent appraisal of the back wall continued as he lowered his glass again.

The two bartenders watched him nervously, with hesitant, dreading glances toward the door. Finally one of them mustered up enough courage to speak, and stepped toward Cohen.

"Listen, mister, we don't want no trouble in here, and—"

"We aren't makin any for you," Cohen interrupted, drawing on the cigar and exhaling without apparent concern.

"We don't want any fightin' in here!"

Cohen watched the stream of smoke. "Tell that to the boys outside."

"We're just workin' men," the bartender began again, a plea obvious in his voice.

"Good. Just do your job, get me another bottle, and stay the hell out of the way."

Resignedly, the bartender retrieved another bottle from the back bar, placed it before Cohen, and retreated with his partner to the far end of the bar. Cohen splashed more whiskey in a glass and waited.

He heard the sound of numerous boots on the porch steps, listened to the batwing doors slam open, noted the sound of men filing into the room to stand silently against the door. One pair of boots clomped across the room, and Cohen glanced up for the first time.

"Bartender? Bring another clean glass down here."

After a moment's hesitation the bartender scurried forward, complied with the request, and retreated as quickly as he had come. The infantrymen behind him were parting to make a path, and Cohen jerked the cork free from the fresh bottle and poured without looking at the man placing his wide palms on the bar beside him.

"Have a drink, Sergeant."

Hatcher's hand closed around the glass, and all eyes were on the two sergeants, who stood side by side without looking at each other.

"Don't mind if I do," Hatcher replied. "Here's mud in your eye."

Cohen nodded, raised his glass, and drank. "What's on your mind?"

"Seems my boys back there don't like the smell of horseshit. Kinda stinkin' up the town, they say."

"That a fact? I thought that smell was crotch-rot. The kind you get from diggin' too many ditches."

Hatcher shrugged and splashed more whiskey into the two glasses. "Matter of opinion, I guess. Seems to be only one way to find out."

"Yup, I suppose so," Cohen replied, dusting an ash from his cigar. "What's the rules?"

"Same as always. Even sides, no knives or guns. Anything else goes."

"Sounds fair enough. Who pays the damages?"

"The loser, same as always."

"You boys got enough money to cover the costs?"

"Won't be needin' any. Got anything else to add?"

Cohen nodded. "One thing. You and me go head to head."

"I'd kinda figured on that."

"*After* the fight is over. Could be we might need a tiebreaker. Besides, we've damned near got a full bottle to drink here."

Hatcher studied the proposal. "Could be we'll need one at that. Toe to toe, first man down is the loser?"

"Sounds fair to me," Cohen said, topping off the glasses one more time. "Let's you and me knock these two drinks back at the same time. First glass to hit the bar, and the fight's on."

"I'll go for that."

The two sergeants raised their glasses, hesitated, then tilted their heads back and drank. The room was stone-silent, with all eyes upon them, and then the empty glasses slammed down on the bar at the same time.

As if the sound of glass on wood were a starting gun, which in fact it was, the room instantly filled with shouts and grunts as the two sides rushed toward each other and met in the center of the room, with the remaining engineers peering in through doors and windows.

Neither Cohen nor Hatcher turned to watch the fight. Seeminly oblivious to the battle raging behind them, the two sergeants continued to drink, shoulder to shoulder, each taking a turn to pour, with neither of them saying a word to the other. The tough-fisted infantrymen and brawny, thick-bellied engineers were quite evenly matched, with equal numbers of both ranks falling victim to well-aimed punches. Chairs and tables were broken in the tumbling sprawl of men being knocked from their feet while others, locked in bear hugs, wrestled to the floor to continue punching, gouging, biting, and kicking. Footing became slippery from spilled drinks, blood, and sweat, and the gasping heaves of tortured lungs filled the stale air. The tide of the brawl surged back and forth, carried on drunken rage, and the fallen were littered about the room or were crawling away with blood dripping from eyes, noses or mouths. With sufficient strength regained, many of them struggled to their feet again to rejoin the fray.

Still, neither Cohen or Hatcher had looked around. The whiskey bottle before them was nearly empty, and after the final pouring, Cohen shoved the bottle down the bar in a skidding slide. The sounds of combat behind them were lessening, and when nothing more could be heard except the occasional solid *thunk* of knuckles on flesh, Cohen turned the half-empty glass in his fingertips and spoke around the cigar lodged in the corner of his mouth.

"Well, what do you think, Sarge?"

Hatcher chewed his cigar contemplatively. "Sounds like it's about over."

"Yes it does. Shall we take a look?"

"Might as well. Damned near out of whiskey anyway."

The two men turned simultaneously and leaned back against

the bar, resting their elbows on the polished wood. Approximately twenty men remained standing, leaning against walls or unbroken tables, sucking in great gasps of air and mopping blood from their faces with the backs of sleeves. Eyes were bruised and swelling shut, lips were split and twisted into grotesque shapes, and purple-black splotches decorated their cheekbones and jaws.

Cohen nodded as he counted. "Ten red-legs and ten blue-legs. Looks like a draw, Sarge. How do you make it?"

Hatcher had been counting as well. "Same. I got a couple more sittin' up than you do, but I guess that don't count."

"Nope. Gotta be standin'. Guess it's up to you and me now," Cohen said, tilting his glass and draining the last of the whiskey.

Hatcher matched the move, then placed his glass carefully on the bar. "Looks that way. Center of the room?"

"Center of the room," Cohen replied, setting his glass down. Both men stripped their tunics off as they moved away from the bar.

When both of them were stripped to the waist, they kicked the debris out from beneath their feet, turned, squared away with fists raised, and began to slowly circle each other. Then each of them threw a punch in the same instant. Cohen's cracked along Hatcher's jaw, and the engineer's slammed home to the side of Cohen's head. They both drew back and circled again cautiously, neither of them showing any ill effects from blows received.

Two more punches were thrown. Cohen took one alongside the rib cage and landed one on Hatcher's chest, just above the heart. Again, neither man went down. Then the doors to the Last Ace slammed open again, and Kincaid and Edgerton stepped inside.

In the presence of two officers, both sergeants dropped their hands to their sides and snapped to rigid attention. Fallen and exhausted soldiers around them were scrambling, or attempting to scramble, to their feet while Edgerton surveyed the room. As senior, it was his place to speak first.

"Well, Lieutenant Kincaid, I'd say our men have met in less than formal circumstances."

Kincaid nodded, glancing at his men to make sure none of them were seriously hurt. "That's my observation as well,

133

Captain. By the look of things, I'd say our bet is off."

"Yes, a pity too. I was really looking forward to a drink of dragoon whiskey."

"I'm sure a captain in the Corps of Engineers would have paid off with only the best," Kincaid rejoined. "At ease, men."

The men slouched to weary positions of rest, as did Cohen and Hatcher, but with military correctness.

Edgerton studied his sergeant closely. "I think I speak for Lieutenant Kincaid as well as myself, Sergeant. I have seen nothing of what's transpired here tonight. Do you agree, Lieutenant?"

"Absolutely. Sergeant Cohen has my word on that, as does Sergeant Hatcher."

"Excellent. Now I'd like to ask Sergeant Hatcher a question."

"Please do, sir."

"What was the upshot of this little sparring session between you and Sergeant Cohen?"

"We made an agreement, Captain. If our men fought to a draw, him and me would settle it. We figured they fought to a draw."

"I see," Edgerton said, his lips pursed in thought. "And still no decision has been reached?"

"No, sir, it hasn't. With your permission, sir, we'll settle the matter here tonight."

"Sergeant Cohen?"

"Of course. We were just gettin' warmed up and findin' the range."

"A noble endeavor, but it is imperative that we get back to the site, unfortunately." A twinkle came into Edgerton's eyes as he looked at Kincaid. "Are you still amenable to the size and amount of our personal, shall we say, agreement, Lieutenant?"

Kincaid smiled and nodded. "Of course, Captain. As much now as before."

"Then it's settled. Tomorrow afternoon at five o'clock the two sergeants here will have an opportunity to square accounts. I'm certain that the rules have been established, so we'll go along with them. Is that acceptable to you gentlemen?"

Both men nodded in agreement and Cohen offered his hand to seal the bargain. Hatcher grasped it firmly, without reluctance.

134

While the two sergeants were pulling on their shirts again, Edgerton stepped toward the pair of white-faced bartenders. "Which of you fellows is in charge here?"

The older man wiped his hands on his apron while stepping forward without enthusiasm. "I am. I represent Herman Crocker, the owner of this establishment."

"Would you please convey a message to Mr. Crocker for me, sir?"

"I will," the bartender said. "And my message as well."

"That is as it should be. Please ask your employer to make an assessment of the damages sustained here tonight. When a sum has been arrived at, he is to send a messenger to the construction site at Ryan's Ravine to talk with me personally. A collection will have been made from all parties involved in this little tussle, and retribution will be offered at that time."

"I'll tell him, but he ain't gonna like it."

"The fortunes of war, sir, the fortunes of war. Now, would you be so kind as to place two bottles of your finest whiskey on the counter, one for myself and one for the lieutenant."

The bartender eyed Edgerton suspiciously. "You intend to drink 'em here?"

"No we don't. We'll take them with us." The captain glanced around once more and said with a smile, "I rather suspect you're about to close for the evening."

In the absence of moonlight, shielded from above by a heavy cloud cover, Cole Creek resembled an inky black snake pursuing its slithering path toward the unfinished dam at Ryan's Ravine. The water, spilling and gurgling over the logs already in place, was audible in the eerie silence of night, in combination with the croaking of frogs and the sharp screech of crickets' wings being rubbed together.

Another sound, kept low to avoid detection, was the strained grunting of three men dragging a small raft toward the stream. A fourth man walked behind them, gingerly carrying a wooden box. When the log raft touched the water, the three men retreated and the fourth placed his box on the contrivance.

"You sure this is gonna work, Orin?" one man asked, stooping beside the man walking the box into position. "They've got a guard by the dam, you know."

Orin Tate smiled in the darkness. "Like a charm, Toby. Like a charm."

"If it does, ain't ol' John Cole gonna be a little pissed about us goin' against the wants of him and the others?" Toby persisted.

"To hell with them," Tate replied, taking a length of fuse from one of the other men and affixing it to a blasting cap, which he then inserted in a hole drilled in a stick of dynamite. "All him and the rest of 'em want to do is sit on their butts and bitch. I tol' that soldier boy his dam wasn't goin' in, and I meant it. Cole always wants to do things right, by the law and all that shit, but old Orin Tate says the law ain't worth a fuck unless it works to your advantage."

The wooden box on the raft was furnished with a lid, which Tate opened now to reveal a bundle of sticks of dynamite in the larger of two interior compartments. Tate gave the fuse attached to the stick of dynamite a gentle tug to make sure it was secure, then placed the fused stick in the center of the bundle inside the box. The fuse he carefully arranged in the other compartment and passed its end through a small hole in the lid, which he then placed on top of the box and tied in place with a length of baling wire. A short section of fuse protruded from the hole in the lid. He stepped back, surveyed his handiwork with a satisfied smile, and said, "In about three minutes this little beauty is going to solve all our problems for us."

Another man leaned close and whispered, "You sure that guard ain't gonna see that fuse burnin'?"

Tate chuckled softly. "Hell no. That's what the box is for. The fuse burns inside. The only thing he might see, if he was lookin' close—which he won't be—is a teensy bit of smoke."

"But what if he does?"

"That won't matter either. If he comes close to this box, he won't have time to do anything, and if he comes too close, he'll be blowed all to hell along with the fuckin' dam. Got a match?"

The other man produced a match from his vest pocket. Tate struck it on his thumbnail and shielded the flame with his cupped hands until he was sure it was properly lit, then touched it to the end of the fuse protruding from the box. There was a hesitation, a sputter, then white-hot ignition, throwing off yellowish-white light and shooting sparks. Tate carefully tucked the fuse inside the box, then beckoned to the others behind him.

"Come on, boys. Help me push 'er in."

136

The raft slid easily on the slick grass, and Tate waded to midstream to position the bundled logs properly in the center of the current before splashing ashore and retreating a short distance away with the others.

"That should be timed just about right," he said pridefully, watching the raft glide silently down stream. "Three-minute fuse, and that old girl should be there in two, maybe two and a half minutes."

The hissing sound of burning fuse was quickly lost to them, as was the raft, swallowed up in the darkness.

The guard, bored with his assignment and thinking mainly of the pass into town that would be his the following night, cradled his rifle in his arms and stared into the gloomy night.

Nearly two minutes had elapsed before the raft nudged up against the dam with a solid thud. Water coursed around the box attached securely to the raft's forward section. Even though the sputtering, hissing sound was muffled by the box and diminished by the sound of rushing water, the guard detected a strange odor and an unfamiliar noise. He walked toward the water's edge to peer into the darkness at the face of the dam, and he could make out a black object he had never seen before. Curious, he walked onto the dam to get a better look at what appeared to be a black box sitting on top of a bunch of logs floating on the pool that was nearly eight feet deep behind the dam.

When he finally isolated the smell of burning powder, he froze with eyes locked open in terror, wanting to run, but his legs would not function. When they finally did, it was too late.

A mighty roar split the night sky with an orange-red blast, and the guard, logs, and water cascaded into the air.

The dam disintegrated in a great rush of water, sending logs and mud coursing downstream at flash-flood acceleration. In a matter of a very few seconds, there was no more dam at Ryan's Ravine, and Cole Creek flowed along its free and easy course across the plains.

eleven ─────────────────

In the weak light of dawn, with Kincaid and Edgerton standing by his side, Major Sacke stared at the raw earthen banks where his dam had been. The look on Sacke's face was that of a man wishing to be alone so he could cry in privacy, and he nervously adjusted his glasses while biting his quivering lower lip to maintain control.

"Those sons of bitches," he murmured in a barely audible voice. "Those dirty sons of bitches."

Kincaid watched the major and actually felt sorry for the man.

"Maybe it's time to give up, Major," Matt said softly, as if they were standing on the grave of a loved one.

Sacke blinked his eyes several times while his blank gaze drifted to Kincaid. "Give up?"

"Yes, give up. Enough men have died, enough hatred has been generated and enough disturbance created to entirely satisy the needs of one ill-advised project."

The lieutenant's words seemed to jolt Sacke from his mourning. "Did you say, 'ill-advised,' Lieutenant Kincaid?"

"Yes, that's what I said."

"I designed this project, Lieutenant. I promoted it back in Washington, helped push its acceptance through Congress, and now you have the nerve to tell me it's ill-advised?"

Kincaid listened to the first notes of hysteria in Sacke's rising voice and noted the wild look in his eyes. "On paper, what you proposed might have looked feasible, even sensible, but in practical application it is a total failure. The sooner you accept that fact, the better off everyone involved will be."

"This is not a failure! I won't let it be a failure! And any delays or alterations of schedule that might create the impression of failure are the direct result of incompetency on the part of yourself and Captain Edgerton."

Edgerton's eyes hardened. "How do you mean that?"

"I placed the two of you in complete charge of the project, against my better judgment, I might add, and you have failed."

"In what way?" Kincaid asked.

"The captain here should have the dam completed by now, and if it had been constructed to the specifications of my design, it would have been strong enough to survive that blast last night."

"Your dam would never have been strong enough to withstand even a heavy rain, Major," Edgerton said icily, "let alone a charge of dynamite."

As if he hadn't heard the captain's words, Sacke directed his wrath at Kincaid. "And you were in charge of defense. Your man assigned to guard this dam must have been asleep at his post, or no one would have gotten close enough to plant a charge."

"In the first place, the man assigned to this post was killed last night, and if he was sleeping, he must have been on the dam itself. In the second place, it was your man, not mine."

"What?"

"Yes. If you remember correctly, one platoon of my soldiers was *ordered* into town last night. With that platoon missing, my second platoon was stretched too thin to provide adequate patrols over the entire area. In light of that, some of your men were assigned to nonmounted patrols. The dam site happened to be one of those."

The death of one of his men had little apparent effect on Sacke, but having the argument turned against him prompted instantaneous, defensive rage. He jabbed a finger wildly at

Kincaid and said in a quivering voice, "You, Lieutenant, are hereby ordered to catch the Indians who did this. I don't give a damn how you do it, but by God I want it done!"

"Fine, Major. And I would follow that order, if the dam had been blown up by Indians. But I'm afraid it wasn't."

"How—what—are you out of your goddamned mind? Who the hell else would have done it?"

"I can't give you a specific name right now, but I will soon. Before I joined you here this morning, I took a little walk upstream. A sled or raft of some sort was dragged to the creek last night and launched well above the dam. The markings in the grass and on the banks are plainly visible, and the men who put the raft in the water were wearing boots, not moccasins. Farther back, I found the markings of shod hooves. Beyond that, I don't think the Sioux have enough knowledge of dynamite to devise a scheme as effective as this one. Whoever did it was well-schooled in the use of explosives, and I'm certain those people were white men, most likely homesteaders from downstream, who violently oppose this project in the first place."

"Then, by God, catch them! Catch somebody? We're dealing with the destruction of government property here, man!"

"That may be true, but when I catch them, they will be prosecuted for the death of a soldier, not for the destruction of a worthless dam."

"Worthless dam!" Sacke screamed, and the contortions of his face made it obvious that he was totally out of control. "There are hundreds of soldiers around this goddamned place, but we only had one dam!"

"And one too many, in my opinion, Major," Edgerton said evenly.

Sacke spun toward his executive officer. "And it is because of that opinion that I am relieving both of you of command as of now. I am taking complete charge of this project." The major's eyes narrowed to tiny slits. "Captain Edgerton, you are ordered to put the timber-cutting detail to work immediately. They will work from dawn till dark, and any man who shirks his duty or lies down on the job will be court-martialed. That includes you, Captain."

The wild, demonic eyes were on Kincaid again now. "And you, Lieutenant, will eliminate your senseless patrols and have your entire command assigned to the protection of the timber-cutting detail and construction site proper. I want those men

140

on foot so they can fight like infantrymen are supposed to fight, and forget this nonsense of prancing around here on horseback." He glared at each of the men in turn for long moments. "Are there any questions?"

"What's the point in asking a question when you know the person you're asking it of is capable only of providing ridiculous answers?" Kincaid asked.

"That's insubordination, and I'll have no more of it! I'm leaving now, and I'll expect my orders to be carried out to the letter. Also, I will expect a salute from you two *junior* officers."

Edgerton smiled laconically. "I'll only salute you one time, Major." The captain paused for effect. "And that will come immediately after your court-martial, not one minute before. You asked if we had any questions, and I do have one, if I may."

"Yes? Get on with it?"

"Does insanity run in your family?"

"You—you—bastard!" Sacke spluttered, before jerking his shoulders around and stalking away with stiff, stumbling strides.

After Sacke had gone, Kincaid shook his head and looked at Edgerton. "I think the poor son of a bitch has gone mad. Is there any way you can relieve him of command?"

"No, Matt, there isn't. He's just got too damned much influence with our commanding general. As I told you last night, he's just about reeled out enough rope to hang himself. I'd say we both watched him slip his neck in the noose just now."

"Do you plan to follow his orders?"

"Of course, and you should as well."

"Isn't that taking a tremendous risk with your men, as well as mine?"

"Matt, his order stated that your men must be standing on the ground. He said nothing about them not standing beside a horse, did he?"

Kincaid grinned and Edgerton clapped him on the back as the two officers turned and began walking toward the encampment.

It was nearly noon when Windy swung down from the saddle and walked to where Kincaid stood talking with his two second lieutenants.

"Howdy, Matt. Got a minute?"

Kincaid glanced over his shoulder. "Glad to see you're back, Windy. Just give me a second to finish up here."

After Kincaid had given his final instructions, he turned and walked toward the creek so he and Windy could be alone, out of earshot.

"Looks like Major Brain Sacke, Commanding, should have hired some beavers to do his work for him, Matt. I saw some of his logs downstream and kind of figured his dam was gone."

"Yes it is. Somebody blew it up last night. I want to talk with you about that in a minute. But first, how did things go with Simms?"

Windy was in the process of cutting off a chew of tobacco, which he popped into his mouth from the blade of his bowie knife, and returned the weapon to its sheath before answering.

"If what he told me ever gets to the wrong ears before we can do something about it, we're going to have another Sand Creek Massacre on our hands."

"Sounds serious. What did he tell you?"

"First off, our proud friend Black Eagle is a half-breed."

"I'll be damned."

"Followin' right behind that, him and Jason Cole have a one whole hell of a lot in common."

"Such as?"

Windy worked the tobacco, pursed his lips, and spat. "They both have the same mama."

"What?" Kincaid asked, both stunned and astonished.

"One and the same. Grace Cole is the mother of both boys. Her name is Cloud of the Moon now, and she's the one I was trackin' some twenty years or so back. Black Eagle's father, Stalking Crow, is the one who took her."

"Is she still alive?"

"Far as I know."

Windy proceeded to relate his entire conversation with Simms, and Matt listened intently.

When Windy had finished relating what Hunting Fox had told to the agent, Kincaid asked, "Does Black Eagle know who John Cole is?"

"No, that's one thing his mother never had a chance to tell him. Black Eagle cut and run as soon as she told him the truth, and he hasn't spoken to her since."

"I wonder if he would have attacked the Cole homestead if he had known."

"Maybe so. He's pretty damned mixed up in his thinkin' right now, and he could look on the place as the source of his shame. Wouldn't be surprised if he killed his half-brother, Jason, outright if he could get his hands on him. Other than his mother, Jason is the only real link he has between himself and the white world."

Kincaid's brow furrowed and his eyes went to the horizon in the direction of the Cole homestead. "You're not often wrong, Windy, but you are this time."

"In what way?"

"There is another link as well."

"Who?"

"Melinda."

"By damn, I am. Plumb forgot about her. Must be gittin' old to forget a beauty like that." He squinted at Kincaid. "Obviously you haven't."

"No, I definitely haven't. If Black Eagle does find out exactly what his white heritage is, do you think he'll try to kill them?"

"Probably so. He's got so much hate in his heart right now, and if he's thinkin' like some of the pissed-off warriors I've known in the past, they would likely be the ones he'd want to kill most."

"And what if Cole finds out his wife is alive?"

"Then we've got that massacre I was talkin' about."

"Jesus Christ," Kincaid said softly. "I can't see how this situation can get much worse."

Windy shifted the chaw from one cheek to the other. "I can't either, Matt, but I'm thinkin' it's gonna. You said you wanted to talk to me about the dam blowin' up?"

"Oh, right. I was so surprised by what you just said that I almost forgot. The ones who did it floated a raft downstream with some dynamite aboard, and I found enough sign along the creek to rule out Indians, even if they did know how to use the damned stuff. Out of all the homesteaders we've met around here, who do you think would be the most likely to do something like that?"

"Simple. Orin Tate."

"Why do you say that? I know he was the most vocal of the group, and because of his threats he'd be my first suspicion as well, but we can't implicate a man on words alone."

"I'm not sayin' he did it, Matt. I just said he's the one most likely to have done it. When a man works as an explosives expert for a mine a good part of his life, he's bound to know a little bit about blowin' up things."

"Are you referring specifically to Tate?"

"Yup. Tate was at Slim Barkley's place when we got there the other day. They'd been blowin' stumps on a piece of ground Slim wanted to clear, and he mentioned Tate's value to him and the other stockmen around there as a powder man. He also mentioned Tate's experience in the mines."

"I see. Then he's probably our man. I want him for murder. A soldier was killed on that dam last night. Not one of ours, but one of Sacke's."

"Too bad. Speakin' of Sacke, I noticed the timber detail workin' again when I rode in this mornin'. Is he gonna start this damn fool idea of his up again?"

Kincaid nodded. "Yes he is, and with a vengeance. He's taken full charge of construction and he's put the crews on extra shifts. They should be laying new logs again by nightfall."

"At least you can count on him—he's always stupid. With the dam gone, the Lakota wouldn't have any real reason for attacking again, and that'd give us time to get a little bit of this mess straightened out. But with them building once more, Black Eagle will attack again, sure as hell. He's in too deep to back out now."

"If he does, when do you think he'll strike?"

"This afternoon, most likely. With the dam gone now, he'll probably want to hit us before we can get started building again. Besides, he'll notice you don't have your patrols out, like I did, and he'll be able to take you by surprise. Whey ain't they out?"

"Sacke's idea. Direct order for my men to guard the timber detail and construction without patrolling the area. I would have refused, but Captain Edgerton asked me to go along with it."

"Edgerton?" Mandalian asked with as much surprise as his dour expression could muster.

"Edgerton. He's all right, and he's on our side." Kincaid paused, thinking hard. Then he snapped his fingers and his head jerked toward Windy. "You're about the best drinkin' man in this territory, aren't you, Windy?"

"Been known to pour while others were sippin'. What about it?"

"Edgerton and I each brought back a bottle of the best whiskey we could find last night. Sacke is a drunk who just doesn't fall down in public, and we'll use that weakness against him. There's going to be a grudge fistfight between Ben and Sergeant Hatcher this afternoon at five o'clock, and I want Sacke so drunk by that time that he couldn't find his asshole if he used both hands. If we get started now, we can make it, and I think Sacke will drink with you because he doesn't know you well enough to hate you like he does the rest of us."

Windy wrinkled his mouth to spit while saying, "Now there's a back-door compliment if I ever heard one."

"No offense intended, but it's true. That will give me a chance to get things set up for a possible attack, and using the fight with a big crowd of soldiers gathered around, we might be able to draw Black Eagle into a trap. I'll get the whiskey while you put your horse up, then you start on Sacke and I'll coordinate things with Edgerton."

Windy allowed an easy smile to crease his face. "This had better be damned good whiskey, Matt. I hardly ever drink with a man I don't like, and never with a man I can't stand."

"Who knows?" Matt said, grinning. "You two could turn out to be old drinkin' pardners."

"Yeah, and I might kiss a snake's ass, too."

Fifteen minutes later, Kincaid met Windy at the rear of the headquarters tent and passed the bottles across while speaking in a whisper. "I talked with Sacke and told him that since he was in command, my scout would only relay to him personally some urgent information you had regarding the success of this project. He kind of liked that part about you reporting directly to him, so make it a good long report."

Windy sighed wearily, gripping a bottle in either hand. "You know I ain't much on talkin', Matt."

"With Sacke, all you'll have to worry about is the first five minutes. After that, he'll take care of the rest. Just keep him drinking, and most importantly, tell him you've changed your mind and that you think this plan of his about building a dam here is the best idea to come along since salt on a steak."

"I might have to get drunk myself to handle that," Windy said, moving toward the entrance.

When he neared the tent flap, Windy said respectfully, "Major Sacke, sir? Chief Scout Windy Mandalian, reporting as requested." Since he had never said 'sir' to anyone in his life, the words left a flat taste in his mouth and he was anxious to pull a cork and get on with the drinking portion of this ordeal.

"Come in, Mr. Mandalian. I've been expecting you."

Ducking, Windy stepped inside, tucked one bottle under his arm, and offered an unpracticed salute, which Sacke returned enthusiastically from where he was seated by the desk, while his eyes strayed to the twin bottles.

Windy hefted one with a glance at the label. "Best damned drinkin' whiskey in the territory. Kind of thought the best damned officer in the territory might like to have a little drink of 'er while I give my report."

"Well...I am on duty, Mr. Mandalian. I..."

"Fine with me, Major," Windy replied, turning as if to set the bottles outside.

"One moment, please." Impulsively, and apparently without control, Sacke's tongue swept across his lips and he reached behind him for two glasses. "Perhaps it wouldn't hurt if I made an exception this time. Just one, of course, mind you." He smiled weakly. "In the spirit of friendship and of obtaining information vital to the successful completion of this project. Please pull up a chair and I'll pour."

It was a quarter to five when Windy stepped again into the sunlight. He blinked to adjust his eyes to the brightness, took a sidestep to correct a slight stumble, then focused on Kincaid and Edgerton standing twenty yards away. He moved forward and held up the two empty bottles before tossing them aside.

"That was a rotten assignment, Matt," Windy said, controlling a slight burp, "but we got 'er done."

"Is he thoroughly drunk?"

"Is a pig's ass pork? He thinks I'm still in there talkin' to him."

Kincaid grinned. "Good work. From the looks of things, you didn't do too badly yourself."

"Hated ever' damned minute of it. No place to chew and spit," Windy replied, drawing out his cut-plug and cutting off a chunk.

Matt laughed and turned toward the cluster of men grouped behind them around a cleared, roped-off, square section of ground. Hatcher was taking his shirt off on the side of the makeshift arena occupied by the engineers, while Cohen pulled his off on the other side. Bets were being exchanged between the two sides, and Kincaid could detect an air of camaraderie, rather than hostility, between the two outfits.

"It looks like they're about ready to go, and if our hunch is correct, the trap is baited and waiting for any takers. If you look closely, every man has a rifle, butt down on the ground before him and held out of sight, and one company of engineers and a platoon of Easy Company are missing. You wouldn't be able to tell that if you weren't looking closely."

Windy squinted, and closed first one eye and then the other, before saying, "Aw, to hell with it. I'm gonna have to get a mite closer."

When they moved toward the assembled mass of soldiers, they saw the ranks parting and the two combatants moving toward the center of the ring. Stripped bare to the waist, they were awesome men, and they resembled two prized fighting bulls moving slowly into the arena. Sinewy muscle rippled across their wide, deep chests, and the corded muscles of their necks bulged out to meet broad, sloping shoulders. Their fore-arms hung hammerlike by their sides, and each flexed his powerful fingers in preparation for the punishment soon to be meted out and received. As two rams might watch each other before lunging forward to crash their heads together, so too did Hatcher and Cohen watch each other with brooding faces and expressionless eyes.

Once inside the ring, the ranks closed behind the two men, sealing them off from escape, even had one or the other desired to quit, which was, of course, unthinkable. There was no referee, no one else in that bare space so limited and confining, than a pair of soldiers prepared to give their all for personal honor and pride of service.

They moved forward simultaneously and each shook the other's hand, then they backed away, assumed their individual choice of defensive posture, and began circling each other, stalking, looking for a weakness, an opening.

Suddenly, Cohen feinted with a left to the body, bringing Hatcher's guard down, them came up and across with a mighty left hook that crashed against Hatcher's temple. The engineer blinked twice in response to the crushing blow, while count-ering with a powerful overhand right that caught Cohen on the point of the chin. Neither fighter appeared hurt, but it was obvious that they had learned respect for each other as they backed away and circled again.

Hatcher was the next to make a challenge, jabbing twice

with his left hand, then coming in with a right to the ribcage, before backing away with two more of Cohen's left hooks slamming against the side of his head.

As the fight progressed, the onlookers were stunned to silence in between blows, but when the hero of one side landed a solid punch, his backers yowled with delight. The blows exchanged were, even throughout five full minutes of battle, with neither man indicating fatigue or pain. The effects of the fight were visible, though; Cohen had an open and bleeding cut along the side of his right cheek, and Hatcher was bleeding freely from his nose. A mouse was rising under the engineer's right eye, his jaw was swollen, and his chest was red with welts from punches received. Cohen, with one eye beginning to close and the skin broken on his left hand, had black splotches appearing just beneath his heart, and there was a raw abrasion across his left shoulder where a punch had grazed in passing.

Another five minutes elapsed, with heavy, devastating punches being thrown by both men. Then Hatcher rose to the balls of his feet and lunged forward, putting all his weight behind a mighty blow. Extending his arm full length, he caught Cohen again on the point of the chin, and the infantryman stumbled, staggered backward, and raised his hands to ward off the rain of blows to follow. Hatcher was there, moving in for the kill and aiming for the head, while Cohen bobbed and weaved from side to side in a desperate attempt to regain his full vision.

Hatcher was so eager for the knockout punch, so determined to win with one decisive blow, that he forgot to guard his midsection and Cohen, his eyes clearing, landed a vicious left hook to the liver. Hatcher's expression went blank, and he bent at the waist and began back-pedaling.

Cohen was upon him immediately, raining punches to the head and body while Hatcher tried to clutch and hang on. It was obvious by now that both men were tiring and the fight would be won or lost within the next minute.

Kincaid had been watching the fight with extreme empathy for both sergeants. He'd witnessed many grudge fights between rival units during his years of army service, but he had never seen one so brutal, nor one fought between such equally matched opponents. During the last couple of minutes he had thought fleetingly of stopping the fight and calling it a draw, but he knew better. He would have been held in contempt by fighters and onlookers alike, and it would have been considered a sign of weakness of his part, not an act of mercy.

Windy leaned toward Kincaid and said dispassionately, "I'd like to have a colt out of either one of 'em, Matt."

"It can't go on much longer, Windy. One of them has to fall."

"Don't think so," was the scout's reply. "Unless one of 'em gets killed."

"That's a very likely possibility, the way they're going."

Kincaid's eyes left the arena momentarily to scan the horizon, searching for some sign, any sign, of the attack that he considered to be imminent. The line of rolling hills that began a few hundred yards away revealed no clues, and the tall grass shifted silently on the rising evening breeze. After one final sweep of the skyline, his attention went back to the fight and he saw the two men break from their clinch and stagger away from each other. Leaden arms were raised wearily, and the two sergeants resumed their wooden-legged, half-stumbling, circling tactic in anticipation of an opening. Both men raised their right fists to strike at the same time, waiting only for enough strength to deliver another blow.

The booming report of a revolver exploded behind them, and the two sergeants froze in position, like marble statues of Greek warriors suspended in time. All heads turned toward the headquarters tent and they saw Major Sacke standing there, weaving unsteadily, a half-filled whiskey bottle in one hand and a smoking Scoff in the other. He was hatless, his glasses were askew, and there was a twisted, maniacal look on his face.

"What the hell is going on here?!" he screamed. "We haven't got time for you loafers to sit around!" Sacke stumbled to one side, caught himself, and glared at the assembled troops again. "That's my dam and I want it built now! You're all against me and I don't give a shit! My name is Major Brian Sacke, Commanding, and by God I will command! Get back to work, you lazy sons of bitches, or I'll shoot you where you stand!"

Kincaid started to move forward while Sacke weaved, raising the bottle to his lips. The he stopped suddenly. The rumbling echo of many running horses reached his ears, and his head snapped toward the horizon once more. Where there had only been gently wafting grass before, the skyline was filled with a hundred or more charging ponies breaking the crest and

149

closing fast. The Sioux war chant, mixed with the crack of rifles filled the air, and the rumbling became even louder.

"Get to your positions, men!" Kincaid screamed at the soldiers behind him. The sharp command jolted them from their immobility, and the infantrymen scrambled to swing up on their mounts while the engineers ran for trenches that had been dug earlier in the afternoon.

Incoming rounds snapped past Kincaid's ears, tearing holes in the tents behind him, but his only concern was the direction of attack chosen by Black Eagle. As he had expected, a second wave of screaming warriors surged over the rise to the southwest, and white puffs of smoke drifted lazily from their rifles as well.

Then he remembered the major. Turning, he ran toward Sacke to drag him to cover.

Wild-eyed, Sacke stood there, brandishing the bottle in the air and waving his revolver unsteadily while screaming in a high-pitched voice, "Get back to work, damn you!"

"Get back, Major! Get back inside the tent!" Matt yelled, angling to place his body between Sacke's and the incoming fire. With two strides to go, he heard a thudding, smacking sound, and he watched Sacke's eyes fill with shock as the Scoff and the bottle dropped from his outstretched hands, and saw him lifted off his feet to be thrown backward through the tent opening.

Kincaid ducked instinctively and continued on. The major's motionless boots protruded outside the tent, and dropping to his hands and knees, Kincaid crawled forward. The screams, the deafening roar of gunfire, and the angry yells behind him sounded like the gates of hell had suddenly opened up and all the demons residing there had been set free.

Inside the tent, with his eyes still open and his glasses lying crushed beneath his head, Major Sacke stared blankly at the ceiling while his uniform turned a wet reddish color as blood seeped from a massive hole in his chest.

Kincaid lowered his head and swore softly under his breath. Major Brian Sacke was no longer commanding.

twelve _____

When Kincaid emerged from the tent, he drew his Scoff from its holster, stooped to pick up the dead major's revolver, and snapped off three quick shots at the Indians swirling before him. His third platoon was mounted, charging into the battle, and he could see Easy Company's bugler, Reb McBride, seated upon his horse, his bugle poised, while watching his commanding officer. Glancing toward the creek, Matt could see no evidence of the engineering battalion, which pleased him as he fired twice more, seeing one Sioux topple from his horse.

Kincaid hesitated, waiting a moment longer for the Indians to become fully involved in their battle with the entrenched engineers and the platoon of mounted infantry, then he looked quickly at McBride and raised and dropped his hand sharply.

The bugle instantly went to McBride's lips and its shrill music rose above the surrounding din. Simultaneously, Kincaid saw the first platoon burst from the treeline, surging forward at a dead run, while the engineers lying in wait deep inside the diversion channel crawled to the lip of the ditch and pushed their rifles' muzzles out before them. In a matter of seconds,

Black Eagle's warriors were coming under fire from three different angles.

Numerous Indian ponies and warriors were spilling to the ground, and as he emptied the last chamber in the pistol in his right hand, Kincaid thought he caught a glimpse of their chief, still mounted, circling and shouting orders in the midst of the fray.

Quickly holstering his own weapon and shifting Sacke's Scoff to his right hand, Kincaid fired. He thought he saw the chief's shoulders jerk at the same moment, as if under the impact of a bullet, but he couldn't be sure. Then Black Eagle disappeared from view, obscured by the clouds of gunsmoke and the horses and men milling frantically around him.

The dragoons had no time to reload once they'd emptied a weapon, so now those who weren't firing were swinging their Springfields like clubs. By this time several army mounts were riderless as well, and racing about aimlessly in the swirling melee.

A group of Sioux warriors who had lost their mounts now charged the diversion channel on foot in an attempt to escape the withering crossfire. The engineers, their weapons empty, leaped from the ditch, brandishing their shovels. They wielded them not like axes, chopping and swinging, but with wicked forward thrusts, like bayonets. The wide, sharp leading edges of the shovels were formidable, and Matt saw one warrior pitch forward as his head rolled grotesquely away from him, trailing blood from severed veins and arteries. Two more went down with shovel blades in their stomachs, and those remaining were picked off by the engineers who still had ammunition. Three of the engineers were killed by the rushing warriors, and that was the last Kincaid saw before he turned his attention back to the main battle.

As he raised his revolver to fire again, Matt saw a peculiar sight that drew his eyes away from the sights of the gun in his hand. One young soldier, kneeling by his dead mount, with one hand resting on its outstretched head as if to provide futile comfort, was rapidly firing his Scoff at the warriors charging him, and two spilled from their mounts.

Recognizing Greer, Kincaid rushed forward, firing as he ran, and knelt beside the private and his horse. A brave leaned down to club Greer with an empty Spencer while Matt dropped a second Sioux, and from the corner of his eye Kincaid saw the private grasp the warrior's arm, jerking him from the back of his running pony. Instantly, Greer was upon the rising Indian, whom he felled with a backward whip of his revolver barrel before firing a bullet through the warrior's head.

When Greer turned back, Kincaid could see tears streaming down the young soldier's cheeks, and his face was pale and drawn, but his teeth were gritted in determination as he raised his pistol to fire again.

Sensing the only means of escape, Black Eagle rallied his warriors toward the diversion channel, and their ponies cleared the ditch in a sailing jump, while engineers beneath them fired upward or swung shovels at horse's hooves. Off to Kincaid's left, he could hear the throaty roar of Windy Mandalian's Sharps, and the last warrior over the ditch plummeted downward, his pony's neck twisted backward, its hooves flailing. There was no question in Kincaid's mind as to the Indian's inevitable fate if he landed in the ditch alive.

As the last faltering shots aimed at the fleeing warriors died away, a heavy calm settled over the encampment, which was littered with dead and wounded on both sides. Kincaid turned to Greer, who had knelt again by his horse's head and was crying shamelessly, making no attempt to hide the tears. He moved to the private's side and touched his shoulder lightly.

"You fought well, Private," he said softly. "You proved yourself a man, and you should be proud."

Greer looked up slowly and his eyes were swollen from crying. "They killed my horse, sir. That made me mad, but I'm not proud of killing them." He looked down at the motionless mount again. "They just shouldn't have killed my horse."

"None of us is proud of killing them, but we had no choice. They are just as wrong as we are. If Major Sacke had listened to reason, and their leader had not been filled with hatred and revenge, none of this would have happened. As they say, it takes two sides to make a fight. I guess two sides met today."

"I don't like killing, sir. I don't like it at all."

"And neither do I, son, neither do I." A memory, a thing he had seen, several sketches or drawings, somehow came to Kincaid's mind in response to Greer's words, and a plan rapidly formulated itself in his mind. "Give me a little time, Private, and maybe I can get you out of this. Right now, though, I've got to see to our wounded."

"Thanks for coming to help me, sir," Greer said, again without looking up.

"No thanks needed. You would have done the same for me."

Kincaid started to move away, then stopped and turned back.

"Private?"

Greer looked up slowly. "Yes, sir?"

"I just wanted to point out one thing that you might not have noticed."

"What's that, sir?"

"You don't stutter anymore."

A weak, almost surprised smile spread across the young man's face. "Thank you, sir. I guess I don't.".

When the final tally was made, Easy Company had suffered three dead and four wounded, while the engineers had lost ten men with fourteen wounded. When Kincaid found Edgerton, the captain was on his knees and wrapping a bandage around a wounded corporal's chest. When the bandage was securely in place, Edgerton rose and followed Kincaid toward the headquarters tent.

"Did you know that Major Sacke is dead?" Matt asked.

"I thought he might be. I saw him get hit. I don't like to speak ill of the dead, but a hell of a lot of good men have been killed here because of him." As if sensing what was going through Kincaid's mind, the captain paused and looked across at Kincaid. "Matt, you're not feeling responsible for his death, are you?"

Kincaid shrugged. "Yes, I guess I am. If he hadn't been drunk—which was my idea, by the way—he might not have—"

"I don't want to hear any more of that kind of shit," Edgerton said sharply. "If you hadn't gotten him drunk so we could implement your defense plan, we very well might have lost all, or most, of this command. You did the only thing you could do, and if I'd been smart enough to come up with it myself, I would have done so. You pulled our fat out of the fire, Matt, and I give you my most sincere thanks for that."

"Your engineers fought pretty damned well themselves, Steve. We couldn't have pulled it off without them."

A look of satisfaction crossed Edgerton's face. "They did

do pretty well, didn't they? I'm damned proud of them, Matt. Damned proud."

"What'll you do now?" Kincaid asked as they stopped short of the tent, where Sacke's boots still stuck out.

"I'm going into town and wire Washington, just as soon as we get things straightened out around here. In that message I'll detail the folly of this entire operation and tell them I'm pulling this battalion out of here, with or without authorization to do so."

"That's a violation of procedure and might cost you your captain's bars, you know."

"Who gives a shit? If that's the price I have to pay for using sensible judgment, then I don't want any part of this goddamned outfit anyhow."

"That's the way I'd feel," Kincaid replied. "Can I run a thought by you and maybe ask a favor in the process?"

"Name it. Anything you want, you've got it."

"There's a young private in my outfit by the name of Greer. He isn't cut out for battle, even though he fought well today. After this fight, we'll go on to another and still another, and I don't think he'll be able to handle it in the long run."

"I can understand that. I'm not sure I would be able to, either," Edgerton said honestly. "What are you getting at?"

Kincaid watched the captain's face closely. "In the planning of things you're going to build, do you have any need for sketching, drawing, things like that?"

"Sure as hell do. I could use somebody who can do renderings now, as a matter of fact, but they're damned hard to come by."

"I've got one for you," Kincaid said.

"Who?"

"Private Greer. I've seen some of his work back at the post, but I'd forgotten all about it until today. As I said, he's damned good, even though he's never had any formal training. I'd like to see him transferred to your command."

"And I'd like to have him. But we'll be pulling out tomorrow or the next day," Edgerton said, his eyes locking on Kincaid's. "There wouldn't be time to have any transfer orders cut."

"We won't wait for any. When you go, he goes with you, and I'll take care of the paper bullshit later."

"That's a violation of procedures, Matt," Edgerton said, his

155

eyes twinkling. "And it might cost you your first lieutenant's bars, you know."

Kincaid grinned. "Who gives a shit? If that's the price I have to pay for using sensible judgment, then I don't want any part of this goddamned army anyhow—or words to that effect."

The two officers' mutual laughter was broken off when Windy walked up. "Excuse me, Matt, but I thought you might like to know. I counted thirty-seven Lakota dead. They took a pretty rough thumpin', and I don't think we'll have to worry about them again tonight. But of course you'll post a guard anyway."

"Thanks, Windy. We've got a detail digging graves now, and we'll bury the dead at sunset. In the morning we'll have to take the fight to Black Eagle, if he's got any fight left, which I assume he does."

"He does. He's got his back to the wall now, and he knows he'll be hanged if we take him alive."

"Yes, I'm sure he would be. It's a shame, but—"

He was interrupted by the solitary tattoo of a lone horse approaching at full speed. All three men looked toward the sound. They saw what appeared to be a stockman, bent low to his horse's withers and urging every bit of speed he could muster from his tiring mount.

"Can you make out who that is, Windy?" Kincaid asked, squinting and shielding his eyes with a hand against the glare of the lowering sun.

"Looks like young Cole to me. And from the way he's ridin', I'd say this ain't just a friendly visit."

They watched Jason rein in his plunging mount, ask directions from a group of soldiers, and spur his horse toward the headquarters tent. Even before the horse had stopped, the young homesteader was sliding from the saddle and staggering toward Kincaid.

"Lieu—lieutenant. I—I've—gotta talk to you," he panted, sucking in air as he tried to speak.

"Just hold on a second, Jason. Get your breath first, and then tell me what you've got to say." Kincaid was outwardly calm as he spoke, but concern for Melinda Cole filled his mind.

When Jason Cole had regained his breath, he turned to look at his sweat-drenched horse with its foam-flecked mouth, heaving sides, and the pink flesh showing inside its flared nostrils. "Let me loosen this cinch strap first," he said, throwing a stirrup over the saddle and working the leather strap expertly. After Jason had shifted the saddle several times to break the sweat seal between the blanket and his horse's back, Kincaid summoned a soldier to walk the horse out and cool it down.

"All right, Jason," Kincaid said as the horse was led away, "I'd like to hear what you've got to say. Is there some trouble at home?"

"No, not at home exactly, but we've got trouble for damned sure. Last night, Orin Tate's place was burned to the ground by the Sioux. Today he's—"

"Excuse me a second, Jason. Was Tate there when the raid occurred?"

"No, don't guess he was. Him and three of his hands came by our place sometime late yesterday afternoon. They were leading a pack horse, and Orin said something about having a little powder work to do. He hires out to various places, so we didn't think anything about it. Why?"

"Did you notice that Cole Creek was running at full flow when you rode up here?"

"Yes I did, and I was damned surprised, to tell you the truth. Did you fellows finally give up on it, or are you just lettin' water out?"

"Yes, we did give up on it, and yes, the water was let out. I'll tell your pa about that later. Now, what were you saying before I interrupted you?"

Cole slapped the dust from his chaps with his Stetson as he spoke again. "Orin has spent the whole day going from place to place. He's madder than a wet hen, as you might imagine, and he's come up with sixty men, and tomorrow morning, just before daybreak, they're going to hit the Sioux reservation and kill every Indian in sight."

Matt and Windy glanced at each other before Matt spoke again. "Is your pa in on this?"

"He hasn't got any choice but to go with 'em because all the homesteaders in the area had made an agreement to help each other out and abide by the majority opinion. Right now, Orin's got everybody fired up, and Pa's the only one who's speaking out against the ambush. The opinion's against him, so he hasn't got any choice."

"And that's why he sent you here?"

"Yes. He's got enough hate in his heart to kill a hundred Sioux, but not women and children from ambush, or any other

157

way for that matter. He was hoping I could get to you fast enough so that you could get there in time to stop it. Even at that, they might not listen to you, but they sure as hell won't listen to Pa."

"They'll listen," Kincaid said firmly, and looked at his scout. "How long will it take us to get to the reservation, Windy?"

"Five hours at least. That's good, hard, steady ridin'."

Kincaid fell silent, calculating for several seconds. "If we left here at midnight, then, that should put us there just before dawn."

"'Bout that."

"That'll have to do. My men need some rest. They've been working hard all day and just fought one hell of a battle. We'll leave at midnight."

Windy dug the chew from the side of his jaw with a finger, tossed it aside, spat to clear his mouth, and said, "No matter what time you get there, Matt, it might be too late."

"Why?"

"I don't reckon all of Black Eagle's warriors were here today. Medicine Hawk must've burned down Tate's place, and he'll be waitin' in ambush for any white men to come after him. If they plan to get there just before sunrise, that means ridin' in the dark. If Black Eagle and his warriors are still on the prowl, and if they get together—which they will—there ain't no sixty homesteaders been born yet that'll get out of a mess like that. I told you things could get worse, Matt."

"Yeah, you sure as hell did," Matt replied dryly, turning back to Edgerton. "Steve, we don't know for sure that Black Eagle won't attack here again after we're gone. How long will it take you to break camp?"

"We can be out of here at midnight, Matt, and gone by the same time you are. We'll set up defensive positions on the outskirts of town and wait for the next eastbound train to come through."

"Good. If you're gone, I don't think they'll come after you. The dam obviously won't be built, their burial ground will be safe, and the creek will run where it always has."

"Fine," Edgerton said, moving away. "I'll get things started now and talk to you before we go."

Kincaid looked again at the scout. "Windy, you've got to get back to the reservation and warn Simms. Have him find—"

Matt started to say "Mrs. Cole," but caught himself in time. "Find Cloud of the Moon and Hunting Fox, and make sure they're safe. You probably should get started now, because it might take some time to find them."

"Good as gone, Matt. See you in the mornin'."

The moon slid through the heavens, a brilliant silver disk, timeless, entirely removed from the scene of carnage it illuminated below. Its brightness caused night shadows to stretch long behind the soldiers as they hurried here and there, carrying tools, supplies, personal belongings, and other paraphernalia toward the waiting wagons.

Matt Kincaid watched the heavenly body glide along its orbit with effortless grace, and he wondered about the restrictions of mankind. He was tired, and he rubbed his eyes with the palms of his hands. Why? he wondered. Why had so many died for something so futile? At midnight everyone would be gone, and after a season or two, nature would reclaim the land and no one would ever know the strife that one ill-begotten decision had wrought upon the mortals who had engaged in combat there. Was it all meaningless? Time stretched to eternity and all things had but a limited time allotted them to accomplish whatever they had been created to achieve.

He and his men had fought gallantly for something completely nebulous, nothing more than a concept, and several of them had died for a cause in which they may not even have believed. As the stream had taken away the logs that were intended to block its natural right, men's dreams had sucked them into the cold arms of death. As he sat there on a box, deep in thought, he likened the Garderville Dam Project to the fight between Cohen and Hatcher; nothing had been accomplished, neither man had won, and the moon came up as it always did, and still would have, regardless of whether one man had won or not. And tomorrow the same futile battles of humans against humans would begin again. If only—

His reverie was broken by a tentative throat-clearing behind him.

"Pardon me, sir. Could I talk with you a moment?"

Kincaid turned and saw Private Greer standing behind him. "Certainly, Private. You'll be leaving soon, I guess?"

"Yes, sir. And I just wanted to thank you. Captain Edgerton talked to me and he seemed like a nice man. I'm anxious to get started drawing for him, and I wanted to say that I won't let you down. If there are two things in life that I can do well, one is to draw and the other is to calm down horses."

Kincaid smiled warmly in the dim light. "I know, Private. I have every confidence in you. Have you always been able to draw?"

"Yes, sir. I never learned it from anybody, it just came naturally."

"Where do you come from?" Kincaid asked.

"Pennsylvania, sir."

"Why did you join the army?"

Greer hesitated. "'Cause I didn't have anywhere else to go."

"How do you mean?"

"My ma and pa died when I was little, and my uncle took me to raise. He didn't want to, but he was stuck with me. Anyway, he was pretty mean. I don't mean to talk bad about him," Greer added quickly, "but he was for a fact."

"I'm sure he was, Greer," Kincaid said. "You're not talking bad about him. Is he the reason you joined the army?"

"Yes, sir. I—I lied about my age. I'm really only sixteen. You can tell that to the Captain if you want to, sir. I don't want to lie anymore."

"You tell him if you want to, but he won't hear it from me."

"Thank you, Lieutenant. My uncle used to beat me when he'd catch me drawin', and he'd say it was the work of the devil. He was pretty religious. At least I guess he thought he was. Anyway, I was so scared of him and other people that I started to stutter. I never did it before he started beating me."

An increasingly heavy weariness was coming over Kincaid. "Well, I'm glad that's over for you, Private." He offered his hand, which Greer accepted enthusiastically. "I hope everything works out well for you with the engineers."

"I'm sure it will, sir. But there is one thing I'm going to miss about the mounted infantry."

"What's that?"

"The horses, sir. I really love the horses."

Kincaid smiled patiently. "Mules need love too, Greer. Give 'em a hug and a kiss for me."

After the young private had left, Kincaid sat watching the engineers strip and fold their tents, and he marveled at how fast the encampment was dissolving before his eyes. What had once been a miniature tent city was now rapidly becoming open prairieland again, and once more the transitory nature of man's existence entered his mind. Except for the flattened grass where the tent floors had been, and the beaten-down ground from the bootprints of many men, the grandiose scheme to build a dam at Ryan's Ravine would have been imperceptible to the casual observer.

"Excuse me, sir. I have to load that box on the wagon."

Kincaid looked up at the soldier standing above him.

"Oh." Matt rose quickly and stepped aside. "Pardon me. Is that the last of it?"

"Yes it is, sir. We'll be gone in ten minutes."

Kincaid looked around, and indeed, there was nothing left except the sound of Cole Creek rippling in the background.

"Matt?"

Kincaid glanced toward the tall figure approaching him with an extended hand, and he recognized Captain Edgerton.

"Yes, Steve," Kincaid replied, grasping Edgerton's hand. "Looks like you're about ready to move out."

"We are. I just wanted to say goodbye and give you my heartfelt thanks for everything you've done."

"You're welcome, but I don't feel that we accomplished a goddamned thing."

Edgerton looked toward the line of wagons waiting in the distance. "You accomplished more than you could imagine, Matt. Those men over there are alive right now because of you and the soldiers of Easy Company. Don't ever forget that."

"I won't dwell on it, but thanks for the observation."

"You know, it's a funny thing, Matt," Edgerton said. "Tomorrow I'll be on a train and gone from this miserable place. But you? Tomorrow you go into battle again. I'll tell you one thing," the captain added, shaking his head. "I'm just damned glad I can add and subtract and can't shoot a gun worth a shit."

Kincaid smiled with a glance toward his men, mounted and prepared to move out. "Neither can I, Steve, but don't tell them that."

Edgerton chuckled, clapped Kincaid on the shoulder, and walked toward the line of wagons. Halfway there he stopped, turned, and called back.

"Hey, Matt!"

"Yeah, Steve?"

"You said something the other night about engineers being perfect assholes?"

161

"Yeah, I remember!"

"I have a confession to make. We're not perfect!"

"I know, but you're still assholes!"

The laughter of both men faded across the vacant ground as each turned toward his command.

thirteen ─────────────

He could feel the strength and warmth of the horse under him as he rode through the biting chill that always came in that hour just before dawn. White puffs of steam came from the mount's nostrils, and the heat of its body warmed the saddle, causing Kincaid to grip its sides more tightly with his legs.

Perhaps it was the thought of leading his men into another needless battle, but whatever it was, he felt totally alone, even though he was riding at the head of two platoons of soldiers, with young Jason Cole at his side.

They had paced their mounts well throughout the night, and now, with the first tinges of gray touching the eastern horizon, they were well onto the Oskalla reservation, angling toward the agency, still some distance away. It had been a silent ride for the most part, with only the creaking of leather, the soft jangle of equipment, and the swishing of grass beneath hooves to break the moonlit quiet. All of them were weary with involvement in a conflict of dubious merit, and there was an overpowering sense of dread concerning the battle that would envelope them with the coming dawn.

Deeply immersed in contemplation, Kincaid didn't realize at first that Jason was speaking softly to him.

"I'm sorry, Jason, I was thinking and didn't hear what you said. What was that again?"

"I said there must be quite a feeling of satisfaction in being the commanding officer of a group of men like those behind us. To be leading them and be completely in charge."

"That depends on where you are leading them," Kincaid said, offering a weary smile. "There's damned little satisfaction to be enjoyed from a mission of this kind."

Jason fell silent, as if wondering whether what he was going to say next should be said at all. He glanced once at the tall, handsome soldier beside him before making up his mind. "I can see why she thinks so much of you, Lieutenant," he said quietly.

"Who?"

"My sister, Melinda."

"Oh," Kincaid replied, feeling a twinge of embarrassment. "I think the world of her, too."

"She and I are real close, and she told me all about the two of you." Kincaid remained silent until Jason added quickly, "Well, not everything, I suppose, but just about everything."

"That's nice. A brother and sister should be close."

"We are, like I said. With Ma being dead and all, and Pa trying to make a go of the homestead, we had to spend quite a bit of time by ourselves while we were growing up."

Kincaid thought about Jason's offhanded reference to his dead mother, and he wondered what Cloud of the Moon looked like, and what would happen if the family was reunited. It had occurred to him that that reunion might not be possible at all after so many years and so many complications. Black Eagle was equally as much her son as the young man riding next to him—a son whom she had raised and been with since his birth, unlike Jason Cole. Kincaid wondered if she would even recognize her white son, and if she would choose to continue her life as an Oskalla Sioux.

"That must have been rough," Kincaid said.

"It was at first, what with Pa thinking she was still alive and never accepting the fact she wouldn't come home to us. He still hasn't given up hope, and sometimes, late at night, I've heard him praying for her safety."

Kincaid wanted to escape a conversation that he found increasingly uncomfortable. It disturbed him, the thought of a life once nearly destroyed, its memory sealed away in the heart, now possibly being exposed to a new and greater disappointment. The night sky was lifting now, as the grayness along the horizon yielded to a pink fringe, and he felt even more weary than he had before.

"Should be a beautiful sunrise," he said. "It would be nice if we could just—"

They both heard it at the same time—the sound of many rifles being fired at once, coming from a great distance away. It was reminiscent of corn being popped in a pan on the stove, and Kincaid's eyes darted in that direction.

"I hope your father and his men haven't ridden into an ambush," he said, straining his ears to locate the exact position of the battle and estimate the number of weapons being fired. "That should be somewhere near the agency."

Jason Cole was listening as well, and a look of deep concern crossed his face. "It sounds like they have, Lieutenant. Are we going to help them?"

"Yes we are, but we don't want to fall into a trap of our own," Kincaid replied, twisting in the saddle. "Sergeant Cohen? Send two scouts forward, one to the right and one to the left. After they get a distance in front of us, we'll follow behind at a gallop."

"Yessir."

While the orders were relayed, Kincaid turned back and watched two soldiers streak away from the column and fan out at diverging angles away from the main body. When they were some two hundred yards distant, he raised his arm and swept it forward while giving his mount its head. The popping sound rapidly became the crashing explosions of rifles blasting away, while the sun hung just beneath the horizon and then surged into the sky.

On the crest of a rise, the scouts reined in and signaled with weapons held overhead that they had the enemy in sight. Kincaid motioned for the columns to break ranks and form a running firing line, which they did in a manner reminiscent of a hand-held fan being opened. Even the drumming of hooves on hard soil could not drown out the cacophony of shots being exchanged in a wild, pitched battle, and from the lay of the ground before them, Kincaid could see that Cole and Tate had very likely ridden into a classic Indian ambush. A small band of warriors was often used to lure pursuing enemies over the crest of a hill at a pace that made those in pursuit think victory was within their grasp. Waiting ahead and out of sight on the other side, the main body of Indians would lie in wait for their enemies to arrive on weary mounts, overconfident and unaware of the sudden disaster that would befall them.

As they neared the rolling prairie swell, Kincaid was certain that the entire band of warriors was engaged in the battle, and he felt no real concern now with regard to a second ambush. The Sioux, he reminded himself, were as confident of victory as were those whom they had lured to a swift and certain death. Kincaid signaled Reb McBride to sound the charge just as they burst into view, in the hope that the shock effect of the bugle call and their sudden appearance would create confusion among the Indians.

When his horse pounded over the crest, he saw the home-steaders clustered in a group along an old dry wash and firing at the Sioux, who swirled all about them. It was obvious that they were badly outnutmbered and that they were under attack from all sides, with no more than minutes, if not mere seconds, left before their position would be overrun. The shrill, piercing call of the bugle split the dawn air moments before Kincaid fired the first shot from the Scoff in his right hand. Upon his signal the other soldiers fired as well, as the wave of horses and men raced down the slope.

Caught totally by surprise, the Sioux wheeled their ponies and aimed and fired at this new adversary bearing down on them, while breaking off the engagement with the homestead-ers. With resurgent hope, the beleaguered defenders fired into the fleeing warriors, and it was the Sioux who were now under attack from two sides. They broke for open ground, but in a practiced maneuver, Easy Company's two platoons split away from each other, with one heading off in a flanking move to the north and the other to the south. The homesteaders, with the pressure of battle relieved, were swinging into their saddles and rallying to form a third unit to bore into the center of the melee. On fresher mounts than those of the soldiers, the Sioux were breaking out of the pincers move, and Kincaid wisely called off pursuit while yelling at his two second lieutenants.

"Have the men take up prone positions on the high ground! I'll get those civilians!"

He pulled his horse's head around and galloped straight at

the homesteaders, mounted now and riding toward him. It was with great relief that he saw John Cole alive and unhurt, with the exception of a bleeding temple where a bullet had grazed his head. His eyes swept over the group of men in search of Orin Tate, but the man was nowhere to be seen. The tall grass was littered with dead horses and fallen men, and Kincaid reined in before the group led by John Cole.

"Are you all right, John?" Kincaid asked.

"Yeah, I'm all right," Cole replied, gingerly touching his torn scalp. "They ambushed us. We're damned lucky you came along when you did."

"Yes, I'd say you are. Where's Tate?"

Cole glanced toward the dry wash. "He's over there. He was the first one killed."

Kincaid's eyes drifted to the silent figure lying beside a dead horse. "I'm sorry about that, but he would have been hanged anyway. He killed a soldier last night when he blew up the dam."

Cole's expression was impassive. "I'm not surprised. In fact I thought he'd do something like that. I noticed the creek running full this morning when we crossed it, and I suspected something had happened to your dam."

"Not *my* dam, John," Kincaid corrected him. "The government's dam."

"Whatever. Do you think those Sioux will make another pass at us, with you here?"

"Hard to tell. Get your people and move to the high ground. I'm going to try and talk with Black Eagle under a flag of truce."

"Hell, that's kind of a waste of time, isn't it? Seems to me about the only thing those people understand is the talkin' end of a gun."

"There's some good in everybody, John. Black Eagle is no exception. Now move your people up with my troops so we can be ready if another attack does come."

"One thing, Matt," Cole said, reining his horse around and jabbing the barrel of his Winchester toward a figure sprawled in the grass beside a horse that was just able to lift its head and switch its tail, but nothing more. "We got the leader of this bunch."

"Do you know his name?"

"No I don't. But he's dead, and that's good enough for me.

167

I was hoping it was Black Eagle when I pulled the trigger, but now I see that it isn't. One more thing, Matt," Cole added, lifting his reins to stop the horse. "I want you to know I didn't want any part of this. It was all Tate's idea."

"I know. Jason told me. Have you got a handkerchief or anything white?" Kincaid asked, stepping down from his saddle to retrieve a lance lying on the grass.

Cole dug in his hip pocket and came up empty. "Nope. I was in kind of a hurry when I left home this mornin'."

Jason had been silent throughout the entire conversation, but now he stripped off his cream-colored shirt and passed it across to Kincaid. "Here, Lieutenant. Use this."

"Thanks, Jason," Matt replied, affixing the shirt to the blade of the lance before climbing back into his saddle. "Both of you go on up—"

"Lieutenant?"

"Yes, Jason?"

"I'd like to go with you, sir. This is our fight more'n it is yours."

Kincaid hesitated, studying the young homesteader. "Are you sure?"

"Positive."

John Cole reined his horse around once more. "Well, by damn, I'm sure not stayin' behind. Let's the three of us go."

"All right," Kincaid replied with a shrug. "My troops will be keeping us covered, and we'll wait on that next rise."

"Do you think Black Eagle will honor a flag of truce, Lieutenant?" Jason asked, turning his mount in beside Kincaid's.

"I think so. If that Indian lying over there is who I think he is, he's the one who encouraged Black Eagle in this foolishness. I think Black Eagle might be seriously wounded himself. The handwriting should be on the wall for him."

"Who do you think that is?" Cole asked with a nod toward the corpse.

"Medicine Hawk. You said he was the leader of this attack. If Black Eagle wasn't in charge, Medicine Hawk would have been. Come on, let's go."

The three of them rode slowly to the crest of the prairie swell and waited there as Kincaid waved the lance back and forth to attract the Indians' attention. They could see them gathered in a group possibly three hundred yards away, and Matt watched them until another, smaller group of riders caught his attention. He could count three horses moving toward them at an angle between Kincaid and the amassed warriors. A lone brave separated himself from the Sioux war party and rode forward as well. Kincaid quickly identified Windy Mandalian in the group of three, along with a smaller white man and a woman riding bareback on a pinto pony.

When the single warrior caught up with Windy's group, the four of them rode together until they were within fifty yards of Kincaid and the Coles, then the small man and the woman stopped while Windy and the Sioux rode ahead.

"Mornin', Matt," Windy said cheerfully, cradling the Sharps in the crook of his arm.

"Hello, Windy," Kincaid replied, but his eyes were on the Sioux. He noticed an absence of warpaint, and there was more sadness than hostility written on the Indian's face.

"This is Hunting Fox, Matt," Windy said, nodding his head toward the young Sioux. "Rightful chief of the Oskalla Lakota. He didn't have anything to do with all that's gone on the past few days." The scout glanced at the two settlers before looking at Kincaid again. "He is Black Eagle's half-brother. Or I should say, *was* his half-brother."

"Was?"

"Yeah, was. Black Eagle died at the agency building last night. In case you're in the mood for some sad stuff, he died in his mama's arms."

Kincaid felt a twinge of remorse as he remembered firing his pistol at the warrior he'd thought was Black Eagle.

"I'm pleased to meet you, Hunting Fox. I'm sorry about your brother."

The Sioux's face was impassive. "Thank you, Lieutenant. My brother was wrong, but he thought he was right. My people wish no more war with the white man. I have learned that Medicine Hawk is dead as well, killed in this battle. The others who followed them are willing to accept their punishment."

"I see," Kincaid replied, thinking while he spoke. "Are you, as chief of the Oskalla Lakota, prepared to take responsibility for the others? Enough men have died, and as far as I'm concerned, you, as chief, should be the one to punish those who have brought disgrace to your people."

Hunting Fox nodded somberly. "I will do that," he said while his gaze drifted to Cole's face. He watched the white man in momentary silence before saying, "I am sorry for what my father has done to you. She is yours now. Go in peace with her." Then the proud Indian lifted his hackamore, turned his pony, and was gone, riding slowly toward the warriors gathered in the distance. He raised his hand as he rode by the woman and the agent, but he did not stop, nor did he speak to them.

Cole was visibly puzzled, and he glanced across at Kincaid. "What was he talkin' about?"

"You'll find out soon enough, John," Kincaid said, watching Simms and Cloud of the Moon waiting in the distance.

"Can I talk to you alone for a minute, Matt?" Mandalian asked.

"Sure, Windy," Kincaid replied, and the two men walked their horses a short distance away.

"I talked with her last night," Windy said when they were out of earshot, "and she wants to come back, but she ain't sure John'll want her. With Black Eagle dead, she has no more ties with the Sioux. I told her she doesn't even need to tell Cole about having an Indian child, but she said she would, when the time was right."

"How is she?"

"Fine. She's an unusual woman. She doesn't hold any hatred for the Sioux, but she's still a white woman and would like to go home to her husband and family."

"Then let's get them together."

As they rode back to where the Coles waited, Kincaid could see the elder Cole studying the woman, who was dressed in a tan buckskin dress, with her raven-black hair woven into a long pigtail behind her head. Even at that distance her radiant beauty was readily apparent, and there was a haunting sense of loneliness about her as she watched the group on the knoll. Loneliness that bespoke yearning and separation; the urge to break forward and close the gap of time.

Kincaid turned his horse in beside Cole's, and Windy pulled up on the other side. The scout studied Cole for several seconds before inclining the barrel of his rifle toward the woman. "Took me twenty years to find her, John," he said softly, "but there she is."

Cole's jaw dropped open in disbelief, and his lower lip trembled while he stared at the woman across from him. "Is that—is that—"

"Yes it is, John. She's waitin' for you, but she doesn't know if you want her back or not."

"Oh God. I—I can't believe—"

"Believe it, John. She wants to come home." Windy watched Cole closely. "Do you want her back?"

The elderly homesteader gave no reply; he lashed his horse with the reins and raced away toward the woman whom he hadn't seen in half her lifetime.

SPECIAL PREVIEW

Here are the opening scenes
from

EASY COMPANY AND

THE BLOODY FLAG

the next novel in Jove's exciting
High Plains adventure series

EASY COMPANY

coming in January!

one   ────────────────────────────

There was a faint whisper of breeze filtering through the timber surrounding him, and the tall fir and spruce trees blocked out much of the sunlight, creating an atmosphere of late-afternoon darkness. Where the sun's rays did filter through, they splashed upon the forest floor and warmed the thick carpet of needles spread like yellow blankets upon the ground. He could hear the distant gurgling sounds of a swiftly moving stream, and occasionally he caught the glint of sunlight on water when a branch far above shifted on the restless wind. Were it not for the mound of stones at his feet, he would have felt a sense of peace and tranquillity known only to those completely at home in the forest.

Windy Mandalian had once run traplines in the stream just beyond the glen, and the man lying at his feet, beneath the pile of stones, had once been his partner. That was before the outbreak of the Indian Wars and his call to service as an army scout.

As he stood there in nature's silence, leaning against the trunk of a huge spruce, motionless with the exception of a chaw of cut-plug working slowly in his cheek, he could very well have passed as a member of one of the Indian tribes he had fought so long.

With his tall, wiry frame encased in fringed buckskin, and the rugged features of his face accented by the dominance of an aquiline nose, he appeared to be as much a creature of the forest as the white-tailed doe that was now timidly entering the glen from the downwind direction and leading her fawn to water. Nothing escaped Windy's perceptions, and his eyes shifted to the spotted fawn standing in a patch of sunlight, its long ears ever in motion and its shiny black nose twitching to search out some alien scent. Long, spindly legs were tensed for a bounding leap the instant a danger signal sounded in its brain. Then the doe, confident of their safety, moved forward once more, and the pair of deer walked silently toward the stream.

The scout smiled inwardly in response to their fruitless precautions, which is what they would have been, had he chosen differently. He was renowned for his deadly accuracy with the big Sharps now cradled in the crook of his left arm, and there was no questioning his skill with either the heavy revolver sagging from one hip or the broad-bladed bowie knife sheathed against the other. He shifted his weight, spat, and glanced down again at the final resting place of his old friend, and his mind went back to the afternoon when he had found Scotty Griffin. It had been six years to the day since he had placed the last stone on the shallow grave, and this was his sixth pilgrimage to the burial site just north of Wyoming Territory and nearly twenty miles beyond the Canadian border.

He and Scotty had enjoyed a successful trapping season, and they would have left the following day, their pack horses loaded down with pelts of beaver, otter, and muskrat. While Windy had retrieved their traps from the north end of the stream, Scotty had worked the southern lines. But when Windy returned to camp, a sense of uneasiness had filled his mind. Griffin, an experienced trapper and woodsman, should have returned earlier, the result of having less ground to cover, but there were no indications that he had returned.

The fire rocks were cold, his bedroll was in place, the pelts lay stacked in preparation for loading onto pack saddles, and the lean-to had not been stripped of its protective boughs, as was a traditional practice. An hour after setting out on horseback, Windy found the reason why. Scotty Griffin lay dead, with an arrow through his chest and another buried deeply in his thigh. Where his wiry, sandy-colored hair had been, there was nothing but a blood-red dome of exposed flesh, still wet and sticky to the touch. From the black-and-blue markings on the arrow shafts, Windy assumed Griffin's killers to be Cree Indians, but in the thick carpet of needles he could find no other markings to confirm his assumption.

The loud, squawking call of a blue jay landing on a limb high above his head brought Windy from his reverie. Leaning his rifle against the tree trunk, he stooped to replace some rocks that had tumbled from the mound during the previous winter. As he gently stacked the moss-covered stones, he thought again of Griffin's two children. A boy and a girl, now eight and six respectively, they were freckled-faced and sandy-haired, just like their father had been. Old Scotty would have been proud of them, Windy thought, replacing the final stone and noticing the depression in the ground where the grave had sunk through the years. That subtle indication of time's passage, in combination with the evening shadows now gathering about him, caused Windy to rise quickly, pick up the Sharps, and stride away with steps equally as sure and silent as those of the doe and her fawn.

A sense of urgency had come over him, the sudden need to quit Canada, ride to the Clearwater Indian agency in northern Wyoming, arrange for the sale of the hides, and have the money given to the guardian of Scotty's children, as he had in each of the past six years.

A short distance away, four horses glanced up from their grazing as the scout approached. Two were pack animals laden with hides dried and cured in the sun, the third bore a burden of traps and chains, while the fourth—a magnificent, tall roan—had a worn but sturdy saddle upon its back. Windy swiftly pulled the picket stakes from the ground, tied the three pack animals in tandem, and then swung up onto the roan. He would pass one more night at the camp he and Scotty had used for so many years, and set out at dawn the following morning for home. That meant he would have to unpack the hides that night and reload them in the morning, but the cargo was too valuable to be left at the camp unguarded, this close to the end of the season. A full month's work had gone into the trapping, skinning, and tanning, and were the pelts to be lost, there would be no time to set the lines again.

With the Sharps again cradled in his arm, his keen eyes searched the forest ahead of him as he guided his mount through the thick timber in the cool evening twilight. With cunning born of years in the wilderness, Windy had sensed three days earlier that he was being watched, and he had seen the imprint of moccasined feet along the riverbank near several of his traps. When he was nearly two hundred yards from his camp, he noticed the roan pricking its ears and glancing curiously off to the right. Instantly, Windy raised the rifle and swung the muzzle in that direction while peering intently into the gloom. Hearing a muffled grunt seconds later, he pulled the hammer back with his thumb and raised the weapon to his shoulder. After a short pause, a stoop-shouldered figure stepped out from behind a tree and stood staring at Windy, his hands held harmlessly by his sides.

Windy watched the man over his rifle sight, his finger pressed tightly to the trigger and but a few ounces of pressure away from sending a bullet crashing into the other's chest.

"Who the hell are you?" he asked in a tone indicating no fear. There was something about the elderly Indian that he thought he recognized, but in the failing light he could make no positive identification.

"Have you forgotten your old friend?" came the soft reply in a slightly tremulous voice.

"Not if you *are* an old friend. I'm gonna ask you one more time—who the hell are you?"

"Swift Otter."

The scout searched his mind, and when the name finally registered, a slow smile spread across his face. "If that's really you, you should know my name. Tell me what it is before I lower this old tom-tom here."

"Some call you The Snake, but Swift Otter calls you Windy Mandalian. I have spoken."

"Well, I'll be damned!" Windy exclaimed, lowering the Sharps from his shoulder and easing the hammer forward while the smile became a grin. "Didn't 'spect I'd ever see you again. What the hell are you doing here?"

A finger went to the Indian's lips. "Speak softly, my friend. All who are about you do not come in friendship," he said, soundlessly advancing to lay a hand on the roan's withers and

178

look up at Mandalian. "We will talk later, but now your life is in danger."

Again, instinct prevailed as Windy's head turned with a slow searching motion. "At my camp?"

"Yes. They lie in wait."

"How many?"

The Indian held up three fingers.

Windy nodded. "How're they armed?"

"Rifles. Leave your horses here. I can take one with a war arrow. You can have the others."

Windy swung from the saddle, dropped the reins to the ground, and ducked beneath his mount's head to grip Swift Otter's bicep. "Thank you, old friend. Do you know their positions?"

"Yes. They are young, but they are not wise. One is by the big rock—I will kill him. The others are behind the fallen tree with the black hole."

Windy mentally judged the placement of the hollow log to the south of his camp, and the huge boulder to the east. "Good. I'll have farther to go than you. Wait until you hear my first shot before firing your arrow."

The old Indian nodded, trotted to the tree, picked up his bow and quiver, then vanished into the forest. Feeling a warm sensation spread through his chest, Windy watched the old warrior for several seconds before crouching and stealing away in the other direction with the Sharps held before him. The moon, a silver disk, had risen above the treetops, and he worked his way through the ghostly shadows of the darkened timber for nearly five minutes before dropping to his stomach and inching forward.

At first he could not see them, concealed as they were behind the log, then he saw a slight movement and his eyes focused on the nearest warrior, who was lying prone with his rifle aimed around the end of the log.

Knowing he would have been dead at that moment, had it not been for Swift Otter, he smiled slightly and silently thanked his old friend. Then his face turned deadly serious and the rifle stock came up to his cheek.

"You fellers waitin' for somebody?" he asked in a voice just loud enough to be heard.

There was a startled rustling in the grass, and moonlight

179

glinted off a rifle barrel being turned swiftly. The Sharps belched flame and the Indian flopped over backward in a violent twist. The second warrior, positioned at the other end of the log, fired at Windy's muzzle blast, but the scout had rolled away while jacking another shell into the chamber. A slug slammed into the ground where he had been seconds before but the Sharps was at his shoulder again, and his second shot blasted toward the orange-yellow burst of flame across from him. There was a sharp, gurgling scream, and Windy fired a third time, then waited while the forest absorbed the crashing explosions and silence settled over the campsite. Where before the night creatures had been calling, there was now an empty void.

Windy waited in the darkness, his rifle before him at the ready and prepared to fire at any movement or sound from the approximate position of the far end of the log. None came, and after nearly five minutes the scout cautiously rose and advanced. He glanced once at the first Indian, who was obviously dead, then moved forward to turn the second one over with the barrel of his rifle. The man's head had been nearly blown away, and there was a gaping hole in the side of his chest. Having heard no sound from the direction of the rock, Mandalian crouched behind the log and aimed his weapon toward the large gray object. After waiting nearly a minute, he heard the, *caaahhhooo, caaahhhooo*, sound of a calling night owl, which he answered before rising again. He knew Swift Otter's victim had fallen as surely as had his own.

They met near the ring of fire rocks and gripped each other's forearms firmly. "You saved this old hide, Chief," Windy said earnestly. "Sure as hell you did. I'd be dead right now if it wasn't for you. Thanks."

"As would I, if it had not been for you and your friend seven seasons ago."

"Has it been that long?"

Swift Otter nodded as their hands dropped away. "It has." His fingers went up and gingerly traced the four ragged scars, running down his cheek and across his chest. "I was no match for the great one."

Windy vividly remembered seeing a lone Cree warrior fighting a grizzly bear, armed with nothing but a knife and courage. He and Scotty Griffin had stumbled upon them by accident. The grizzly had Swift Otter's leg clamped in its viselike jaws

180

and was shaking him violently, as all grizzlies do when they have their prey set up for the kill. Windy had shot the bear, and he and Griffin had taken the Cree chief to their camp and nursed him back to health.

"I'm glad we came along when we did, Swift Otter. That was a long time ago and I haven't seen you since. How have you been?"

The Cree shrugged. "For an old one of my many seasons, I can ask no more."

"You're tough as an old wolverine, Chief, and always will be," Windy said with a chuckle. "How did you know I was here?"

Swift Otter nodded toward the log. "I heard them talking of counting coup on the greatest prize of all. I knew it had to be you."

"Well, I'm flattered, but I'd say they were more interested in my pelts."

"No. All of our people, as well as the Arapaho, Lakota, Crow, Blackfoot, and Cheyenne know of you. Those who would make war—and there are many among the young ones—believe that having your scalp hanging from their coup belts would bring them great medicine. They do not care that winning such a prize as this would make them more like old women. They would not tell the truth of their victory anyway."

"Then there were no others with them?"

"No. Those three were cowards and do not deserve to be called Cree warriors. They will cause no more trouble for my people."

Windy dug out his plug of tobacco, sliced off two chunks with his bowie knife, and handed one to the Indian and nestled the other in his cheek before saying, "Then, in that case, let's build a small fire, make some coffee, and talk."

"It is good. I'll go get your horses and my pony."

"Thanks, Chief. I'll have some coffee ready when you get back."

When the coffee had boiled and each man held a steaming cup of the strong brew in his hands, while sitting crosslegged beside the small blaze, Windy studied the old chief carefully.

"How are things with your people, Swift Otter? Does the Grandmother in England treat you well?"

"She did, but she does not now."

"How do you mean?"

181

"There is much trouble in Canada. In the Shining Times we were allowed to do what we wanted to do, as long as we didn't get in the way of white people. Canada has much land, and we were always able to stay by ourselves. But now the young ones will bring the Grandmother's soldiers down on us."

"Why?"

"Because of the Métis and the ignorance of the young."

"The Métis?" Windy asked with a cocked eyebrow, while blowing the steam from his cup. "They're breeds, aren't they? Half French and half Plains Cree?"

Swift Otter nodded and sipped his coffee, and Windy went on, "I know a little bit about them, and if my memory is correct, their leader is a feller named Louis Reil and he fights under what he calls 'the bloody flag.' Supposed to be a big white cloth smeared with blood or some damned thing. As I understand it, he's supposed to be fighting to set up a separate province here in Canada."

"He is. And he has promised my people safety and citizenship in his new country if we fight by his side. I have told those of my people who will listen that he will fail and that we will be driven from our homeland. The young hear only what they want to hear, and they have chosen to fight on the side of this Louis Reil."

"Have there been any battles so far?"

Swift Otter nodded sadly. "Many. Small and meaningless, but there is a great one to come."

"When?"

"They tell me nothing of their plans. There is a Cree warrior who calls himself Chief Rides Big Horses, and he is the leader of those who do battle on the side of Reil. Rides Big Horses is no rightful chief, but he drinks firewater and fights like a mountain cat. He cares not for the future of our people, only for the face that his accomplishments bring him. He is a taker of women, a killer of children, and a disgrace to the Cree people. I know of no one more cunning and vicious."

Windy paused to think, and scratched the back of his head while saying, "Correct me if I'm wrong, but I thought Reil had run from Canada. Some say he's hiding out in the States."

Again, Swift Otter nodded. "He is. The Métis chief who gives Rides Big Horses firewater is called Johnny Singletree. He will lead them into battle."

"Johnny Singletree? Never heard of him."

"Then the gods smile upon you. He is worse than Rides Big Horses. He is like the dog who bites all, including himself."

"Rabid?"

"If that's the word."

"It is. What happens if Johnny Singletree and Chief Rides Big Horses aren't successful in winning against the Grandmother's soldiers?"

Swift Otter's gaze held on his cup momentarily, then drifted up to Windy's face. "Then we will have two choices: to be killed, or leave our homeland."

"And there's nothing that can be done? I'd stay and help if I could, but I've got to get back to the outpost. I told the Blue Sleeve captain I wouldn't be gone more than a month, and I'll barely be able to make that now."

"Thank you, my friend," Swift Otter said with a weak smile. "But there is nothing you could do, even if you could stay. We can only hope for the best. And now I must go," the Cree said, placing his cup aside and rising with some difficulty, favoring the leg that had been broken in the grizzly's mouth.

Windy stood as well, and they clasped forearms once more across the fire. "Thank you for what you did here tonight, Swift Otter. I'll never forget it."

"It would be best if you did, my friend. We are even now, and who knows what lies beyond the lowering of the moon?"

"Nothing between you and me, that's for damned sure," Windy replied, shrugging off the old Indian's concern while digging an extra plug of tobacco from his saddlebag. "Here, take this with you. I'd offer more, but that's the last of it."

There was a guarded tenderness in Swift Otter's eyes as he accepted the plug, which Windy knew to be a violation of his training as a Cree warrior.

"You are generous."

"Naw. That shit's so old it dries your mouth out trying to work up a spit."

Swift Otter nodded and turned toward his pony before stopping and turning back. "What has happened to your friend?"

"You mean my partner, Scotty Griffin?" Windy asked. "He's dead. Killed just over there, six years ago."

"Do you know who did this?"

"No. There were two war arrows in him when I found him. Looked like Cree arrows to me, but I can't rightly say your people did it."

Swift Otter watched the scout in silence momentarily, as if making up his mind before saying, "I can."

Windy's eyelids narrowed and his body tensed slightly. "You can? How and who, if you can tell me?"

"It might be best if I don't."

"Knowin' who done it means a lot to me, Swift Otter. More'n you could ever realize."

"I know that, and I will tell you," the elderly Cree said while nodding toward Windy's Sharps, leaning against his saddle. "Your friend, the one with the curly hair?"

"Yes?"

"Did he have a rifle like that?"

"Yes he did, and there weren't too many of them around at that time."

"Was he scalped?"

"Yes he was," Windy replied firmly. "What about it?"

"There was a young Cree warrior who returned to our camp six seasons ago. He was boastful and proud. He had a fresh scalp hanging from his coup belt and a rifle in his hand exactly like that one."

Windy caught his breath. "Was the hair on the scalp kind of kinky-like and sandy-colored?"

"It was. I knew it was the scalp of your friend when I saw it."

"Tell me the warrior's name and where he is. I'll go after him right now. Those pelts over there"—he gestured impatiently—"and the army be damned."

Swift Otter shook his head. "Where he is, I do not know."

"Why?"

"Because he has gone to do battle at the side of the Métis."

"Then what's his name?" Windy asked through gritted teeth. "I'll catch up with him sooner or later."

"I'm sure you will," Swift Otter said with a tired smile. "His name is Chief Rides Big Horses."

With those words, Swift Otter turned away, swung up onto his pony's back, and vanished from the ring of firelight. Windy Mandalian stared into the darkness for long minutes before sinking slowly to the ground and leaning against his saddle. Deep into the night his eyes were locked on the lowering coals, while his hands absently worked a stone across the blade of his bowie knife.